THE EXPANSE BETWEEN US

THE EXPANSE BETWEEN US

N.R. SCARANO

Paperback ISBN: 978-1-964112-02-2

Cover by Inkwolf Cover Design
Character Art by A.M. Davis (@amdavis_author)
Formatting by Nicole Scarano Formatting & Design

CONTENTS

AUTHOR'S NOTE

This book was previously published as a Kindle Vella, but it has been re-edited and formatted for this book. This romance was written under my pen name N.R. Scarano and is meant for mature audiences. If you don't like this style of romance (or even if you do!), please see my books with Nicole Scarano on the cover instead. Nicole's books are still meant for mature audiences, but the romance is zero-low steam.

If you would like to go into this story blind, feel free! But for those who like CWS, here they are:

This romance contains violence, language, subtle references to emotional abuse by a parent, and hot chilly pepper love scenes. Everything is between consenting adults

Thank you for reading this note, Princess.

CHAPTER 1

DRIVER

The moment my eyes find her, I notice two overwhelming distinctions. The first, and most obvious, is her beauty. I've never seen such a work of art displayed in the flesh before. She's a woman that men would wage wars over. Her grace is what songs are composed of. The soft curve of her lips will haunt my dreams in the darkest hours of the night. Perfection is too weak a word for such divinity, and my soul would eagerly become her slave, if only to taste her beauty once in this lifetime.

And the second? She is a fucking bitch.

"Ladies and gentlemen, may I have your attention," I say as I settle before the crowd. I always address the passengers before a long-distance flight so they can put a face to the pilot holding their safety in his hands, and within the hour, we'll launch into deep space for our return trip home.

I've been a pilot since before I could walk. My father owned an interplanetary shipping company, so I grew up in a cockpit. When I turned eighteen, volatile political unrest erupted, creating a hostile environment for pilots like my dad. The death toll soared as insurgents attacked cargo and passenger ships with the same violence that they assaulted the war vessels with, leaving wreckage and bodies alike strewn among the stars, so I left our family business to join the military. Having been raised in space, I had an upper hand on the planet-trained soldiers, and combined with my towering height, quick reflexes, and powerful body, I rose through the ranks with alarming speed. By the time I was thirty-three, word of my accomplishments had spread throughout the galaxy. I took pride in my newfound fame. I was a hero among men, my ego as inflated as my prestige, and I should've known it would be my downfall. My heroics made me a target, and in an attack that lasted over seventy-two hellish hours, I emerged broken.

I required months of surgeries to reconstruct the right side of my body. Medical technology is at its pinnacle, so within a year, I had a fully functional right leg, and my ribs had been rebuilt. My damaged organs had been replaced, and while I walk with only the barest hint of a limp, my flesh will always bear the scars. The damage has scared more than one woman off, but the harshest blow was my release from the military. Bestowed with the highest honors and awards for the bravery and sacrifice that saved my men, I retired from active service. Humility taught me a painful lesson, and I faded away from the public eye to become a civilian pilot. Now, at forty years old, I'm the most sought-after Mors Expanse navigator. The rich and famous revel in the idea of a war hero guiding their ships, which is what brought me to this moment with this breathtaking creature. She's the heiress to the Ambrose fortune. Her ancestors founded the Federation that currently rules our system, making Serling Ambrose one of the richest women in our galaxy. When I learned she was on this flight to the capital planet, Corr'us Sanctum, I'd assumed she'd hired me. Wealthy women often salivate at the chance to travel under the command of a war hero, but the contempt etched into her stunning features informs me she believes I'm the dirt caught in the soles of her designer boots. I've rarely seen such hostility directed at me from a stranger, but after surviving an attack that almost destroyed the entire right half of my lower body, her disdain has little effect on me. It tells me, however, that it was Imperator Ambrose himself who chartered this transport. Serling is his sole heir, and it seems the man wishes a pilot known for not only his skill but also his battle training to guide his only child home.

"Welcome aboard The Bellator," I say, scanning the crowd. I'm careful not to avoid her gaze, and the enigma that is Serling Ambrose baffles me. Her beauty strangles my heart until it can't beat, but her venom freezes my blood into icy shards. She is both welcoming and painful to be around, and it takes seconds to realize my eye contact irritates her. Her position in society is so far above mine that even my gaze offends her, which is perhaps why I hold her stare as I speak. I should be more respectful considering the exorbitant fee her father paid to ensure her safe passage, but I didn't risk my life for over a decade to protect the galaxy just to be treated like dust by a woman who looks barely thirty.

"I am Driver Thorne, and I have the pleasure of serving as your pilot for our journey to Corr'us Sanctum," I continue. "I expect this flight to go smoothly, but I would like to seize this opportunity to remind you that our trajectory takes us through the Mors Expanse. The deadliest part of the known galaxy, this stretch of space is unavoidable. I've charted the most direct path through it, and having flown this route countless times, I have every confidence that our trip will be smooth sailing. I would be remiss if I didn't warn you of the incredible dangers that accompany the Expanse, though, so there will be no unscheduled stops. No changes to the plan. No redirects. I request that you follow the rules and listen to the staff, especially in the event of an emergency. Your safety is of our utmost concern, and we wish your time aboard The Bellator to be pleasant."

I finish my welcome speech with a pointed glance at Serling, and if her scowl is any indication, this next month will be anything but.

CHAPTER 2

DRIVER

War was kinder than Serling Ambrose. One week has passed since our flight launch. At least three remain until we reach Corr'us Sanctum, and while I knew having the Ambrose heiress onboard would place a strain on the crew, I would rather plunge headlong into battle than endure her presence.

There's a reason this ship's name means warrior. Only a few pilots are authorized to navigate the Mors Expanse, and while the ships we fly are luxurious, they are built for warfare. Their hulls are manufactured to withstand both natural and technological assaults, and they're equipped with military-grade weapons. The heavy defenses and highly trained personnel are required for a run of this intensity, and our fees are exorbitant. The Mors Expanse is a perilous stretch of space. Planets, storms, radiation, and countless other disasters plague it, and pirates often hide on its outskirts, hoping to rob travelers before casting them into the treachery of a cosmic storm. The Expanse is thousands of miles wide; the width requiring days to traverse, but its length spans millions of miles. Circumventing the Expanse lengthens the month-long journey into eight for the wealthy and eleven or more for those who can't afford passage on the advanced cruise liners. But when time is of the essence, crafts like The Bellator are chartered to slice through the galaxy's death. My ship is the most expensive to hire. It boasts the best defense technology and luxury interior, but at its core, it's still a warrior. It was created for battle, as is its crew, which is why learning Serling reduced a staff member to tears has my blood boiling.

I would rather charge into a bloody fray than go toe-to-toe with this twenty-nine-year-old, but I refuse to let her bullying go unchallenged. Since I've never seen her on a Mors Expanse run before, I assume she chartered an eight-month luxury liner for the cruise that carried her away from home. Those ships cater to the insanity of the wealthy, but I won't allow her to walk on my crew. We are days away from the Expanse. Days away from the most difficult flight known to man, and I can't have her attacking my team. We're here to protect her, to deliver her to her father in one piece. Nowhere in our contract does it say we have to let her eviscerate us.

I locate Serling on the pool level and calmly stride through the doors, the crystal water far too peaceful for how I feel. I realize I need to tread carefully with this conversation. The Imperator could ruin me with a single nod, but this isn't his daughter's first offense. For an entire week, she has complained about everything from the food to her quarters to the engine noise. She has insulted crew members, mocked other passengers, and refused to adhere to even the simplest of rules. But I've been her greatest object of violence. I don't know what I represent to her that inspires such visceral hatred, but the bitterness she aims at me is unwarranted for someone who's a stranger. If I were anyone else, the hostility of such a gorgeous creature would cripple me, but it only brings out my pity. This woman is so delusional in her wealth that she cannot fathom the meaning of human decency.

"Miss Ambrose." I cross my arms over my broad chest as I

settle beside her lounge chair, and I instantly regret my hasty decision to address her here. I'm a tall man at six foot five. I tower over her reclining form, which gives me the perfect vantage to see every inch of her glorious skin, and she has all but three small triangles of it bared to me. Her bathing suit—if one can call what she's wearing that—is a material I've never seen used in clothing before. The bikini is more string than garment, and the swaths of fabric concealing her nudity adhere to her like paint. I would've assumed it was airbrushed on, except she shifted when she heard me approach, and it slid over her breast slightly. I try not to look at her body, refusing to let her see how that painted illusion is affecting me, but fuck, the way she looks lying before me is obscene. The triangles covering her breasts are barely there and intensely tight, doing nothing to hide her peaked nipples. The section between her thighs is equally narrow, and one swipe of a finger is all it would take to bare her. The bikini's color matches her midnight-black hair, and I grind my teeth in annoyance. I'm angry at my body's reaction to how stunning she is. I detest how, for a split second, I wonder what would happen if she twisted sideways and allowed her nipple to fall out of her top. But what I hate most is she knew I planned to speak with her. She knew I was hunting her down, and she purposely met my assault head-on with a power play of her own.

She looks up at me, knowing exactly what she's doing as she slides one leg against the other, and I shut my body down, staring at her with a blank and unaffected glare. Her manipulation won't work on me. It only makes me hate her more.

"Might I have a word with you?" I say, my voice calm and controlled, and I can tell my lack of response to her sexuality infuriates her.

"If you must." Her seduction vanishes as the hostility takes over, and I genuinely wonder what inspired her to despise me this much.

"In private." I gesture to the door. Other passengers sit a few chairs away, and I would rather not confront her with an audience.

"Here is fine," she says, refusing to give me an ounce of control in this conversation.

"Very well." I step closer, angling my body to prevent the others from overhearing. "I was informed that you had words with one of my crew members. The things said were both untrue and uncalled for, and your actions caused them to become visibly upset. I understand we're here to make your trip as enjoyable as possible, but this run is incredibly dangerous. I need my crew sharp and alert for the week it'll take to cross the Mors, and I cannot allow you to disturb the people who are working hard to ensure your safety."

"Tell her she should grow thicker skin," Serling says, completely unphased by my words, and I stand by my initial assessment. I would rather stride headlong into battle than deal with this arrogant woman.

"I don't know what kind of ships you've traveled on, but on The Bellator, I require respect to be extended to everyone onboard, staff included."

Anger flickers through her as she glances at me. "I've traveled on many ships, and all of them surpass this pathetic excuse for luxury. My father will be disappointed when he hears what his money purchased." She stands with a challenge, and her significantly shorter stature forces her to look up, her features stained with defiance. "Maybe I'll tell him you threatened me." Fire burns in her eyes, and she arches her back, pushing her barely contained nipples into my line of sight. But I refuse to take the bait. I don't react. I don't move. I simply stare at her face as if she's nothing more than a blank wall.

"Maybe I'll ask him to ruin you," she taunts. "What's a war hero compared to the founding family of the Federation?"

"Please remember to watch your words around my staff," I say, ignoring her empty threats. "We're honored to have an

Ambrose on board, but I won't stand for cruelty right before we take on the Mors. Thank you for understanding and flying with us. Enjoy the pool, Miss Ambrose."

I turn and exit the airlock before she can claim the final word. Reprimanding a founding family heiress was undoubtedly foolish, but I don't know how much more of this woman I can endure before my civility expires.

SERLING

"You will come home, and you will perform
your duty."

One sentence. Ten words. That's all my father's message held. Two simple commands. A single line of text. That's it. Uninspired. Small. Seemingly inconsequential, yet that one communication caused my stomach to clench. It's unnerving how ten words can change everything. How they can strip you down into nothing and ruin your entire life. I keep waiting for the dread to subside, for the pain in my gut to lessen, but it's been over a week since I received his demand, and the pain has only worsened. Anxiety gnaws at my insides, making it difficult to eat, to sleep, to function, and this morning I was so upset, breakfast made me nauseous. I barely made it to the toilet before it came back up.

Mortified by my own disgusting weakness, I sat on the restroom floor and sobbed. I'm not the type to wallow in the filth of a bathroom stall, though, so when a crew member found me and fussed over my location, I lost it on her. I never let people see my weakness. Especially not some low-level crew member who will probably sell my secret to the tabloids for a pretty payout. Who knows what that bitch would say when selling my fear to the news, and always a master of cruel words, I cut the woman down to size.

Of course, she ran to the pilot and turned me into a villain. I know he hates me. I see his disgust every time he stares at me with his nearly black eyes, but I don't care. He doesn't matter. He never will. Driver's an inconsequential interruption in my decadent life, and normally I ignore men who are nothing. I barely even look at them, but this pilot? This man with his towering height, death-black hair, and body forged in battle brings out the worst of my malice. I want to eviscerate him. To destroy him until he is bloody beneath my heels. I don't understand why I need to make him suffer. Maybe because my pain is so great. Maybe because he reminds me that everything I crave is being stripped away. Of how the fate awaiting me in Corr'us Sanctum is the one I'm the most afraid of.

CHAPTER 3

DRIVER

S ir?" One of The Bellator's navigators steps into the cockpit and sweeps a hand over his data screen. The information transfers to my monitors, and my chest instantly tightens.

"We've been tracking this storm," he continues. "It was close to our current trajectory, but it was small enough that we believed it wouldn't cross our path. It tripled in size overnight, though, and is now gaining on us. If nothing changes, we'll be on a collision course with it as soon as we hit the Mors."

"Radiation levels?" I lean forward, studying the information on my screen.

"Projections indicate it'll surge beyond our shield's protection. If this storm continues to grow at its current speed, the radiation will seep through our hull."

"Shit." I rub my eyes in exhaustion. "I really don't want to plot an alternate course." Nothing about this flight has been easy, and while storms are always a threat, this is the largest I've seen in years.

The Mors Expanse is constantly shifting, but a few sections have proved to be safer crossing points than the rest. We've mapped most of our current trajectory out, but if we depart from it, we'll have no directions for Headquarters to follow. We'll have to create a path as we go, meaning if we lose communication with Corr'us Sanctum at any point, they'll never find us.

"It looks like we have about twelve hours before we need to decide," I say. "I want all hands on deck tracking this storm, and I'll alert Headquarters. Hopefully, we'll get lucky, and it'll move fast enough to bypass us."

We are not that lucky. Eight hours into our twelve-hour window, the storm doubled again, and it picked up an asteroid field that's miles wide. It also slowed down, its mass hovering directly in our path. We'll hit it within a few hours, and between the flying debris and radiation, we won't survive direct contact.

"We have a decision to make," I say as I finish explaining our situation to the crew and passengers. I don't normally include passengers in flight discussions, but with the brutality of this storm, they need to understand the severity of this threat. The choices we make will affect everyone. "We have three options. The first is we turn back. We're only a week out, and The Bellator is stocked for the month-long journey with a large reserve of emergency fuel and rations to support the numbers onboard beyond our projected travel time. Retreating won't be an issue, but that'll ground us until the storm clears. You'll also need to charter new flights to Corr'us Sanctum. Unfortunately, Headquarters won't refund your tickets because of the waivers you were required to sign to travel through the Mors Expanse." The crowd grumbles at that information, but I expected this reaction. The rich love to bemoan extra expenses despite having more money than they know what to do with.

"Our second option is to wait in the hopes the storm passes,"

I continue, but when people nod in agreement, I raise my hands. "There are downsides to remaining here. We're currently hovering on the edge of the Expanse. Sitting here indefinitely will eat at our fuel reserves. We can afford to waste some, but at a certain point, it'll force us to turn around. This will also leave us exposed to pirates, and while The Bellator is one of the largest and most well-equipped battle cruises, we cannot fight a horde. If we wait, my recommendation is only for a few days since there's no predicting if the storm will clear or if it'll increase in size."

"If both options end with retreat, shouldn't we turn around now instead of wasting time?" a passenger asks.

"That's a valid point," I say. "But we would risk turning around only to discover the storm passed quickly. It's why I brought the decision to you. I want everyone to be comfortable with how we proceed."

"I don't want to meet up with pirates," a beautiful blonde chimes in. "But I think waiting here for a little while won't hurt. I have a photoshoot scheduled shortly after we dock in Corr'us Sanctum, and I hate to miss it."

"We can afford to wait a few days," I say. "The Bellator's defense team will be on high alert. Protecting you and this ship is our main priority."

The crowd erupts in murmurs of agreement. It seems everyone on board recognizes the second option is the favorable choice, but just when they move to voice their final decision, Serling steps forward. Her arms are folded over her chest, and her black travel suit highlights all the right—or the wrong, depending on how you look at it—places. She pins me with her glare, and it's like the devil reincarnated inside this gorgeous woman.

"You said there were three options," she says coolly, and it strikes me she's the only one in this crowd unbothered by the threat we face. For a split second, I wonder if she's truly that skilled at hiding her emotions or if she wants danger to befall us.

"You only mentioned two, Mr. Thorne. I would like to hear the third…" she pauses, and I can tell by the way she inhales that she's readying to threaten me with her position. "Being that my father paid for this trip, I should make the final decision. Not them."

There it is.

"Respectfully, Miss Ambrose, this isn't about money but the safety of this ship and its passengers."

"The third option," she demands, and I grind my molars in irritation. Her disregard for others makes me want to leave her stranded at the nearest waylay station to become someone else's problem.

"We take an uncharted course through the Mors," I answer. "Our current route is the shortest distance through the Expanse, and it's the only one mapped by Headquarters. I've successfully flown it dozens of times, but straying into the unknown could push us into dangers far greater than the one this storm poses."

"But it wouldn't delay our trip," she says.

"It undoubtedly would. We would need to swing far off course to avoid the storm, and the Mors is unpredictable. One misstep could strand us in treacherous space with rapidly dwindling fuel reserves."

"Well, I think it's still a better option than sitting—"

"It doesn't matter what you think." I step forward, my sudden closeness forcing her to look up at me. "It doesn't matter who your father is. We decide as a group."

"Maybe we should wait a day or two," the blonde model interrupts, but Serling throws her a death glare, and the girl recoils.

"I agree." I stare Serling down as I speak, watching her anger boil over, and it worries me she wants to charge headlong into the deadliest stretch of space. What is she running from that's making her reckless? Or is she so out of touch with reality that she feels invincible? Money will do that to people, especially the beautiful. It makes them believe they're untouchable, even by nature. "I think we should give the storm a few hours, and now that you've heard my opinion, let's vote."

A notification pings, and I pull up the communication thread on my screen. It's late, and normally I'm asleep by now, but the storm's growing intensity won't let me rest. Instead of lying in my quarters staring at the ceiling, I opted to study every chart and article written about the Mors. Despite Serling's opposition, the crew and passengers voted with me. They chose to wait for a few days before we decide between turning back or forging an alternative path, and I want to be prepared. Unfortunately, little is known about the Expanse save for its bloodlust, so these hours of studying have done nothing but make my eyes burn.

I scan the message, worried that at this hour it's an update on the ever-increasing storm, but it's a noise complaint from the passengers' quarters. The crew tried to address the situation, but it was to no avail. They're requesting I handle it, and I rub the sleep from my face. I'm sure the guests have turned to alcohol to ease their anxiety, but I'm the pilot. I am leader and law aboard The Bellator, not a babysitter to the rich and famous.

I drag my tall frame off the chair and glance down at my mostly bare body. My shorts do nothing to hide the disfigured flesh, and knowing the scars will undoubtedly freak the passengers out, I begrudgingly pull on my uniform. It's too late for this shit, and if the crew is requesting that I handle the disruption, it means the disturbance has gotten out of hand. I pray a fight hasn't broken out. I can hold my own, but the wealthy don't love it when a man like me humiliates them in a drunken brawl.

Music and rowdy voices greet me the second I slip through

the airlock to the passenger quarters. Alcohol is definitely involved, and I understand why the noise complaint traveled up the chain of command. The volume is obnoxious, and an older couple hovers in the entrance of their private suite waiting for me.

"Thank goodness you're here," the husband says. "We tried to ignore them, but it's become unreasonable."

"I understand," I say with a gracious smile. "I'll take care of it. Have a good night."

I give them a respectful nod and continue to the common room. Just as I round the corner, a drunk couple stumbles past me, a whirlwind of limbs and laughter as they kiss. They don't notice me as they stagger down the hall, clothes falling off their bodies, and I remind myself that I'm no longer a commanding officer in the military. I can't barge into this party fueled by rage and force these passengers to fall in line. They expect a certain amount of groveling and bowing from men like me, but with a storm of this magnitude approaching and the Mors hovering on our doorstep, civility will be a test of my willpower.

"Ladies and gentlemen," I say, using my controls to override the sound system. The room plunges into silence, and the crowd turns toward me with expressions of bewilderment. "I'm glad you're enjoying your time here aboard The Bellator, but due to the late hour, we've received a noise complaint. Feel free to continue the party, but I must ask that you be respectful to those trying to sleep."

"Come join us, Mr. Thorne," the blonde model from earlier slurs as she emerges from the crowd, and I don't miss the suggestive tone of her words. "I'll get you a drink." Her drunken body moves seductively, but I remain firmly where I stand. I'm well aware of my sex appeal when clothes cover my scars. Passengers often flirt with me, but it's a line I never cross. Passengers are and always will be off-limits to me and my crew.

"You won't get him a drink," Serling's cool voice says before

I can decline, and she emerges from the crowd like a demon in the night. She's wearing a plain black dress, but on her, it's exquisite. It's designed perfectly for her figure with barely-there straps and an open back. The hem is just long enough, the waist cinched to hug the curve of her hips, the top low and loose, ensuring her nipples would slip out if she bent forward. The garment blends seamlessly with her black hair, and the simple gold jewelry strangling her throat matches the gold heels that wrap around her ankles. She is breathtaking in her cruelty, and I instantly know she was the instigator behind this party. She's why my crew couldn't shut it down, and every ounce of patience leaves my body. I understand why she's so beautiful. It counters the ugly soul that beats in her chest.

"No thank you, I don't want a drink," I say to the model, who looks crestfallen that she's been denied, but she still smiles with flushed cheeks as I address her. "I simply came here to request you keep the volume down as our other guests are sleeping."

I turn to leave when Serling's voice fills the now-silent room. "Stop batting your eyes at him, Meli," she says with cool disgust. "It's pathetic."

I don't acknowledge her words. I won't give her the satisfaction, but then I hear the model, Meli, make an embarrassed sound.

"He's a washed-up soldier," Serling continues, determined to humiliate us. "And he's old. Watching you flirt with him makes me cringe. Have some fucking self-respect."

"Meli, can I walk you to your room? Perhaps it's best to turn in for the night?" I extend a hand to the girl as I pin Serling with a dangerous expression. I've made grown men cry with this stare, and it brings me a small thread of satisfaction to watch her bravado falter.

"Um…" Meli glances at Serling as if seeking permission, but all she finds is icy hostility. "Yes, thank you." She takes my arm, and without another word, I lead her from the room.

"Fine," Serling spits at our retreating forms. "Slum it with the old man. It's humiliating, but I guess some people enjoy trash. Don't say I didn't warn you when he can't get it up to fuck you."

SERLING

"Slum it with the old man," I call after Meli and Driver. "It's humiliating."

Neither of them looks back as they leave, but every other pair of eyes study me. They watch to see what I'll do next, who I'll target next, but they're inconsequential. A group of useless airheads drinking the night away as we barrel into danger. The moment Driver leaves my sight, the fight leaves my body, and suddenly I want nothing more than to get out of this dress. I'm far too sober to deal with this many intoxicated people.

I don't know why I said those things. I don't know what about that pilot fills me with such hatred, but the second he looks at me, I want to rip him to shreds. Perhaps it's because he's the first person to challenge me. Most men cower before my wealth, chasing what my name could do for them, but never loving me. Most refuse to even disagree with me. But Driver Thorne? He pushes all my buttons, and it brings the devil out of me. I want to eviscerate him, to flay him open until he is bleeding on the floor at my feet, and I hate that man more than I've ever hated anyone. I don't like the reason for my visceral reaction to him, though. I don't like what it means, because when I look deep inside myself, my anger isn't with him. It's with what he represents. He's something I can never have, and he isn't old. He's only eleven years my senior at forty, and everything about him makes my body come alive. He towers over me with hands built for power. His black hair is just long enough for my fingers to thread through, and I want to grip it tight as I stare into his almost black eyes. He is all height and dominance and intelligence, and it enrages me. He represents the freedom I'll never have, and so I punish him for it. I hurt him, because if I cause him pain, maybe I won't hurt as much.

CHAPTER 4

DRIVER

An alarm shatters the early morning hours, and I jerk awake. Panic floods my chest as I register what this warning means, and I scramble out of bed to lean over my personal monitors. The storm held steady all night, but it suddenly surged back to life. It has tripled in size again, and with a knot of dread coiling in my stomach, I realize it changed course. It's headed straight for us.

"Shit." I grab a shirt and pull it on as I race out of my room. The pilot quarters are located just off the cockpit, and I slide into my station seconds later. The advanced equipment of my controls shows the true magnitude of the storm, and for a single moment, panic owns my body.

"Sir?" A navigator rushes into the cockpit.

"How did this happen?" I initiate the emergency protocol.

"I don't know. We monitored it all night. There were no changes, then suddenly, it shifted. It's moving fast." He comes up behind me and brings a satellite image to the forefront of my screens. "See here." He points to a bulging mass that has extended outward from the main storm cell. It's miles away still, but it's curling alongside the ship to surround us. "We can't retreat with this flanking us. If we don't move now, the storm's center will trap The Bellator."

He plays a simulated progression for me, and my stomach drops as I watch how quickly it'll consume us. We can't move forward, nor can we fall back. Our only escape is to plunge headlong into the uncharted miles of the Mors. The Expanse might be dangerous, but all our other options are fatal.

"Shit." I minimize the projection and pull up my controls. "Move every passenger to the emergency hangar. No one stays behind in their rooms, you understand? I want everyone strapped in and accounted for."

"Yes, sir."

"I'm going to contact Headquarters and alert them to our change in course. Make sure the crew straps in as soon as the passengers are secure."

"Will do, and, sir? Have you ever flown in a situation like this? Perhaps when you were in the military?" His voice is terrified, and everything within me wishes I could lie to him.

"I've been in tough spots, yes. Have I faced a storm of this size? No. I don't think anyone has."

SERLING

The alarm won't quiet, and I move to the observatory windows. Space is hauntingly dark, but unlike the last time I gazed out through this thick pane of glass, I notice a gentle haze in the distance. I squint at the unusual color, trying to make out what it is, but it's the endless alarm that clues me in. It's the storm, and if I can see it…

I turn on my heels and race to the lift, leaving the solitude of the observatory behind. I couldn't sleep last night. My cruelty churned in my stomach, making me nauseous, and despite my overly spacious suite, I felt claustrophobic. I took to wandering the lonely halls of the ship and discovered this observation deck. The vastness of space makes me feel inconsequential, and that insignificance calmed my anxiety. I lost track of time as I studied the intimidating expanse of death before us. I've never seen the Mors before, and that my father chartered this flight through it tells me all I need to know about my standing with him. He wants me back; my duty more important than my safety. He refused to wait another eight months for a cruise to fly me around this dangerous stretch, which is why, when Thorne suggested charting an alternative course, I voted for that option. If my father wishes I travel through the deadliest part of the galaxy, I might as well witness all the destruction it has to offer.

The lift delivers me to the flight deck, and I step out in search of the pilot. He should be made aware that the storm is visible to the naked eye. With the radiation that close, we should move, but The Bellator is still hovering motionless in space.

"Excuse me, where is Mr. Thorne?" I ask a crew member as she races past.

"Miss Ambrose, please follow the emergency instructions," the woman calls over her shoulder, ignoring my question. "Make your way to the guest hangar and strap it."

"But where is—"

She disappears around the corner without a backward glance, and I scan my surroundings. The ship is an orchestra of chaos, but I assume Driver is in the cockpit. I ignore the woman's advice to join the other passengers and pick my way through the pandemonium. I make a few wrong turns, but I eventually locate him as he runs the preflight checks.

"Mr. Thorne?"

"What?" he snaps without looking at me, but then, as if suddenly recognizing my voice, his head whips around. "What the fuck are you doing here? You should be in the—"

"I was on the observation deck, and I could see the storm." I cut him off. "It's moved closer."

"We know," he spits out as the engines roar to life. "Go downstairs, Miss Ambrose."

"Sir," a male voice comes from the communicator. "We're in position. Ready when you are."

"Shit." He looks back at me, all hints of the professional gone. "You won't have time to get downstairs. Sit down."

"What?"

"I said sit," he shouts. "Wedge yourself in that corner and don't stand up. This flight will get turbulent, and I can't have you falling."

"I do..." I start to argue. I refuse to sit on his filthy cockpit floor in my designer dress without a safety harness.

"Now, Ambrose!" He thrusts the throttle forward, The Bellator surging to life, and my skull smacks the wall as we launch for the Mors Expanse.

DRIVER

"Ambrose?" I shout over my shoulder as I hear her land hard. "Ambrose? Shit! Serling, answer me."

"Some pilot you are," she spits. "When my father hears of your disregard for my safety, he'll crucify you."

I smirk as I push the Bellator to her limits. The woman is fine. "Stay seated. The next few minutes will be rough."

I'm shocked when she listens, but the roar of the engines

makes conversation impossible. I haven't pushed a ship this hard since my days in the military, but the storm is increasing with every second. Our window of escape is closing fast, and if we miss it by so much as an inch, the radiation will flood The Bellator. The faintest contact is fatal, and even if we survived the initial breach, the sickness would ruin our bodies. As vehemently as I hate the woman at my back, I can't allow her to die of radiation poisoning. It's a brutal death, and not even the devil deserves that end.

Minutes bleed into an hour with alarming speed. My muscles ache with tension. My skin is slick with sweat, and I can tell by my navigators' voices that the crew feels the stress as acutely as I do. Evading this storm as we enter the Mors Expanse's unfamiliar territory requires a level of concentration and skill I haven't had to rely on since the battle that ruined my body, but this is why I'm the best. This is why the wealthy pay my inordinate fees, because no matter how close the storm moves. No matter how hopeless our situation seems, harm never befalls this ship. I'll make sure of it.

"Ladies and gentlemen," I say over the ship's speaker system. "I realize this past hour was stressful, but we've successfully evaded the storm. There's a possibility it'll catch up with us, but my team will monitor it closely. You're now free to move about the ship, but I request that you remain alert. We've officially entered an uncharted territory of the Expanse. Headquarters is aware of our course deviation. We'll be in regular contact with them about our situation, but I must remind you that even if we were on our original path, the Mors is dangerous. Please follow all safety precautions and crew instructions."

I end the transmission and lean back in my seat. The stiffness in my neck has seeped into my skull, forming a dull ache, and I twist my spine in search of relief.

"If you had followed my suggestion and entered a different

section of the Mors instead of waiting, we could have avoided this nightmare," Serling says, stealing my peace. There'll be no reprieve from this headache with her present. "Fleeing that storm almost killed us, and for what? So you could side with the stupidity onboard and appease their—"

"Miss Ambrose," I interrupt. "You've never flown the Mors, so I realize you don't understand, but traveling through even the charted courses is deadly. It's why you're currently sitting on the floor of a warship and not a cruise liner. Very few pilots have the clearance to fly the Expanse, and many have died attempting this run." I stand, crossing the cockpit until I tower over her defiant form. "Changing course is not something we do... ever. Storms rarely grow this aggressively, but the Mors is always dangerous. I didn't side with the others because I was appeasing their stupidity, as you call it. I opted to wait because taking an alternate path is a last resort. One that could very well kill us."

She opens her mouth to argue, but I step into her personal space, silencing her as I crouch before her. "We're committed to this course of action now, but I don't like it. From this moment on, your luxury trip is over. We're in hostile territory, and I'll be damned if I let anything happen to this ship. That includes you, Miss Ambrose. You wanted this option. I just hope you're prepared for the severity of its reality."

"I understand the risk," she snarls, always demanding the last word, but I don't have the time to argue with a spoiled brat.

"Miss Ambrose, please return to the passengers' quarters. We'll notify you of any updates." I open the cockpit's airlock, signaling this conversation is at an end. For a moment, she seems to search for another advantage in this argument, but realizing she's lost this round, she steps for the exit. Her concession is a minor triumph, but our battle is far from over. I don't doubt that her silence is a strategic move and that when she strikes back, it'll hit me in the most excruciating way.

"Have a pleasant—" I start, but my voice dies when she glances out the window behind me with a terrified expression.

"What's that?" Her words falter.

For a split second, I assume her distraction is a ploy to gain the upper hand, but her fear forces me to move. I spin on my heels, but I barely register the object flying for us at an ungodly speed before my world explodes.

CHAPTER 5

DRIVER

Blood drips down my neck. That's what my brain fixates on as I regain consciousness. Alarms blare. My body aches. The Bellator's movements are severely erratic, yet the only thing my mind can process is the oozing dampness. It tickles as it slides over my skin. I should wipe it off. I should sit up. But I can't. Blood drips down my neck, and…

I jerk awake, sitting up so fast my head screams in protest. I'm sprawled across the cockpit floor as alarms clutter the air. Sparks spit dangerously from where the wall paneling ripped off and severed the wires, and the ship moves in a way that tells me we're experiencing engine failure.

I push to my hands and knees, a curse on my tongue as pain engulfs my body, but I force myself to move. My arms give out twice before I reach my chair, but I refuse to yield. I crawl through the chaos and pull myself up to the controls, and the sight that greets me settles terror in my chest. I've been unconscious for fifty-four minutes. For almost an hour, I lay on this floor as The Bellator catapulted deep into the Mors Expanse. Navigation is shot to hell, so I have no clue where we are. Communications are down, which means even if I did, I couldn't alert Headquarters. We're lost in the most dangerous stretch of space on a ship that's experiencing catastrophic systems failure. The engines are burning. Life support is operating at critical efficiency, and the escape pods were destroyed...

"What the...?" I lean forward because that can't be right. It's impossible, yet the alarms all warn the same thing. So much more than the escape pods are gone.

An explosion rips through the ship before I can fully make sense of what I'm seeing, and The Bellator pitches wildly. The force throws me from my chair, and a rib cracks as I slam into the controls. I roar in pain, my voice lost under a deafening alert.

WARNING:

IMPACT IMMINENT

"Fuck." I ignore the agony in my chest and climb into my seat, strapping into the harness as I pray the engines retained enough power to avoid a crash.

WARNING:

IMPACT IMMINENT

A planet comes into view as the ship spins, and I shout in frustration as I do everything in my capacity to evade its gravitational pull.

WARNING:

IMPACT IMMINENT

My attempts are useless. This vessel's damage is fatal, and

there's no escaping the inevitable. I hit the comms to address the crew, but the dead controls signal they were destroyed. I can't warn them. I can't help them. All I can do is pray we survive the impact. The Bellator's hull is heavily reinforced, but with the explosions ripping through her belly, I doubt she'll endure. This is her end. The foreboding in my chest tells me it's mine as well.

Everything after that happens in a blink of an eye. An explosion pushes the ship into the planet's gravity, and it's the strongest gravitational pull I've ever experienced. It drags us down, the ship's ruins breaking apart as we burn through the atmosphere. The air is alive with warning sirens. My chest is alive with panic. We're gaining speed, and as I watch space give way to sky, I come to terms with the fact that these are my last moments. I don't expect to survive the collision, so I stare out the window, appreciating the beauty of the blue sky. I try to enjoy the majesty of my final view, and then the Bellator crashes on an unknown alien planet in the vast hostility that is the Mors Expanse.

The crash doesn't kill me, but it doesn't knock me out either, so I remain conscious for every excruciating detail. The impact, the fires, the pain. It's unbearable, and I don't know how long I sit strapped to my seat, unable to move. It might have been an hour. It might have been days. I lose track, for all I can focus on is the agony, my aching war wounds reminding me of my mortality.

I don't understand how I survived, yet my suffering informs me I'm very much alive. The Bellator was not so lucky. She'll never fly again, which means I'm trapped on an unknown planet that's hundreds of miles from the last location I sent Headquarters. They won't know where to search, and the savage vastness of the Mors will ensure rescue never finds us. My body shudders as I inhale, the weight of our reality terrifying, and the fear drives me to my feet. The Bellator is well stocked, and if we ration creatively, we may be able to stretch the provisions. My biggest concern is the Med Bay, though. People were undoubtedly injured or killed in the crash. I broke at least one rib. We need that sector of the ship intact if we're going to survive.

I unsteadily exit the cockpit's airlock and limp to the navigator and crew bays. They're located a half level down from the cockpit, requiring me to move through two airlocks and down a short flight of stairs that aggravate my right leg, but I need to find the crew. We need to make a plan and help the injured...

I freeze in my tracks as I arrive at my destination, a new breed of terror worming into my soul. There's a massive hole in the ship's hull, and not one human is in sight. I don't want to believe it. I can't. But I have to. An explosion ripped an extensive wound in the wall beside the navigator's bays and sucked every single member into the darkness of space. My entire crew is gone.

I stumble to the controls and pull up the employee and passenger logs. We equipped every person on board with a small monitor to track them and their vitals in case of an emergency, and a tear slips from my eye when I see the crew list. Every one of them is dead. With blinding panic, I pull up the passengers' trackers, and I can't stop the devastated roar that pours out of me at the sight of the manifest. All of them are gone. Every last human life has been extinguished. Not a single heartbeat registers on the monitors, signaling a catastrophic loss of life, and I sink to a seat as my body goes numb. Everyone died. Everyone. I'm the sole survivor of this crash, and I collapse forward with my head in my hands. Why didn't it kill me too? Why did it let me live when it stole every other life?

A strangled and ugly sob escapes me. I don't understand how this happened. What crashed into us after the storm, and why am I the only one it spared? I was responsible for these people. It was my job to protect them, to guide them safely home, and I let them die. I failed them. Perhaps that's why I survived this crash. Dying is too easy a punishment for my failure.

Beep... beep... beep.

I jerk upright at the sound. A heartbeat. The monitor is registering a heartbeat. There's another survivor, and with shaking fingers, I pull up their profile. I read the name, and then I read it again because I don't believe my eyes.

Serling Ambrose is alive.

SERLING

Every breath is a lesson in pain. The air is like knives to my lungs. Something sharp digs into my spine, but I can't move. I can't lift my head or bend my legs, and I'm choking on my own breath as I lie flat on my back. All I can see is blue sky. We must have crashed on an alien planet, but all I remember is I was standing with Driver when a projectile suddenly hurtled for the ship. It was silent and fast, none of The Bellator's sensors detecting it, and that alone warned me what it was. It wasn't organic, nor was it the dangers of the Mors. It was military; the design reminiscent of a missile, and in that terrifying second before impact, I knew it hadn't come from the pirates who hover on the Expanse's outskirts in search of unsuspecting prey. I've heard enough about pirate attacks to know they rarely operate with expensive tech. They use recycled materials and rely on the element of surprise. They target less fortified ships, but the Bellator is a warrior among the stars. It's the reason my father chartered the legendary Driver Thorne. Pirates would never risk an assault on such a fortress, which leaves only one other explanation. Someone of incredible means and motive targeted this warship with surgical precision. The only question my pain-riddled brain cannot answer is who was the target? Was it Thorne? It wouldn't be the first time radicals tried to eliminate him. If the gossip is to be believed, he still wears the extensive scars from that infamous attack, and he'll be a threat to insurgents as long as he lives. Or was I the mark? Was someone trying to end the Ambrose line?

I groan as I try to sit, but the warmth coating my skin spreads with the effort. I can't tilt my neck down, but even if I could, I'm afraid to look at my chest. I know what that sticky liquid is, and I'm afraid to see proof that I'm dying. No one is coming for me. When the missile hit, Driver flew in one direction and I in the other. The cockpit sealed automatically, a safety measure to ensure the pilot survives to evade the threat, and as I lay screaming on the floor, I knew I had to get out of the open.

Explosions ripped through the lower levels of the Bellator, forcing her to spin with wild movements. I had noticed the pilot's quarters off to the side, and I crawled on my stomach to Driver's room. There was plenty inside that could kill me, but it was a smaller space, and using his mattress as a barrier, I wedged myself under his desk. I passed out at one point, my head slamming into the wall as an explosion launched us into hyper-speeds. I can't be certain, but I think the ship also made a long-distance jump. Her speed fluctuated, but even trapped in his windowless room, I knew it was too fast. We were barreling into the Mors Expanse on a burning ship.

I lost all track of time, but my gut told me that any hope of salvation vanished hours ago. Based on the ship's unguided movements, Driver was dead, and with one bone-jarring explosion, The Bellator succumbed to this planet's gravity. The impact ripped the ship apart, flinging me from the pilot's quarters and onto a rocky surface. Razor-sharp protrusions dig into my spine, and despite the tears and terror, my body refused to pass out. I've been awake for every brutal second of this crash. I survived the impact, but I wish I hadn't. I heard the force of The Bellator hitting the ground. I felt the impact in my bones. No one survived that, which means I'm alone on an alien planet in the most dangerous stretch of our galaxy, bleeding out with what I fear is a broken back.

My hands shake as the tears come. *Are you happy, Father? Is this what you wanted?* Maybe the missile was meant for me. Here ends the Ambrose dynasty. Serves my father right for gambling with my life in the name of duty. I hope the Federation rots in—

"Serling?" a male voice breaks through the silence, and I grimace. I'm dying, yet the universe insists on punishing me until my last breath. I don't want to hallucinate his voice. Not now. Please, by all that is holy, let me die in peace.

"Serling!" he screams. "Where are you?"

My breath catches in my throat. He sounds so real. How is that possible?

"Serling Ambrose, answer me, goddamn it!"

My god, he is real. "Here…" I whisper, my inaudible voice raw and weak.

"Fuck." His voice moves further away. He's leaving. He can't leave.

"Here…" My mouth barely works. "Please…" I don't hear him anymore. He's probably a figment of my imagination, but if there's even the smallest chance that Driver's alive, I need him to find me. So, I ignore the pain, the blood, the fear, and I scream.

"I'm up here!"

DRIVER

I laugh when I see her name on the screen. A full-bellied, *'Are you fucking serious?'* kind of laugh. The universe must hate me, for not only am I one of the sole survivors of a catastrophic crash, but the powers-that-be cursed me with her. A navigator, a medic, or a member of the defense team is essential to our survival on this strange planet, but Serling Ambrose? That self-centered heiress will be the death of us.

I'm ashamed to admit that for a fraction of a second, I contemplate leaving her to fend for herself. I don't want to risk my life for such an ungrateful human being, but as the monitor beeps her heartbeat, I know I can't leave her. I've never left anyone behind, and I refuse to start now, even if being stranded with her is a punishment I don't deserve.

Serling was standing beside me when that object hit the Bellator. I believe I know what I saw in those seconds before impact, but I should find her before I dwell on that terrifying reality. If she's injured, she may not have much time.

The hole in the navigation level's hull killed the entire crew as it sucked them out into space, so if she's still alive, it stands to reason she never left the pilot's airlock. I didn't see her on my walk down from the cockpit, which means she most likely crawled into my reinforced room. Serling may be an awful person, but I have no doubt the woman's smart. If she was conscious, she would've found a safer location than the open halls.

I limp to my quarters, but the sight that greets me steals my breath. My room is gone, ripped apart at the seams, and if she was in there... I shudder at the thought. Her heart still beats, but for how much longer? The crash destroyed this section of the ship, scattering what had once been my home across the rugged landscape. If she was here when we crashed, she was undoubtedly thrown out onto that treacherous terrain. Not even someone I hate deserves to leave this life like that.

"Serling?" I move through the ruins and step out into the open. The light brown rocks are sharp and uninviting as they slowly morph into a cliff a few yards from the crash site. There's no vegetation or wildlife in sight, but the area offers a host of blind spots. Between the rocky protrusions and the debris, she could be anywhere.

"Serling!" I shout as I carefully pick through the chaos. "Where are you?"

I fall silent as I search, but only stillness answers me. My body screams in agony as I climb over the uneven surface, but I don't stop moving. I scour the wreckage for any sign of human life, for drops of blood, for a glimpse of her midnight black hair, but I find nothing.

"Serling Ambrose, answer me, goddamn it!"

But she doesn't answer. Only the sound of the wind reaches my ears, and I turn back toward the crash. Maybe I was mistaken. Maybe she made her way to the passenger emergency hangar.

"Fuck." The second that theory pops into my head, I know it's a pipe dream. None of the passengers survived, which means she'd be dead if she had hidden down there. No, she's here, but where? If she's unconscious, I might not find her in time. The sharp rocks digging into my feet as I climb are ruthless. I can't imagine what they did to her body when she fell.

"I'm up here!" A weak voice shatters the air, and I freeze.

"Serling?"

"Up…" her faint voice breaks, but it's enough. It sounds from both behind and above me, and I study the cliff with a sinking sensation. She's up there somewhere, and if the impact compromised her spine, moving her to the ship could kill her.

"I'm coming!" I race across the rocks with adrenaline-fueled momentum. "Hold on, I'm coming."

"Here." Her voice is even weaker than before, but I hear it and adjust my trajectory.

"Keep speaking." I climb as fast as my pain allows, but she remains silent. "Come on, Serling, speak to me…. Please."

Her failure to respond terrifies me, and I force my speed to increase. It takes another ten minutes of searching, but just when I've lost hope, I spot manicured nails hanging over a ledge.

"Serling!" I vault up the last few feet and inhale my shock when I see her. She's lying on her back, her hands shaking by her side, but she's conscious. Her terrified eyes find mine, and blood oozes from where her flesh presses into the rocks. I try not to react at the sight. I don't want her to panic at my facial expressions, but her rigid form settles fear in my gut. I don't like how much blood is spreading over the stones.

"You're okay," I lie, pulling myself next to her to grab her hand, and tears spill from her eyes as she watches me. "Can you move?"

"No," she mouths.

"No, as in it hurts, or no, as in you physically can't?"

Her tears worsen at my question, but her fingers tighten around mine, proving at least her hands work.

"Good girl. Where does it hurt? Is it your back?" She

squeezes me again. "Shit... We need to get you to the Med Bay, but I can't move you if your spine is broken." I start to retreat, but her grip tightens. "I'll return with a medical transport, I promise."

Her tears come faster, and for a second, she's no longer the spoiled heiress I despise but a young woman terrified by her pain. She's still wearing that revealing designer dress, but it's torn and ripped and soaked in blood. It barely covers her body, which gives me a gruesome view of her injuries.

"I'll be back," I repeat. "I've never left a man behind, and I won't start now." I attempt to pull my hand from her grasp, but ever the stubborn woman, she holds on tight. She stares defiantly at me and then lifts her head off the stone with a scream of pain.

"Serling, stop!" I try to push her down, but she keeps moving. She sobs through her agony, and unable to bear the sound, I scoop her into my arms. Blood coats my hands as I pick her up, but to my relief, nothing happens as I cradle her against my chest. Perhaps her spine is merely bruised and not broken, but either way, she won't let me leave her. Her entire body shakes as she cries, but she's safe now, and so help me God, I will get her to the Med Bay alive. I may hate this woman, but she will survive. I'll probably live to regret this decision to rescue her, but I'll save her all the same.

SERLING

His face is the first thing I see when I wake, and in those foggy seconds between unconsciousness and awareness, my body reacts to his rugged beauty. His dark hair frames a mature and angular bone structure, and while he isn't pretty like the men who travel the elite circles, his unique features are undeniably handsome. He's the most alluring man I've ever seen, and in my weak state, my mind wonders what it would be like to trace his full lips with my tongue, to feel his incredibly muscular chest beneath my fingertips.

But then I remember how I cried when I thought he was going to leave me bleeding on those rocks. How I clung to him as he climbed down the cliff, and my embarrassment morphs into a violent hatred. I don't let people see my weakness, and if someone is unfortunate enough to witness a breach in my shell, they suffer the consequences.

"You're awake," Driver says as he moves closer, his voice neither kind nor cruel. "How do you feel?"

"How extensive were my injuries?" I ask, ignoring his question, and while he does a good job of hiding his annoyance, I can tell he's taken aback by my directness.

"Thankfully, the Med Bay survived the crash with minimal damage." He crosses his powerful arms over his sculpted chest as he nods to our surroundings. "You are an extremely lucky woman, Miss Ambrose. You were thrown from the ship, yet your injuries were mild. Substantial bruising and a few lacerations that required stitches, but nothing the Med Bay couldn't handle with ease."

"I wouldn't label my situation as lucky," I spit, and it bothers me he doesn't so much as flinch at my tone. Most men would cower and bow and apologize, but he just stares at me with indifference. "How many survived the crash?"

"Two."

"Two?"

He glances meaningly between us, and understanding hits me like a punch in the mouth.

"You're it?" Panic floods me. I can't be stranded here alone with this man.

"I'm it," he confirms. "You've been asleep since yesterday afternoon, so I seized the quiet as an opportunity to assess our situation," he continues, as if I'm a soldier under his command and not the heir to the entire Federation. "Whatever struck The Bellator was aimed at the passenger levels," he says, and the intensity of his gaze makes me wonder how close a look he got at the missile before it hit us. Does he suspect that I'm the reason for this catastrophe? He studies me for a moment as if waiting for me to react, but when I don't, he resumes his debrief. "It killed the passengers instantly, and the subsequent explosions forced us off course. We're somewhere deep in the Mors Expanse, but without navigation, it's impossible to tell where. Even if we knew our position, it knocked out our communications, so we can't contact Headquarters."

"We're stranded here?" I bolt upright despite the pain.

"Yes," he says as if this isn't a death sentence. "The explosions that followed the initial impact ripped a hole in the hull on the navigation level and pulled the crew out into space. The cockpit is reinforced because, in the event of an emergency, survival often relies on the pilot's ability to evade the threat. We most likely survived because we were in a separate airlock from everyone else. I found a few bodies in The Bellator's remains, but no survivors. As for the ship, she'll never fly again, so unless a rescue recovers us, we'll never leave this planet."

"My father will tear the galaxy apart until he finds me," I say.

"I hope so." Driver shrugs. "But I wouldn't bank on it. They don't know where we are. Headquarters knew we were evading a storm, so when we lost contact, they would've assumed we had died. They won't send a rescue into the Mors without proof of survivors, and without communications, we can't signal them."

"My father isn't Headquarters," I say, and Driver's expression of doubt makes me want to claw the look off his face. "He'll find me."

"Well, until then, there are a host of dangers we need to prepare for," he says, placating me as if I'm a child. "The Med Bay sustained minimal damage, but supplies won't last indefinitely. We'll have to be careful how we use them. The passenger levels were destroyed, but the crew quarters and their airlocks are functional, which means we have protected lodgings. It'll take time, but some sections, like the navigation level, can be repaired. We can't fly or communicate beyond this planet, but short-way radios and radar should still work, which will help us map the area. The atmosphere is breathable, but I have no idea what threats the flora and fauna pose. This is the Mors, though, so my money is on toxic vegetation and hostile predators."

"Predators?" My voice breaks.

"Some of the fuel reserves burned in the explosions, but we have a decent store to work with. It would be wise to find alternative means of heat, cooling, and power, though." He ignores my interruption. "The food and water supplies were largely untouched. Since it's just us, that month's supply plus the emergency provisions will last significantly longer if we ration, but it's still best we locate other food sources."

"Do you really believe there are predators on this planet?" I repeat. My mind swirls with all the horrible things he's listed. Low fuel, no communications, me living in the crew quarters, but it's the predator comment I fixate on.

"This is the Mors," he says with exasperation, and I can read in his exhausted body language that I'm the last person he wants to be stranded with. I know he wishes I was a soldier trained to handle the stress of a disaster, and his disappointment in my survival burns shame and rage in my chest. "Of course, there are predators."

DRIVER

I stifle a smirk when I introduce Serling to her new quarters. The room's guarded by functioning airlocks, which means she'll be safe, but the space is only wide enough for the narrow bed welded to the wall, a desk, a dresser, and a cramped shower that doubles as a toilet. I doubt she's ever seen a space this small. Her closet is probably double this size, but the mattress is comfortable, the doors lock, and the bathroom works. I found clothes in her size in a female crew member's dresser, and I hate to admit how much pleasure it gave me to watch her don the uniform. The material is standard issue, and while it's comfortable, it's affordable, something Serling seems to think she's allergic to. I also hate that despite the plain garment, she still looks stunningly beautiful. I've always thought the phrase *'pretty enough to wear a sack'* was bullshit, but observing her examine her accommodations with disgust proves me wrong. Everything about this woman makes my body a traitor to my mind and dignity. She is the devil, yet I want to fall to my knees and worship her. I won't, though. I have self-respect, and if this is how she responds to a clean and safe room, then I dread our upcoming fight to survive. I worry if the predators don't kill her, I might.

"I'll be three rooms down from you, and at night, we'll seal the airlocks," I say. "I'll let you rest since the medication is still healing your injuries, and I'll bring you dinner later. We have a lot of work to start tomorrow."

"Work?" She pins me with a shocked glare, and I wink at her. I can't help it. God, I am going to enjoy making this woman earn her keep.

"Get some sleep, Miss Ambrose," I say as I turn on my heels and exit the airlock before her protests hit my ears. I decide to put some distance between us before she chases me down to argue her way out of manual labor. I know she'll fight me every step, but we won't survive by my efforts alone. The odds are stacked against us, even if we both work tirelessly. There's a chance our days are already numbered, but I'm not the type to accept defeat. The right side of my body bears witness to my will to live.

Something about Serling's fear of predators triggers a concern inside me, though. There are undoubtedly monsters on this planet, but I've faced evil and survived. I've been on planets where the hostile indigenous species were small, so their savagery was no match for mine, but if this world boasts large creatures, we're fucked. The Bellator sustained too much damage to keep an animal of significance out indefinitely, which is why I'm navigating the debris to the defense outposts. I checked the armory while Serling was unconscious, and thankfully, the weapons cache is still intact. The gun and knives are highly effective in combat with human militaries and smaller beasts, but they'll be useless against something large, especially if they have armored shells. I've only encountered one world where the native animals had protective exoskeletons, and that's a memory I would prefer to forget. Our firepower bounced off their hulls, and we lost half our squad on that mission. We never discovered how to kill them, and our salvation came in the form of evacuation. If this planet is home to similar monsters, we stand little chance of survival.

Which is why I stop before the massive exterior guns in one of the ship's multiple defense outposts. Longer than I am tall, the barrels of these deadly weapons deliver a payload strong enough to disintegrate a ship. It's currently welded in position, and I have no clue how or if I can move it, but Headquarters built these to withstand the apocalypse. The Bellator might be in pieces, but this gun in all her glory remains in perfect working condition. Its survival brings me hope. I don't know how, but I'll design a defense utilizing these because I need every monster to know a new alpha predator rules this planet. I didn't survive a seventy-two-hour military assault to die at the claws of monsters. I didn't survive almost losing the entire right side of my body to be defeated by a twenty-nine-year-old devil either, but if I had to bet on what will finally put Driver Thorne in the grave, my money is on Serling Ambrose.

CHAPTER 7

DRIVER

B reakfast." I knock on Serling's door, careful not to tip the tray of food in my grip. She's been in a lot of pain since the crash, which is how I rationalize still treating her like a passenger even though my own damaged body protests my every move, but if we're going to survive, she needs to start pulling her weight. I gave her time to rest and heal, caring for her despite her ungrateful complaining, but that ends today. Babying her will only get us killed since I can't manage all that's required alone. The Federation doesn't exist on this planet. She's no longer an heiress. I won't let her die, but my graciousness ends there.

"Miss Ambrose?" I say when her room remains silent. "You need to eat. We have a long day ahead of us."

A groan comes from inside, and a second later, the door opens. Her black hair tumbles around her face in tangled strands. An oversized shirt hangs loosely to the tops of her thighs, and by the hostility etched into her features, I woke her up.

"Eat this and then meet me in navigation." I push the tray into her reluctant hands. It's piled high with fruit, meat, and cheese. I took inventory of the kitchens while she slept last night.

After dinner, I tried to rest, but the stress of our reality stole my hopes of sleep. I won't be able to relax until our situation is moderately stable, so I used my insomnia to search the pantry. It's stocked with non-perishables, but since we're a luxury warship, we stored a significant amount of fresh foods as well. Our wisest course of action is to eat them first before breaking into the dry reserves. I hope we find edible vegetation on this planet, though, because the supplies won't last indefinitely.

"Why?" she challenges.

"Navigation," I repeat. "In a half hour." I close the door on her annoyed expression and wonder if she'll show up of her own volition. My guess is she'll ignore my request completely or arrive hours too late to be of any real help, and I ponder what crimes I committed in my past life to deserve this punishment.

It's an hour and a half later before she joins me in navigation, but her appearance genuinely surprises me. Serling Ambrose is an intelligent woman, so deep down, she must realize helping me will increase our chances of survival. Still, I wasn't expecting her to show up and had almost removed my shirt to keep from sweating through the fabric. I'm glad I decided against it, though, and opted to push the tight sleeves up my arms instead. I don't want her to see my mangled truth. I shouldn't care what she thinks, but her beauty is flawless. I don't wish to hand her more ammo to use against me.

"We need to seal this." I gesture to the gaping hole in the ship's hull. "We've lost navigation and communications, but this level's other functions are still in working order. We'll need them if we're going to survive, so we should protect the controls from the elements. Can you hold those in place while I weld them?" I nod at the pile of scrap metal I gathered before she decided to grace me with her presence.

"This seems excessive," she says, not bothering to move. "My father is too proud to let his dynasty die out. He'll come for me."

Her words give me pause. Not '*my father loves me*'. Not '*my father can't live without me*'. There's no love in her claim, and for a split second, I wonder if I misjudged her. But then she glances at my sweat-soaked chest with disdain and reminds me of who she really is.

"Yes, it's necessary. Now hold this steady," I order, but when she still doesn't move, I climb off my ladder, grab her arm, and guide her closer. "This isn't just for the equipment's preservation. With this hole, only one airlock protects us from predators entering our living spaces."

As expected, the mention of predators inspires her cooperation, and she seizes the metal sheet. She holds it up obediently, and I resume welding. We work in silence, and to her credit, she refrains from complaining. I wish she would though, because while her mouth is silent, her eyes speak volumes as she glares at me. I don't know if it's my sweat in this humidity, that I'm forcing her to perform manual labor, or if it's purely her hatred of me, but her revulsion is so severe that I almost send her back to her room on two different occasions. I'm not an insecure man, but there's something about her disapproval that cuts deep. Perhaps it's because she's the only other living person on this world, and she can't even hide her repulsion around me.

SERLING

Helping Driver is hell. I can see in his eyes that he's convinced we'll never be rescued, which means I'm stuck in the Mors for the rest of my life with him. But I'm not cut out for manual labor. I'm not a survivalist. I'm not a soldier. *I'm not, I'm not, I'm not.* The list goes on eternally. My arms ache. My back hurts, and this isn't my responsibility. He's the pilot. He's the staff. He should do this, not me.

The endless afternoon soaks us in sweat, and while I hate how my borrowed uniform fits, how it feels, how it smells, how it clings to my clammy skin, what I loathe most is how tight Driver's shirt is. The lightweight sleeves are rolled up to reveal the raised veins weaving down his muscular forearms. The thin material keeps him cool while clothed since he emerged damaged from the brutal attack that ended his military career. He's undoubtedly horribly scarred, and the fabric is meant to hide his flaws, but in reality, it only accentuates his perfections. His every move causes the shirt to tighten around his powerful body. His form is seductive, his movements masculine and intoxicating, and I despise my body's reaction to his. I detest how standing beside him makes me want to run my fingers over his harsh lines and soft curves, but what truly inspires my hatred is that my father will come for me. He has to. He needs me to fulfill my duty, and that means that no matter how I long to know what Driver Thorne's body feels like against mine, he'll always be beyond my reach.

CHAPTER 8

DRIVER

The metal crashes to the ground so hard that the sound hurts my ears. It grates over my knuckles as it falls, peeling the skin back, and small smears of blood bloom across my hands.

"Fuck, Serling, you're supposed to hold it steady," I snarl. She's standing above me on a ladder, holding the last metal sheet in place for me to weld, but she lost her grip. I realize I'm overreacting. This sheet is heavy, and while she's toned, her lithe body comes from exercises performed inside on foam mats while wearing designer activewear. She isn't used to manual labor, and by the damp spots on her uniform, helping me seal this gaping hole has pushed her to her limits. Anyone could've dropped it, but my patience is running thin. Working side by side with her disgust has turned me into someone I don't recognize or particularly like. Her disdain is easily ignored from afar, but this proximity reveals her every glare, every frown, every sigh. She keeps glancing at my ribs as if being this close to my scars has her crawling out of her skin, and I'm tempted to take my shirt off and really give her something to cringe over.

"I am holding it," she spits back, jumping off the ladder. "My hands are sweating because it's fucking hot in here. How do you expect me to work in these conditions? If my father knew you had me working at all, he would skin you alive." She moves across the room and unzips her uniform, shoving it down to her waist. She ties the one-piece garment around her by its sleeves, leaving her bare save for the small white tank top she has on underneath. It's soaked with sweat, making the thin fabric completely see-through, and of course, she isn't wearing a bra. Her peaked nipples stick out through the material, their pink shade unmistakably visible, and I hate how utterly perfect her form is when mine is so disfigured. I wish my traitorous body didn't react to hers. My mind and heart cannot stand Serling Ambrose, but my dick betrays my resolve. I'm mad my flesh is so weak because she is the worst breed of human to grace this galaxy. The gods certainly have a cruel sense of humor because her beauty is flawless, and I can't drag my eyes away from the mesmerizing swell of her cleavage.

"So, your father would prefer you sit in your quarters and do nothing?" I say, forcing those unnerving thoughts from my mind. "Because if you do nothing, we'll die on this planet. I can't save us alone, and even with your help, we might be doomed. But if you're so convinced Daddy is coming, then you better get your shit together and survive long enough for him to rescue you."

"Fuck off," she spits. "I didn't spend millions of dollars to be treated this way."

"Well, I hate to break it to you, Princess, but no amount of money is worth losing an entire crew and ship over." I step closer until I'm towering over her. "I think we both know why we're here. Why we crashed. No amount of money could ever atone for what you brought on our heads." She pales at my words, confirming my guess was correct. Our sensors never registered the missile that took us out, meaning it was military-grade and expensive. It was also aimed at the passenger levels. Whoever targeted us was presumably after this beguiling devil.

"So, get used to it, because this is how we live now. This is how we survive, and if you think that I'm going to wait on you hand and foot, you have a rude awakening coming. You can starve for all I care."

"I'd rather starve than spend one more second in the same room as you." She turns on her heels and storms for the exit.

"Fine by me!" I shout at her back. "We'll see how your tune changes in a week when the stomach pangs get too sharp for you to ignore. I've gone hungry more than once in my life, but I doubt a princess like yourself has ever had to skip a meal."

"Stop calling me that." She whirls on me, and if I were anyone else, the death in her eyes would terrify me.

"Okay, Princess." I smirk, and for a second, I think she might attack my face with her still-manicured nails, but she simply clenches her fists and turns around.

I don't know how I'll attach this final metal sheet without help, but I would rather struggle alone than stand next to her. The hours we spent working were hours too many, and I need a break from her constant scowl.

CRACK!

The heavens explode with a lightning bolt of unnatural size, and I stare out of the hole in the hull with a new sense of fear. It lights up the cloudy sky with violence, and a dark premonition settles in my chest.

"What was that?" Serling turns in time to witness another bolt shatter the air, and her anger morphs into terror. "That's…" she trails off. "Are we safe in here?"

"We should be," I say as rain begins to fall. "Unless any of the exposed wires are still live. If they get hit, it'll fry what remains of our system."

My words force me into action, and I race for the controls. I initiate a hull scan on one screen and an electric diagnostic on another. If any live wires are unprotected, the entire ship could lose power with a single bolt. No food storage, no terrain scans, no Med Bay. And not only could it ruin the system, but it could electrocute us. Normally lightning is a non-issue, but with The Bellator in pieces, too much untreated metal is exposed.

"There." Serling points at the screens, and I flinch in surprise at her nearness. I didn't hear her approach. "There's an overlap between the hull damage and the active electrical grid."

I lean closer, but she's right. Directly over the still functional crew quarters is a missing stretch of paneling. Rain has started to fall, and if the lightning touches down… Serling might boast a host of negative qualities, but she's smart. She found the connection faster than I did.

"We need to repair that," I say, turning toward the forgotten metal sheet, and I'm suddenly grateful she dropped it. If we'd welded it in place, I would've had to search for another piece.

"Wait." She seizes my biceps in her small hands, and the contact surprises me. "You're going out there? In this?"

"We can't leave those wires exposed."

"Why do you keep saying we?"

"Because I can't do this alone." I extract my arm from her grip. "I need your help." I grab the welding kit and throw a coil of rope over my shoulder.

"No." She steps away from me. "I'm not going out there."

"Serling…"

"I said no."

"Serling, if the ship gets struck by lightning, we could die." I step forward and gently catch her biceps to stop her from fleeing. "If those wires get hit, we'll lose power, and we could die. We can survive without lights and possibly the cooling system, but not the Med Bay."

"But WE could get hit and die out there," she argues. "That isn't normal lightning."

"I'll do the hard stuff, I promise." I never expected to beg this woman for help, and I doubt she's ever had someone need her, but desperation shatters all boundaries. "The exposure is on an angle. I can't hold this steady and weld at the same time. I need you to hold it for me, but as soon as we get two corners attached, you can go inside while I finish."

She says nothing, but when she doesn't leave, I take that as her answer. "Here." I shove the sheet at her, and she unties the arms of her uniform from around her waist. She wiggles back into it, zipping it up to her neck before she grabs one edge. I capture the other, and we race through the airlocks toward an exit. The rain falls painfully hard, creating little rivers as it flows off the rocky cliffs, and I pray the surrounding land doesn't flood. I can only divert so many disasters before one finds a weakness in our defenses.

Serling slips on the slick ground, but she catches her footing before she takes me down with her. I can barely see her through the thick rain, but we hug the curve of the ship until we come to an exterior maintenance ladder.

"Climb," I order as I tie the rope around the metal sheet. "I'm right behind you. You'll be fine, I promise."

She stares at me, seeing through my lies. I don't know if we'll survive this. The lightning increases, transforming the heavens into a battlefield, but with a scowl and a curse, Serling climbs. When she reaches the halfway mark, I follow, readying to catch her in case she falls, but thankfully, her grip is strong. She makes it to the exposure quickly despite the height, me close on her heels, and I use the ladder rungs as a makeshift pulley. It's slow going until she joins my efforts, and her unprovoked help takes me aback. By the panic in her eyes, it's not because she wants to, though, but because she's terrified to remain up here. Either way, we make quick work of it. My body burns with exertion, but the ever-increasing storm spurs me onward.

"Hold the rope tight," I say when the metal hits my boots. "I'm going to move along this ledge."

Serling nods her understanding, and I slide across the hull. It's difficult in the rain, but when I finally settle into position, I gesture for her to pass me the sheet. She grunts as she shoves the edge toward me. Fatigue is gaining on her, and I pray she can hold on a little while longer. The lightning strikes the ground closer and closer to our location with every bolt, and we have minutes before we're the target.

After thirty seconds, her grip slips. The uneven weight threatens to knock me off my perch, and while my first instinct is to scold her for not being careful, I bite my tongue as she desperately tries to regain control of the sheet.

"Hold on, Serling!" I encourage over the rage of the storm instead. "Just a few more minutes."

"I can't!" she sobs. "I can't hold it."

"Yes, you can!"

"No, I can't!"

"Serling, look at me!" She glances up, and her expression tells me some of the droplets on her soaked cheeks are tears. "Don't you dare let go. You got this. I know you do."

She shakes her head, but she doesn't let go.

"We're almost there." I push myself to work faster. "You can do this." A strangled sob escapes her lips as a bolt of lightning strikes too close for comfort. I half expect her to drop the sheet and fling herself to the ground, but she remains at my side, arms and voice shaking.

"Just one more corner," I tell her, praying this seal doesn't come loose in the storm because of my carelessness. Another bolt strikes even closer, its raw electric power dancing over my skin, and Serling flinches so hard that I worry she'll fall to her death.

"Get inside!" I push her hands off the metal sheet.

"You're not done," she sobs as she grabs the ladder with uncertainty.

"Go!" I repeat, my deep voice echoing through the sounds of nature at war. "It's too dangerous."

She obeys, but she only makes it a few rungs before glancing up at my immobility. "Aren't you—"

"Go!" The severity in my tone makes her recoil. "I'll be fine to finish by myself. Just get inside."

She doesn't hesitate. She climbs down the ladder as fast as her exhausted body can carry her, but just when she reaches the halfway point, just when I think she's safe, lightning hits the stones ten feet from the ship. Then with a speed my eyes barely register, a thin electric thread separates from the main charge and strikes Serling.

CHAPTER 9

SERLING

A single second. That's all I have, yet everything freezes, and as if life is moving in slow motion, I see my future. The lightning charred the stone, and the thin sliver that exploded from the mother bolt will do the same to my chest. I have a single moment to decide my fate. Do I let nature carve a hole through my body, or do I roll the dice and fall? The rocks might break my bones. They might kill me. They might ignore me altogether. And as the electricity races for my heart, I release the ladder.

I plummet to the earth, my ankles and knees cracking painfully as they crash against the rocks, and I scream. The storm hides my voice, but I do not fall silent. I can't. The pain is unbearable, and I'm vaguely aware of Driver shouting above me, but I can't answer him. I can't do anything but let the agony pour from my lips. My vision blurs as I hover on the edge of consciousness. I don't know how long I lay there. He probably thinks the lightning incinerated me. Serves him right for making me work in such dangerous conditions.

A second bolt strikes too close for comfort, and I finally find the will to move. Crawling on my hands and knees over the rocks until I locate the ship's entrance, I drag my soaked body inside and collapse onto the floor. I should pull myself to the Med Bay and see if the fall fractured my ankles, but I'm in too much pain. I don't want Driver to find me like this, though. My cheeks burn with shame at how I allowed him to witness my tears on the ladder. I haven't cried in front of anyone since I was ten years old. I'd spilled soup on my dress at a political dinner, and my mother's anger burned my small soul alive. I wasn't aware of it at the time, but a famous designer had clothed my family for a profile on the Ambroses that would air galaxy-wide before an important vote. The stain ensured I couldn't be included in any of the photos, something my parents needed me to be a part of, and I'll never forget the verbal thrashing my mom gave me in the bathroom as she tried and failed to clean my outfit.

Our absence forced my father to leave the event to find where we'd disappeared to, and when he saw my tears, he told me I was a disgrace to the Ambrose name. Ten years old, and I was already humiliating the most powerful family in the galaxy. He grabbed my shoulders and swore if I ever embarrassed him again, he would give me something to truly cry about. I've not shown vulnerability since. It's why I was so cruel to the crew member in the bathroom. She caught a private moment of weakness. I don't allow people to glimpse my suffering, and twice now, Driver Thorne has witnessed my fear, my desperation, my shortcomings. I cannot let him discover me on the floor like this.

Gathering my resolve, I push off the ground and walk toward our food reserves. I'm not hungry. I'm in search of something stronger, so I don't bother to read the labels when I locate the liquor. I don't care what I drink, so I grab the first one I find. It burns as I swallow, and even though it makes me gag, I take another gulp the second I can breathe. I repeat the process as I limp to my room, and once I'm inside, I strip the drenched uniform off and throw it onto the shower floor. In between sips, I peel my soaked tank top and underwear off and pull on a clean pair of panties, but I don't bother with a shirt as I sink to the floor. I can't stop crying. It's as if every painful moment from the past nineteen years has surfaced, and my emotions turn ugly.

"Serling!" Driver bangs on my door so forcefully that I flinch, spilling alcohol down my bare chest. "I saw the wet footprints and followed them here."

I say nothing as he continues to knock. I simply sip the liquor and savor the burn.

"Serling, answer me! I need to know you're alive!" He almost sounds worried, and for some reason, his tone severs the last thread of my fraying sanity. I jump to my feet and yank the door open. Relief floods his features a millisecond before he registers my nudity, and he jerks his sight to the floor.

"Fuck." He shoves past me and digs through my dresser until he finds a tee shirt. "Put this on." When I make no move to obey, he clenches his eyelids shut and grabs my soaked head. He nudges it through the hole, followed by my arms, and only once the oversized top covers me does he open his eyes.

"I thought the lightning hit you." He clutches my biceps as if to shake me, but then he notices the alcohol and my glazed expression. "Did you go to the Med Bay? Are you hurt?" I don't answer. "Serling, are you okay?"

"Of course I'm not okay!" I scream in his face, and he releases me as if my skin is composed of live wires. "I'm stuck on this planet with you. You're the last person I would ever spend time with, yet we're trapped here without an escape."

Hurt flickers through his eyes, and for a second, I wonder if he is genuinely concerned about me. Maybe he was worried, but that only inspires hatred since I don't need his sympathy. I can hear myself becoming my father as I rage. Even my thoughts mirror his, which makes me hate myself with a burning passion, and that realization turns my venom deadly.

"I told you I didn't want to go outside." I shove him toward the door. "I told you it was dangerous, but did you listen? No, because you're some big-shot war hero. Fucking arrogant asshole. You almost got me killed. Do you know what would happen to you if your actions killed me? I'm Serling Ambrose. My life is more important than yours will ever be. You aren't even worthy of breathing the same air as me, and I don't do manual labor. I don't venture into storms. You might be stupid enough to risk your life, but I'm not. I refuse to be involved in any more of your schemes. If you need my help, fine, but don't you dare ask me to do anything dangerous like that again. Don't talk to me. Don't order me around. Stay the fuck away from me."

I expect him to argue. He's the only man who doesn't cower before me, and I want him to fight. I need him to yell, to give me an excuse to hurt him, but he simply steps out of my room with sympathy in his eyes. That one kind expression knocks the damn in my soul loose, and I cry like I've never cried before. Ugly violent sobs for him to witness in all their horrendous glory.

"I'll get you something to eat." He takes the bottle from me, his calloused fingers brushing mine, and I suddenly want those hands to hold me. To tell me everything will be okay. That we aren't dying here, but I've dug too deep a grave to ever escape. He may pity me, but Driver will never like me. Not after this. Not after how I've treated him.

"Get some rest." He shuts the door, and I collapse on the bed. Fifteen minutes later he knocks, signaling he has left my dinner on the floor, but I curl in on myself and bawl harder at his care. I hate him. *I hate him, I hate him, I hate him.*

What I really mean is I hate myself.

DRIVER

I barely see Serling over the next two weeks. She refuses to acknowledge or interact with me, and while I could force the issue, I opt not to. From dawn until well after dusk, I work to ensure our survival and fortify the ship. I've made system repairs to the best of my ability. I've reinforced our defenses, but it'll take some creative thinking to move the guns. I still haven't figured out how to utilize them. The constant tasks are exhausting, and I'm too tired to combat her attitude, so I let her ignore me. I'll save my strength for a fight that matters.

I don't allow her to wallow in her room, though. Heiress or not, she pulls her weight, and after the storm, I started leaving a list of simple chores with her breakfast tray like laundry and meal prep. For the first three days after our argument, she refused to complete anything I requested of her, but on the fourth day, I banged on her door until she flung it open and agreed to help. She knows absolutely nothing about cooking or cleaning, so the sanitation of our clothes and living stations is questionable, but at least she's working. I would help her if she asked for directions, but she won't come to me, and I refuse to go to her. Not after what she said. I won't let her die, but that's it. I no longer care to make peace, even if we never leave this planet. I'm fine with her avoidance. In fact, I might prefer it.

"What are you doing out here?" Serling's voice comes from behind me as if my thoughts summoned her, and I grind my teeth as her footfalls approach. She either needs something or is tired of being alone, but I don't have it in me to humor either scenario.

"We've been here for a few weeks," I answer without turning around. "We still have plenty of food, but we're running out of water quickly with this heat. If I'd been prepared, I would've constructed a collection system during the storm, but it seems we crashed during this planet's season change. I'm afraid the rains have ended, so water is our biggest concern."

"That doesn't explain what you're doing outside." She shifts into my field of vision, forcing me to acknowledge her, and I wonder if she ventured out onto the rocks looking for a fight. She's had no one to insult in two weeks. Maybe going cold turkey has her on edge.

"This entire terrain is rocky," I answer, trying to keep my cool. "No water, no vegetation, no animal life. Unless it rains again, which judging by the cloudless sky is unlikely, we'll dehydrate." I glance down at her from my stone perch. The top half of her uniform is tied around her waist, but thankfully her tank top is black this time and, therefore, not see-through.

"Headquarters would've declared us dead when the missile hit. They lost all contact with us, but the ship is programmed to send a distress signal when situations become critical. I don't know if The Bellator did, though, since it was badly damaged. Regardless, they don't know where we are, but they know something catastrophic happened," I continue. "They would've alerted your father to your death. If you're right, and he has decided to hunt for you despite Headquarters' report, his rescue team will require at least a week to prepare and two to reach the Mors. They'll need another week to cross the Expanse to our last known location, and then they'll have to combat the dangers as they systematically search for us. It could take them months to find us. Possibly years, and we're running out of water."

"Years?" Panic fills her voice. "That's too long."

"We don't even know if anyone is coming. Our rescue hinges on whether your father believes the Headquarters' death notice. If he does, we're never going home. If he doesn't, he'll have to hire a team skilled enough to search the Mors. Either option leaves us here for months, if not longer," I say. "The terrain here is rocky. I was curious if the entire planet was like this, so to answer your question, I'm searching for the best direction to find water in."

"We can't be stuck here for years."

I open my mouth but decide against calling her a broken record. Regardless of my feelings for this girl, I was baptized in hardship and bloodshed at an early age. I'm at home in the fray, but this twenty-nine-year-old has never had to endure the intense fear disasters inspire, so for the sake of peace, I keep my opinion to myself.

"Even if we're here for only a few months, we should prepare for the worst," I say instead. "We need to find water and edible vegetation. I climbed the cliff to get a better view and noticed a hint of green in that direction." I point, and she follows my finger. "It's far. Traveling will be risky, and if I locate water, transporting it will be difficult. I don't want to leave The Bellator's safety, but if it doesn't rain, I'll have no choice. There's a lot to consider, but dehydration is our most imminent threat."

"You're going out there?" she asks. "On foot?"

"The ship and her escape pods will never fly again. I don't like it, but we'll dehydrate before we starve."

"Can't we just wait to see if it rains?"

"We have about a week before we're in trouble."

"Then maybe we should wait," she says as her fingers pick at the knotted uniform around her waist. It would be nice if she was worried about me, but I can tell by her unsteady voice that she dislikes the idea of being alone and unprotected. "It might rain again."

"It might," I agree without conviction.

It doesn't rain. A week goes by. Seven full days, but the humidity only increases. I can't wait any longer. I need to leave the ship.

"There's plenty of food, and there's enough water if you ration it," I say as I shoulder my pack. "I'm not sure how long I'll be gone or if I'll find water, so no lengthy showers."

"I know what rationing means." Serling glares at me from where she sits atop the useless control panels. I gave her a crash course on how to work what few functions remain. Short-distance transmissions will keep us in contact until I pass out of range. On the one hand, I look forward to the peace. I need a break from her perpetual aggression. While we waited for rain, she stopped ignoring me. I'm not sure if she was lonely or afraid, but her scowls have been my constant companions this past week.

But leaving her also makes me nervous. I tell myself I'm worried because if she encounters danger, I don't trust her to handle it. I can't stand her, but I don't want her to die. Deep down, though, the reason I'm hesitant to leave is that she's all I have. Like it or not, Serling Ambrose is my sole companion, my only source of help and conversation. We're the only two people on this planet, and while I've endured deadlier missions, I was never alone. The army always had my back, but here in the Mors, Serling is all that stands between me and utter isolation. I'll never admit it, but the thought of losing her paralyzes me.

"Stay inside The Bellator," I say as I move for the exit.

"Why?" she challenges. "It's too damn humid in here."

God, she wants me to strangle her. I could just reach out and grip that beautifully delicate throat in my fist and be done with her. Maybe I'm not that afraid of being alone. "If you must go outside, always keep the ship in sight," I growl, but she doesn't so much as bat an eye at my warning tone.

"Fine, I won't go outside." She swings her legs down and jumps off the controls. For seconds, she hovers before me as if trying to decide whether or not to wish me luck, but the moment passes. Her features harden, and I take that as my cue to leave. A heartless send-off from a heartless girl.

"Miss Ambrose." I turn around when I've walked ten feet from the exit, the morning sun already unbearably hot. "Don't die before I get back."

CHAPTER 10

DRIVER

The rocky terrain slows my progress, forcing me to make camp for the night within the confines of the stones. My war injuries ache from sleeping on the ground, but when dawn finally breaks, I push onward. My pack weighs me down, the exertion overheating my body, and I worry that trying to carry enough food and water will condemn me to dehydration. There's not so much as a wisp of a cloud to offer me shade, and despite my hopes for rain, the clear skies assure me that'll never happen.

By the time the second night falls, I'm still surrounded by stone, but the horizon of color is almost within reach. The closer I walk, though, the browner the swath of green turns, and that concerns me. It warns I won't find what I'm looking for and that I'll need to push further, but with every mile, the mechanics of transporting any water I locate back to the ship become increasingly impossible. Our shuttles were damaged in the crash, and unless this planet proves itself welcoming, it's not safe to move our camp away from the Bellator's fortified remains. So far, we've experienced nothing hostile besides the lightning, but this is the Mors. This planet has an ugly side. We just haven't seen her yet.

It takes another half day of blinding sunshine and unforgiving terrain to reach my destination. With every step, my hope grows until the colors become a recognizable landscape, and my heart sinks at the sight. I understand why the green of this environment presents with a brown tint. I endured almost three days walking through a natural furnace, only to be confronted by this devastating reality. My pack was too heavy. I drank too much water on my journey here, and regardless of how I move forward, that fact remains. Nothing I choose bodes well for me.

"Serling?" I speak into the short-distance communicator. "Are you there?" Silence answers me, and I stare at where I left invisible The Bellator far behind. She should still be in range, so why isn't she answering?

"Serling, do you copy?"

Nothing.

I switch the comms to relay a message and say a silent prayer that she'll remember to check the communication logs.

"Serling, I found a new environment at the end of the rocky terrain, but it isn't viable. It's a stagnant swamp, and by the smell, the water isn't drinkable. I can either come back or press onward in the hopes I'll eventually find a fresh source." I pause for a second, weighing my options as if I have any other choice. "I'm going in."

I activate the scanner and aim it at the oozing ground. The sharp rocks slowly gave way to a putrid swamp, and then about a mile in, trees and plants unlike anything I've seen sprouted from the water. Sparse at first, they became increasingly thick, and that gives me pause. Their unique and dying leaves hide the sun, and if I press onward, I'll have to surrender to the darkness and all its hidden evils. The scanner will help, but it's not a foolproof plan. It reads toxicity levels, which will determine if the water is safe to drink, but it also comes equipped with night vision, heat sensors, and radar. I'll need all three as I wade into this swamp. I don't want to know what lives beneath this poisonous surface, but walking into the shadows blind is a death sentence.

I study the screen as the radar maps out the immediate area. It hasn't registered any life forms other than mine, but I don't entirely trust its assessment. There are creatures in this universe that defy logic, and with my recent luck, this swamp is probably home to such unnatural predators.

"Serling, come in." I try her one last time, but silence is my only answer. I shouldn't let it bother me. It's either a technology issue or her defiance, but my anxiety over her safety surprises me. I dislike her with every fiber of my being, but I guess my hatred is comfortable. It's a constant I can rely on. No matter what terrors this planet throws my way, they'll never compare to how a single glare from her ignites my chest. If something happens to the Ambrose princess, my only constant disappears. I'm in danger if fighting with that beautiful menace is the only normality in my life.

I wait for a full sixty seconds, but when Serling still doesn't answer, I glance back at the scan of the swamp. Radar mapped out the deeper sections, and I slowly pick my way through the shallows. The stench is unbearable, and I pray my breakfast won't make a reappearance. The water smells like decaying flesh mixed with a putrid scent I can't place, and it coats my ankles with a thick and oily slime. The scanner warns the bacteria level is dangerous for human consumption, but I don't need technology to know this water is unsafe.

Yet I forge onward because I'm stubborn. Because I cannot fail. I've survived wars, injuries, and crashes. I've survived Serling Ambrose, and I refuse to let dehydration end my life. So,

I convince myself this swamp is merely the darkness before the dawn, that if I just keep walking, I'll find the promised land on the other side. I cannot retreat to The Bellator and face Serling as a failure. She would be unbearable if I returned empty-handed, and I would rather die out here fighting to survive than wither away from thirst and Serling's virulence.

After twenty minutes, the sparse trees become threateningly thick, and I pause before their darkness swallows me whole. The trunks are a pale brown and look like vines that grew so close together they fused into one plant. They twist into almost violent patterns, and the vines seem to connect below the water's surface. Based on the scans, the roots form a massive nervous system, and instinct warns me to be wary. If this ecosystem is linked, it could operate with a hive-like mentality. If I disrupt something, if I harm a single plant in this swamp, the entire landscape could view me as a hostile invader. For a moment, I wonder if I should abandon this devil's errand. Should I turn around and admit defeat? Dying by dehydration will be slow and agonizing, but is falling victim to this swamp a kinder ending? Judging by the darkness ahead, I predict perishing here will prove an excruciating death.

And with that, I step into the shade.

What little light filtered through the tree line vanishes as night falls. Humidity clings to my skin. Filth coats my legs. The stench is overwhelming, and I have nothing to show for the miserable hours spent within the confines of this swamp. I've found no signs of fresh water or edible vegetation, and as darkness claims the land, I realize this putrid environment offers no safe place to make camp. The swamp stretches endlessly in all directions and could take days to escape. I need to sleep, but without a secure location, I can't surrender to my exhaustion. Too much can go wrong when—

Something flashes across the scanner's screen, and I freeze. For the briefest moment, the radar detected movement below the water's surface. It was a momentary flicker. Nothing more. But something's here with me. I lift my gaze and study the grimy surface, but not so much as a ripple gives the creature away. My heart thunders so loud that I fear it'll betray my location, but the stillness holds. The placid water remains calm. I'm alone, or so the creature wants me to believe. That or my imagination is hallucinating threats, and the scanner merely detected debris floating through the sludge. I pray that I'm alone in the darkness, but I don't trust the silence. Hope for the best. Prepare for the worst.

Careful not to cause ripples, I scan the area, searching for a defensible position. The wet ground is bacteria-ridden, making camping on the swamp floor impossible. The only other option is the tree line, and while the vine-like trunks prick my wariness, sleeping high in the branches is the lesser evil.

I spot a broad tree about thirty feet past where the scanner detected the movement. Its trunk twists and coils around itself as if it's writhing in pain, but the protrusions make for generous handholds. About fifteen feet off the ground, the fused, woody vines separate into a mass of convoluted branches. They won't be comfortable, but they're dry. They offer my best chance at surviving the night, and I pray no carnivores make their home among the leaves.

I use the scanner to stick to the shallows, my boots disturbing the water despite my care. Ripples flow out from my steps, but for a few seconds, I'm the only one unsettling the stillness. The scanner detects no life forms or movement, but just when I relax, just when I believe I'm alone, the water ten feet to my left vibrates.

I stand frozen, waiting for my stalker to make another move, but peace returns. The silence is so loud that my ears ring, and with a thundering heart, I take a step. When nothing happens, I take another. Three steps. Four. Five. The quiet holds. Only my boots disturb the swamp. Six steps. Seven. Ten. I'm almost to the thick tree. Thirteen steps. Fourteen. Twenty.

The water behind me surges to life as something monstrous breaks the surface with the speed of a hunter cornering its prey. I launch into a run, no longer concerned with hiding my location. I push myself forward, using every ounce of willpower not to look at whatever is racing through the swamp with an unholy momentum. Its roar warns the predator is massive, and I can practically feel its hunger as it hunts me.

Twenty-seven steps. Twenty-eight. Thirty. The tree is almost within reach. I'm so close, but the monster at my back is closer. I don't think I'm going to make it. My muscles ache from running through the sludge. My lungs burn. I'm not going to make it.

Thirty-nine steps. Forty. The creature surges for me as I leap for the tree. My fingers graze the rough bark, and with the power and agility the military hammered into me, I grip a vine and pull. My boots dig into the wood. My thighs coil tight like springs, and I jump into the air as the monster's teeth slam shut with a deafening clang.

CHAPTER 11

SERLING

His absence is a blessing at first. Without the constant scrutiny, tasks to complete, and orders given in a deep voice, I can finally relax. The Bellator's humidity, on the other hand, has the brutal opposite idea. She continues to rise, and while my defiance longs to turn on the cooling system, Driver's concern stays my hand. If we run out of water and fuel before my father finds us, there'll be nothing for dear ole dad to rescue. The petty part of my brain loves how devastated he would be to find his sole heir dead because of his impatience. If he'd allowed for a trip around the Mors, I would be lounging by a pool drinking cocktails instead of sweating through cheap fabric and sleeping on a mattress barely large enough to roll over on, but father gets what father wants. It would serve him right to learn that a single impatient decision destroyed his ancient lineage, but even here on this forsaken planet, the will to live has me in her chokehold. Despite this miserable heat, depressing accommodations, and aggravating company, I don't want to die. I need to survive, if only so I can look my father in the eyes and tell him he was wrong.

So, I don't turn on the cooling system, and I ration my water.

I spent hours sweating through my clothes after Driver left, but then I decided to enjoy the peace. Without his constant repairs and construction, I stripped down to my underwear and explored the remaining crew rooms. I found a few surviving articles of clothes that fit me for when he returns and some personal items that'll make my time here bearable. Initially, plundering the dead's belongings settled a rock of guilt in my belly, but I like to think if I'd died and another woman survived, that my luggage might help her. The sentiment is generous for my normal mindset, but crashing in the Mors Expanse is bound to change a person. So, with a silent prayer for the fallen, I gathered the stolen goods and moved them to my room.

For the first three days, I used the scavenged appliances to read the crew's books, listen to their music, and watch the shows they stored on their devices. Last night, I broke into the liquor and drank myself into a blissful state of oblivion as I danced naked, but I woke this morning with a hangover and an uneasy fear tightening my chest. Driver promised to radio when he approached the end of the communications' reach, but I haven't heard from him. I drank my water ration, ate some of the preserved fruit since the fresh is gone, and then checked the system for messages. It's been four days since he left, and I haven't heard a single word. For all I know, he's dead, and I'm alone here with an ever-dwindling supply of water.

That thought, combined with the heat and my hangover, drove me back to bed, where I currently lay in utter boredom. I don't want to read or listen to music. I've always enjoyed solitude, but this is different. Before, I knew I could leave my house and see people. I could call a friend and ask them to grab lunch, but this? This is complete isolation. I'm utterly alone.

I shift from the warm spot on the mattress to a cooler one as I close my eyes. It's too hot to sleep, but I try anyway. I'm tired of this planet. I'm tired of being afraid and sweaty and sore. I'm tired of the loneliness, and sleep is the only escape from this painful existence.

I lose track of how long I lay there, but suddenly, a hand grips my bare hip. I've taken to sleeping naked in this heat, and the muscular hand pulls me against a broad chest. His skin is warm, his calloused hands rough, and a soft moan escapes my lips at how good he feels. It's been so long since a man has slipped into my bed, and as his palm slides over my belly, I push myself further against him. He takes that as an invitation, and with powerful movements, he flips me over and slams his mouth against mine before I can even open my eyes. His kiss owns me, his lips demanding and seductive, and before I know what I'm doing, I wrap my arms around his neck. I deepen the kiss, parting my lips to grant him entrance, and his tongue slips inside, coaxing another moan from me. I've never been kissed like this. It's as if someone set fire to my soul, and I can't get enough. I hook my leg over his hip, desperate to satisfy the craving he ignited, and he bites my lip at the intensity. I pull his hair, needing more, needing everything, and we moan in beautiful unison until he grips my thigh and yanks me closer.

"Be a good girl for me and—"

I jerk awake so fast that my vision blurs with dizziness. I gag at the dream, or rather, who starred in it. It wasn't some faceless man fulfilling a fantasy. It wasn't an old boyfriend or celebrity crush come to visit my dreams. The man invading my sleep was none other than Driver Thorne, and the disgust that races through my body is so palpable that I jump into the shower and wash away the memory of his imagined touch.

DRIVER

The monster's fangs slam closed on nothing but air, but his jaws are so close, I feel the heat of his breath. It roars in frustration as it surges for me, but all I hear is churning water as I climb ever higher. I don't dare turn around for fear it'll slow me down, but based on the thrashing, I suspect the creature is water-bound. That realization offers a modicum of relief, but terror still pulses through me. If something that big exists in this swamp, it points to other hostile predators inhabiting this planet. I pray that disrupting this monster hasn't ignited a chain reaction. I hope Serling listens for once in her life and doesn't go outside.

By the time I reach the branches, the dark waters have fallen still, so I climb onto a nest of interwoven vines and force myself to glance down. I don't want to face the creature hunting me, but I need to know what inhabits this planet. Is it truly water-bound? Is it alone? Have I disrupted a tenuous peace that spells death for Serling and me? I brace for the sight, but the animal is gone. The water is dark where the creature disturbed the mud, but there's not even a heat signature for the scanner to detect. My predator has either abandoned its hopes of an easy meal, or it's waiting patiently far below the surface for me to risk returning to the swamp floor.

Either way, it appears I've temporarily escaped the danger, and I pray the creature is nocturnal. Otherwise, I'm trapped up here. The swamp appeared empty until the daylight vanished, and I hope this monster sinks to the depths in oblivious slumber come morning. Perhaps that's why we saw no signs of life at the crash site. I seal our quarters before we go to sleep, and we never venture outside at night. Without working surveillance, we have no clue what happens beyond our fortified walls, and while I noticed nothing when I camped among the stones, it doesn't mean something didn't notice me.

I shiver at that thought. I doubt I'll find safe water in this swamp. My failure puts Serling in danger of dehydrating, but there's a good chance I'll never leave this putrid filth alive. She'll die an agonizing death alone on that ship. Her father isn't coming for her. She desperately wants to believe he'll save us, but the reality is I'm all she has. I don't want to admit defeat. I refused to when an explosion destroyed half of my body, and I can't bring myself to now, but finding water is a task too large for one man. I need help, but the only person left alive is a beautiful girl who's unable to even help herself. And it's with those anxious thoughts that I fall into a fitful sleep.

What feels like only minutes later, an unnerving screech shatters the silence, jerking me awake. For a panicked moment, I forget where I am. My body aches. I'm soaked in sweat while my throat is bone dry. Dim light filters through the branches, heralding another day. Shapes loom among the shadow-cloaked leaves, but there's no sign of a threat. That sound was too close, though. Too unnatural, and I grab the scanner. Its screen flickers to life, and the second it comes online, it registers a heat signature directly in front of me.

My head jerks up. Something's up here, but I see only shadows. I glance back down at the scanner, wondering if I was mistaken, but the reading hasn't changed. A life force is hovering feet from my face.

With careful movements, I slip my arms through my pack and scan the surrounding branches, but emptiness greets me. I'm alone. Nothing's there, yet the hairs on my neck prick with alarm. I'm missing something, but what?

I focus on the leaves as I shift to the nest's edge. I hang one leg down, readying to make my descent, but the instant my foot falls over the side, movement flashes. Eyes blink open from the shadows. Two black, shiny eyes stare at me for a second, and then, with unnatural speed, a dark creature explodes from its camouflage. Fangs race for my face, and I jerk backward as its unnerving screech fills the air. My carelessness flings me off my perch. For a moment, I'm weightless, and then I plunge into the filthy waters, my pack pulling me down into the darkness.

CHAPTER 12

SERLING

```
WARNING:
BREACH IN TANK 10
```

I groan as the sudden alarm yanks me from sleep.

```
WARNING:
BREACH IN TANK 10
```

Panic electrocutes my chest. Tank ten? That's our water supply, and if there's a breach...?

I scramble out of bed and pull the first shirt I find over my head. I step out of my room, unseal the airlock, and race for the controls. Driver left his tools for me, not that I know how to use half of them, but I grab them anyway as I run through the corridors. Everything seemed fine before he left. I haven't gone near the water storage, so how did this happen?

```
WARNING:
BREACH IN TANK 10
```

The alarm urges me to move faster, and opening the airlock, I race for the tanks. Water pulses out of a pipe in the ceiling, and my stomach sickens. These pipes carry the reserves to different sections of The Bellator. The Med Bay, the showers, the cafeteria. This water is all we have, and it's currently raining onto the floor to disappear into the crevasses. I almost burst into tears at the sight. Every second purges what remains of our supply, and I don't know what to do. I'm not a plumber. I've never worked on a ship, and I suddenly hate myself for my stubbornness. I refused to help Driver with the repairs, and now I don't know how any of this shit works.

I step below the leak and open my mouth. I haven't had a drink since before bed, and if this is the last of it, I won't waste it by watching every drop disappear. The stream is too heavy for me to capture all of it, though. I'm soaked by the time I drink my fill, but at least I'm cool and hydrated for the moment.

The pipe is too high for me to reach, but thankfully, debris clutters the room. I grab a broken storage bin from the corner and drag it below the leak before climbing onto it. I study the pipes, and up close, I realize a connecter came loose. It was probably damaged in the crash and finally gave in to its failings. I might be able to screw them back together, and I jump down to dig through Driver's tools. Finding what I think I need, I re-climb my makeshift ladder and shove the bent pipes into place. Water pelts my eyes, blinding me, which forces me to work by touch alone. It takes multiple attempts, but when I hear them click together, I tighten the connector, straining to maneuver the tool while keeping the pipes sealed. The leak slows to a trickle, but no matter how hard I twist, I can't staunch the flow completely. The ruined parts need to be welded. I saw Driver use the machine, but I doubt I can figure it out. I'm shocked I managed this much, but at least I stopped the worst of it. This slow drip is minor, and I can salvage the water with a container. We already lost too much. We can't afford to lose any more.

I race for the cafeteria, and after five minutes of searching, I locate a storage bin filled with packages of dry grain. I dump them onto the floor and drag the container to the pipes to capture what leaks. The tank ten's level is dangerously low. It won't last more than a few days, and if Driver returns, it'll last half that. Not that he's coming back. He never radioed when he left the communication limit. I worry he's dead, and I'm alone with a water supply that won't last the week.

I collapse to the floor beside the droplets and lose track of how long I let the repetitive drips lull me into depression. I don't want to be the sole survivor on this planet. I hate that I'll die without speaking to another human being again more than I hate Driver. At least with his constant presence, the anger kept my emotions at bay. Rage and combat are easy, but without his aggravation fueling me, tears well in my eyes. It's easier to lash out at my victims than to sit here and acknowledge my terror. It's easier to blame someone than admit my weakness is dragging me down, and it's that thought that forces me to my feet. I storm to the controls and engage the short-distance comms. Driver can't hear me, which is probably for the best, but just the possibility of him receiving my message lights a fire in my belly.

"Water tank ten is almost depleted," I start. "There was damage to the pipes that you failed to notice, so thanks for killing us, asshole. If you're hearing this, I hope you die out there, because if you show your face back here, I'll kill you myself…" I reach for the switch to end the transmission, my outburst making me feel better, but I freeze. He told me to stay inside, and I only challenged the order because I dislike being managed. I haven't set foot outside this ship because I'm not reckless. I merely hate that he thinks he can command me just because he's ex-military.

People long to be me. They crave my wealth, my fame, my power, but if they knew the prison the Ambrose name was, they would flee. Every aspect of my life and image has been carefully regulated. My father allows no missteps, no independent thoughts. It's why he was furious when I left Corr'us Sanctum without authorization last year and ordered me home on a flight through the Mors Expanse. He expects absolute obedience, and while Driver isn't my father, while he's simply trying to keep us alive, he demands the same, and I refuse to be controlled. He wanted me to remain inside The Bellator, but it's my fear of venturing out into the heat that kept me contained... until now. I doubt Driver is coming back, and the reality that he'll never return weighs heavy on our water emergency. My body will shrivel with dehydration in a matter of days if I don't refill tank ten, and I realize it sounds arrogant, but I'm too beautiful to die that ugly. I see only one way forward, and while I dread what I must do, I love that it would piss Driver off.

I lean over the microphone and speak clearly in case he's still alive. "Oh, and I'm going outside. One of us has to find water."

DRIVER

The darkness is oppressive, and I lose all sense of direction as I sink. I can't tell which way is up, but I kick and thrash, fighting the pack's pull. I won't drown in this bacteria-ridden swamp. I refuse to become easy prey for whatever hunted me in the trees, but not so much as a sliver of daylight pierces the surface. Not even the blackness of space is this intense, and panic urges my body to hyperventilate. My lungs burn, but I keep my mouth clenched shut. This water is deadly to humans, and a single swallow could be fatal. I fear the contact with my lips and eyes has already ensured severe illness. A bacterial infection this far from the Med Bay spells death, and that thought spurs me on. I kick harder as my lungs scream for oxygen. For all I know, I'm swimming downward, but I don't stop moving. I fight and thrash and destroy the morning peace, and without warning, my head breaks through the surface.

I gasp for air, inhaling a single lungful before all hell breaks loose. Something moves faster than my brain can register, and fangs snap in my face. That unnerving scream echoes through the trees, and the monster from the swamp's canopy comes into view. I rear backward, barely escaping its attack, and as it lunges into a patch of sunlight, I finally see what's hunting me.

A reptilian-type creature stands on two powerful back legs with razor-sharp claws the length of my hand. It's about four feet tall, and black scales cover its entire muscular frame. They aren't solid black, though. They shimmer in the faint morning light, and I realize why I hadn't seen the monster in the shadows. Its scales blend in with the darkness, perfectly hiding the predator from its prey. Its camouflage is nearly flawless, and it terrifies me how well it blends into our surroundings. How long has this beast been hunting me? Did it happen across me in the leaves by accident or has it been tracking me since yesterday?

The arms that protrude from the front of its chest are reminiscent of legs, and I suspect it's to help it navigate the branches. They're small and thin, but their claws are just as nasty as the talons curving from its feet. They'll cleave my flesh from my bones if it gets close enough, but it seems hesitant to step into the deeper waters. It either can't swim, or it's afraid of the creature that chased me last night. I hope for the former but fear it's the latter. Either way, my situation spells doom. His massive elongated head houses fangs that could snap my skeleton in half, and he studies me with hunger in its foremost black eyes. Three smaller ones sit behind the large pair on each side, ensuring this monster has no blind spots. No matter where I move, he'll see me.

With careful movements, I reach for the knife on my belt. It's military-grade, long and sharp and fitted with jagged teeth.

Humans never walk away from a wound inflicted by this blade, but this creature's scales scare me. They're an expert camouflage, but the way they glint in the low light warns they also serve as protective armor.

Just as my fingers close around the hilt, the creature lunges. He leaps into the water, claws aimed at my heart, but I spin around and lower my head. His talons dig into my pack instead of my chest as he looses that terrifying screech. His power forces me underwater, and I realize what he intends to do. He's going to drown me, and even though it'll seal my fate, I have no other option. I have to lose the pack. It holds all my weapons and supplies. I'm dead without it even if I survive this animal, but I can't fight his strength with the extra weight. I click the scanner to my belt, and then with a tight grip on the knife, I unbuckle the pack and slip it from my shoulders.

My movement enrages the monster, and he brings his fangs down hard. He aims for my skull, but his weight is a sudden blessing. I've sunk too deep for him to reach my head, so he thankfully only tears into my pack. He rips the fabric to shreds as I swim around him. I can barely see in the murky water, so I follow the thrashing until I locate his tail. He's sinking with my eviscerated pack, and his throat and eyes are my best chances at finding his weaknesses. I pray the blade will penetrate the scales, and readying my aim, I launch myself at his back.

The creature shrieks as I stab his face, but the metal bounces off his scales with a jarring clang. He pitches backward, trying to throw me off, and I lose my grip on my knife. We plummet into the dark waters, its screams distorted as we sink, but his thrashing doesn't cease as he tries to knock me off. I hold on with stubborn determination because his back is the only place his fangs and claws can't reach. Bubbles and filth surge around us as its tail flogs me, but I refuse to let go. If he dislodges me, he'll rip me to bloody ribbons, and I would rather drown than let this monster feast on my organs while I'm still alive.

He screams again and then convulses, and that's when it strikes me. This beast can't swim. He's drowning. I press my knees into his sides and choke his neck tighter. My lungs burn, but if I can just hold on, I might emerge the victor. Pain explodes in my arm as his talons rip into my flesh, yet I refuse to let go. He's losing speed as he chokes, but the wounds carved into my arms are deep. I could bleed out before this creature drowns. So, with every ounce of strength left in me, I grip the monster's head and break its neck with battle-trained efficiency.

SERLING

I hover in the doorway, my bravado evaporating now that I face leaving The Bellator. A small bag with a water bottle, a protein pack, and a weapon hangs from my shoulders. Security always surrounded my family, even in the comfort of our mansion, so I'm familiar with their mechanics. My father insisted I learn how to shoot in the event of an emergency, but practicing in a safe setting protected by professional bodyguards and venturing out into the land that probably killed Driver are vastly different scenarios. I lie to myself, saying there are no monsters on this planet and that I'll keep the ship in sight. It's the only way I can talk myself into stepping out into the sunshine.

I barely make it a few steps before sweat drips down my face. The humidity is a furnace, and anger washes over me at how this harsh climate will destroy my perfectly curated skin. No matter where I travel in the galaxy, I must always look an Ambrose, so I spend too much time and money getting my skin, teeth, nails, and hair groomed by the capital's finest beauticians.

I've never experienced sunburn, and I almost turn around at the thought that this will be my first. I hate it here. Everything I know and care about is obsolete and useless. Everything I took pride in is worthless now, and every step down the social hierarchy I take is an insult to my name. Ambroses don't search deadlands for water in the blistering heat.

I turn back toward the ship but freeze before I can retreat to safety. Amboses don't do manual labor, but we also don't die of dehydration. A sunburn is preferable to a shriveled death, so I channel my anger in a new direction. My father is coming for me, and when he gets here, he'll find a savage in Serling's place. He'll lose his shit, and that image makes me smile. I'll have survived hell, and he'll be appalled that I didn't weather this torture with more grace. That thought urges me to walk faster. I hope I get a nasty sunburn. Maybe I'll start tanning so that my skin turns golden, and while I'm at it, I should cut my long hair myself to complete the look.

The defiance fuels me as I climb the rocky cliffs that flank the crash site. Driver headed south toward that green stain on the horizon, so I won't explore that way, but maybe there's something closer he missed. Maybe there's a cave that collected some rainwater or an underground pool in the rocks. Maybe I'm delusional, and the heat has finally cracked my sanity in half.

I'm out of breath by the time I reach the top. Sweat soaks my skin, making my cheap clothes gross, and I collapse on a flat rock to drink some of the now-warm water. When I get off this planet, I'm never drinking water without ice again. Hell, hold the water and make the entire glass frozen. I want to bathe in ice cubes.

When my breathing finally slows, I stand up and scan the horizon. Tan rocks. The same everlasting sharpness for as far as the eye can see. No plants. No animals. No birds, or bugs, or even a cloud. Just beige, jagged, hostile rocks. I can vaguely see the hint of green Driver noticed, but at this distance, it could simply be a mirage. Nothing else sticks out, and I feel foolish for thinking I could come out here and magically find water. I'm Serling Ambrose, the heiress, not a soldier. I'm not a warrior or adventurer. I'm not even a woman strong enough to defy her father. It was stupid to waste water and energy coming out here.

I wipe the sweat from my brow and start my return to the crash site when the cliff behind me catches my gaze. A small canyon divides the twin cliffs, and I would have to climb down the one I stand on and then back up to reach the second. In that dip, I would lose sight of The Bellator, which makes my anxiety spike, but something pushes my feet forward. Before I realize I'm moving, I'm standing at the edge, staring down into the little ravine. Nothing dangerous catches my eye. I think I can manage the trip. I'll be tired, but the sun is still high. Hours of daylight stretch ahead of me, so I begin my descent.

The second climb takes longer than expected. My hands ache, and my fingertips bleed from the sharp rocks. I smashed my knee, ripping open my pants and tearing my skin, and at one point, I sat on a flat rock and sobbed as I ate my protein pack. I've never done anything this difficult. My body hurts. I'm covered in sweat and blood. I want to lie down and give up, but somehow, I make it to the top. I try not to think about the return journey because I'm nervous my muscles won't carry me home. I worry I'll fall and break my legs out here. Dying of dehydration is terrifying, but dying of dehydration under this planet's brutal sun with broken legs is unspeakable. Maybe my father shouldn't rescue me. I might kill him for forcing me to travel through the Mors.

I drink some more as I stare at The Bellator's remains. I tried to ration my sips, but I'm almost out. Not only will I have to climb back under the setting sun, but I'll have to do so thirsty. I curse and force myself to stop drinking, shoving the nearly empty bottle into my pack before surveying the land. I see that stretch of green to the south. It's larger from this vantage, which offers me hope. Maybe Driver isn't dead. Maybe he found a lush landscape teaming with life and is readying to return with fresh fruits and clean water. But since he already ventured in that direction, I turn my eyes to the north. I don't expect to find anything but more unforgiving terrain, so when I see what's waiting behind this second cliff, I scream.

CHAPTER 13

DRIVER

I release the creature's body and let it sink to the depths. The swamp vibrates when it hits the bottom, and hope floods my chest. It's not that far down. My pack should be right below me, and I need the emergency medical kit stored inside. My arm is bleeding badly, and I should get out of the water before other predators smell the death, but without that kit, I'm dead. The blood loss is clouding my brain, and this water undoubtedly has already spread infection through my blood-stream. I won't survive for more than a few hours if I don't find that pack, so with aching muscles, I kick.

I locate the creature's scales after twenty seconds, and tracing the corpse, I blindly search the silt. My lungs scream for oxygen, and the edges of my consciousness dull as my brain suffocates, but I don't give up. I keep kicking. I keep searching, and just when my lungs threaten to explode, I feel fabric. I yank it, and my shredded pack slaps my chest. It's too dark to see how much of its supplies remain, but my fingers find the light, and I flip it on. I position my feet on the animal's back, aim the weak light above my head, and push off. I break the surface forty seconds later and inhale the foul air as if it's the most beautiful fragrance known to man.

When the suffocating haze finally fades from my brain, I kick toward a cluster of gnarled vines surrounding a tree trunk. I pull myself out of the water and sit with shaking muscles in the faint sunlight. My forearm looks worse than it feels, the flesh cut clean to the bone, and with unsteady fingers, I dig through the pack. Not much survived the creature's jaws. One water bottle and two protein packs remain. They won't last the journey home, but diving again is foolish. My blood pollutes these waters. If predators found me uninjured, they'll flock to my scent now. My only hope lies back at The Bellator.

When I don't find the medical kit, panic blurs my vision, but then my fingers close over its solid case. I pop it open and immediately inject my arm with a painkiller and an antibiotic. I need the tech on the ship's Med Bay to properly clean and dress this wound. I also don't know if this generic antibiotic will counter the toxins in these waters, but it's all I have. Medication administered, I grab the pharmaceutical glue and squeeze it against my severed flesh, the fast-drying gel closing the wound in seconds. My angry skin puckers against its hold, but this is as pretty as wilderness dressings get. The day is still new, and I should move before infection incapacitates me. It'll take days to reach The Bellator with this injury… if I don't die within the next few hours first.

With faltering hope, I shoulder what little remains of my pack and stand up, but before I take a single step, a screech echoes through the air. It sounds exactly like the creature I just killed, only with one significant difference. This second animal has a substantially deeper voice, which can only mean one thing. That monster is bigger.

SERLING

I move so fast that I skin my knees on my descent. The rocks are sharper on this side of the cliff, and I've lost sight of The Bellator. I can't afford to fall, but I can't reign in my reckless behavior. When I saw what lay behind this second cliff, I screamed, my reaction visceral. My dehydrated body cried tearless sobs. My voice poured from my lips of its own accord, and then I was racing for the edge, scrambling down as swiftly as my exhausted legs would carry me. I've experienced more emotions since we crashed than I have in my entire twenty-nine years, and I don't particularly like this careless, hyperventilating Serling. She's as foreign to me as this planet.

My boots hit the sand, and I take off running. Five feet. Ten Feet. Twenty. The burning sand kicks up around my legs as I run, and when the scalding beach finally gives way, I collapse.

The sobs that escape my lips are inhuman, the foreign Serling firmly in control of my aching and sunburnt body, but at this moment, I don't care that my voice pours out of me. I don't care that my muscles shake uncontrollably. All I care about is what I found, what currently laps at my knees. Water. I found water. Beautiful, crystal blue water.

I lose track of how long I kneel in the shallows, but when my sobs finally slow, I lay my sunburnt body down in the sand and let the coolness bathe my skin. I laugh at the delicious sensation, and for a blissful moment, I survey my surroundings. A thirty-foot beach stretches from the rocky cliff to the water, but exotic trees and flowers surround the rest of the pool, the imposing cliffs circling this entire oasis. I've never seen vegetation like this, but it's gorgeous in a wild way, so I don't bother with fear. Tomorrow I'll worry if those brightly colored plants are poisonous. Tomorrow I'll worry if this oasis is home to toxic insects or dangerous predators, but today, I'm going to enjoy this tropical escape hidden within the wasteland of these endless rocks. I found water. I won't shrivel and die, and with that exuberant thought, I twist my head sideways. My lips part, readying to drink my fill when I freeze, the calm waves centimeters from my mouth. How could I be so stupid? I know better than this. The first rule of space travel is you always test the atmosphere and the water before you expose yourself to it, and here I lay, coated in its gentle ripples about to drink something that could be lethal.

I scramble over the sand until the waves no longer touch me, but it's already too late. The open skin on my scraped knees will have allowed any bacteria or toxins that live in the pool to enter my bloodstream. The oasis looks harmless, and I desperately want to believe I've found salvation, but this is the Mors. Everything in the Expanse is deadly, and my haste may have killed me. Why didn't I think before I lay down in this pool? Perhaps Driver is right about me. I'm useless.

I should return to The Bellator and scan my blood for infection, but I don't relish the idea of repeating this climb. It's a small price to pay for water if it isn't poisonous, though, and I berate myself for not bringing a tester. I contemplate drinking the rest of my supply so I can carry a bottle back to analyze, but the heat is still suffocating. I'll need what little remains in my pack to make the return journey.

With one final look at the beautiful oasis, I move toward the cliff. My progress is painfully slow, and the sun has almost set by the time I seal myself inside The Bellator. I can barely stand. I crave my bed, but I force myself to visit the Med Bay. Pricking my finger, I watch the machine scan my blood with blurred vision. The report thankfully reads uninfected, and I stare at the medical beds, contemplating sleeping here for the night. I don't have the energy to return to my room, but I can smell myself. If anyone from my former life were here, the humiliation would turn me violent, but despite my embarrassment and exhaustion, I'm happy. I found water, and I won't let my suffering steal this triumph from me.

So, I limp to my quarters and take the shortest shower an Ambrose has ever taken. I drink an entire bottle of water and force myself to eat another protein pack. I almost fall asleep chewing, but I manage to eat it all without choking before I lay my searing bare skin on the sheets and pass out before my eyes even shut.

My shaking body wakes me to a world of hazy delusions. My pink skin is flushed with fever. My throat is painfully dry, and my sight sees only hallucinations. My muscles ache. My head throbs, and I think… What is going… Mother? How did you get here? What happened to Driver? I think Driver's dead, and that means, I'm… I'm… I'mmmmm…

I wake with a start. I'm no longer delirious, but by the way my throat hurts and my body aches from lying down, I've lost time. How long have I lain feverish in this bed?

I roll off the mattress with a groan and stumble to the bathroom. I turn on the faucet, desperate to soothe the desert in my mouth, but when I twist the handle, the pipes rattle but no water comes out.

"Shit." I grab the first shirt I find and throw it on, my pink skin protesting the fabric's touch. My body has never experienced such intense exposure, so I suspect I had sun poisoning. The past few days were a blur of delusion, and at one point, I was convinced my mom was here. That memory makes me grimace. I've learned to never show weakness in front of my parents, and if my mother witnessed me writhing naked on an employee bed while experiencing hallucinations, she would've disowned me. Being stranded has its small mercies, it seems.

I limp to the controls, my body too weak to manage more than a fast hobble. Driver still hasn't messaged, not that I expected that asshole to consider my wellbeing while he's out there dying. He was undoubtedly excited to be free of me, and a hint of satisfaction flutters through my belly knowing he probably regretted leaving me when he breathed his last breath.

My amusement is short-lived, though, when I see the date. Two days. I lost two days to that fever dream. Fear settles uncomfortably in my chest as I remember the way the pipes rattled with emptiness, and I race for the tanks. I was supposed to switch the containers below the drip, and that first bucket will be overflowing.

I skid to a halt in the water storage room, and my heart stops beating. The container is filled to the brim, but the pipe is no longer dripping. The floor is dry, confirming the leak stopped a while ago. The red light on Tank 10 reads empty, and I sink to my knees beside the bucket. This four-by-two-foot plastic bin is all that remains on The Bellator, and defeat settles heavily on my shoulders. All my wealth. All my power, position, and connections, and I'll be defeated by this measly offering of water.

I despise the urge to cry rising in my chest. This trip has tested my resolve more times than I can count, and I hate stooping to pity's temptation. So I blink until the tears disappear and dip my hand into the container. I drink from my cupped palm, afraid of what I must do. Afraid of what's to come. I worry my damaged skin won't survive the heat, but I need to brave the sun once more. The oasis is my last hope. And if its water tests toxic, I have depressingly few days left to live.

Chapter 14

DRIVER

For two days, I pushed myself to the breaking point, barely sleeping despite my exhaustion. That single roar struck a fear in my heart unlike any I've experienced. Not even the attack that ended my military career and left my body broken inspired this much terror. I lay dying during the battle, afraid to meet my end amidst the shrapnel, but it was nothing to that monstrous sound. I do not want to encounter its owner, so I ran nonstop through the torturous terrain.

I traveled through the night, using the coolness to stretch my sole bottle of water for as long as possible, but dehydration is my constant companion. The toxic swamp waters are poisoning my bloodstream. That single dose of antibiotics only temporarily staved off death, but my muscles shake, and my vision blurs. If I don't make it back to the ship soon, it'll be a coin toss to see if dehydration or fever takes me first. Unless that monster finds me.

The Bellator comes into view the afternoon of the second day, and destroyed metal has never brought me such hope. I can almost taste the water just looking at her. I practically feel it running over me as I scrub the filth from my body. The sun caked the swamp's grime to my skin, but by today's end, I'll step within the crash's safety, and then I can shoot an entire syringe of antibiotics into my veins. The thought alone gives me a high.

The hours it takes to reach the ship feel like days, but the second I pass through the outer airlock, adrenaline abandons me, and I collapse to the floor. Exhaustion whispers that I should stay here on the cool tiles, that I should shut my eyes and sleep, but I need antibiotics. Without them, I won't survive long enough to take that shower I can't stop fantasizing about.

So, I drag myself on my hands and knees to the Med Bay, my focus blurring as I search the medication stores. It takes too long to find what I need and even longer to inject the antibiotic into my veins, but the second the syringe empties her payload into my arm, relief floods my system. I sit on the floor since I don't have the energy to move to the medical beds, and I lean my head against the cabinets, knowing I'm finally safe to—

I jerk awake. The light filtering through the windows is softer than before. I must have fallen asleep. My back hurts from sitting on the hard floor, but the medication has done its job. I feel significantly better, if I ignore my stiff skin and ungodly thirst, but now that the infection is under control, I can finally shower. I limp to the crew quarters, suddenly aware of the fact that I haven't heard or seen Serling since my return, but then again, I've been passed out in the Med Bay for hours. Unless she had reason to be in there, she wouldn't have found me, and my guess is the princess is probably hiding in her room, enjoying a leisurely afternoon while I almost die.

I'll search for her after the shower improves my mood enough to deal with her attitude. It'll be nice to lay eyes on another human being after all these days alone, but I wish she was a welcoming person. Serling is a goddess to look upon but the devil to interact with, and when she learns that I returned empty-handed, she'll probably throw a tantrum.

I stumble into my room and peel off my filthy clothes before stepping into the shower. I twist the handle, eager to feel the water rain down on me, but nothing happens. The pipes deep within The Bellator groan and rattle, but the shower remains dry. I step out and twist the sink faucet only to receive the same results. No water comes out, only the sound of shaking pipes.

Fear settles in my chest as I grab a pair of dirty clothes and throw them on before I race to the control room. The Med Bay stocks antiseptic wipes that I can use to remove most of this grime, but they're a last result. We can't afford to waste medical supplies on unnecessary purposes, and even if we could, that's not the issue. If there's no water…

I skid to a stop before the controls and pull up the storage system's interface. The sight that greets me is a death sentence. Tank 10, the only tank with drinkable water, has been depleted. For a minute, I stand there in shock, unable to believe my eyes. That's impossible. Tank 10 was full when I left. I've been gone for a week, but the reserves should've lasted one person almost a month if rationed properly. If Serling used it for occasional showers and scheduled drinking, only a quarter of the tank should be drained. For the entire reservoir to be gone, she would've had to take daily prolonged showers, and a new emotion joins my fear. Rage. That selfish, self-absorbed princess. She wasted all our water. Not a single drop remains. She's killed us, and I realize why we haven't crossed paths. She's probably hiding from my wrath, and even though I hate myself for even imagining it, I picture myself strangling her for the briefest second. Of all the people to be stranded with, it had to be her. It had to be the woman who doesn't give a shit about anyone but herself, and I exit the control room with fire in my veins and thunder in my voice.

"Serling!" I bellow. "Serling Ambrose? Where are you?"

She isn't in her quarters nor was she in the Med Bay or the control room, and if I wasn't so blinded by rage, I would've realized the ship was too still, too quiet. Her absence is eerie, but anger fuels my search, rendering me oblivious. She doesn't get to kill us and then hide from the repercussions. She's spent her entire life escaping the consequences of her selfishness, but her daddy isn't here to save her now. It's time she learns the universe doesn't revolve around her.

"Serling!" I burst into the cafeteria, expecting to find the room empty, but to my surprise, she's hovered over the far counter. She jerks at my voice, and for a split second, she looks relieved to see me until she registers my expression. Her armor of cold indifference resumes control of her features, and that's when I notice her severe sunburn. My anger doubles at the sight of her pink skin. I told her to stay inside, but in her arrogance, she ignored me and ventured out into the heat. The violence of her burn tells me she's recovering from sun poisoning, and her defiance is undoubtedly why there's no water left.

"You had one job," I shout as I stride for her, and her body involuntarily flinches at the severity of my voice, which only fuels my emotions. She doesn't even have the decency to look apologetic. Instead, she wears her arrogance like a crown, still deeming me inferior even after her selfishness signed our death warrants. "I told you to do one simple thing. Ration the water, but you couldn't even manage that. It's gone, Serling. All of our water is gone."

"You're alive—" she starts.

"Do you understand what you've done?" My tone shuts her up. "Do you realize how incredibly stupid you've been? I found nothing out there but a toxic swamp. There's no safe water, and because you're too arrogant to listen, we're dead. Do you know what it's like to die of dehydration? Do you know how torturous a death you've resigned us to?"

She opens her mouth, but I cut her off, unwilling to hear her pathetic excuses. "I'm trying to keep you alive. I'm trying to keep you safe, but I should've let you die. I wish someone else had survived this crash because you are the worst person to be stranded with. You're what's wrong with the galaxy. Your family and their greed, their self-importance and arrogance. You don't care for anyone but yourself, but guess what, Princess? Daddy isn't coming to save you. I saw the missile that hit us. You're the reason we crashed since you were the only one on board worth sending an assassination team after."

"I—"

"Please, just shut up!" I slap the wall beside me. She flinches at the sound before staring me down with fury in her eyes, and her unyielding defiance makes me despise her. Even now, with death at our door, she can't admit she was wrong. "I don't want to hear your excuses. Someone tried to kill you, and Headquarters will have announced The Bellator's crash. Everyone thinks we're dead, and because of you, we will be. I knew you were selfish, but I assumed you weren't stupid. Guess I was mistaken. I've been in disasters before, but I can't believe the arrogance of one spoiled girl will be my downfall. Maybe it's a good thing you're never getting off this planet. I'd hate seeing the Federation under your reign."

I realize I'm being cruel, but I can't stop myself. Two rules. That's all I gave her. Ration the water and stay inside, and she violated both. Not only has her disobedience sealed our fate, but she has the nerve to act like I'm in the wrong. The venom in her features is deadly, and I need to leave this room. If I stay here for one second longer, I'll say something else, and I don't want to die with cruelty as my final words.

I turn to leave, but Serling finds her voice and flings it at me.

"Fuck you!" she screams.

"Fuck me?" I ask as I storm for her. "Do you know what I survived out there? I almost died facing dangers that would make your heart stop, and what did you do? You used all the water because you couldn't stay inside. What's wrong with you that you have to be so defiant? Are you really that self-absorbed that you don't understand the danger we're in? What? Were you bored staying safe? Did you want a suntan like we're on some holiday? You are unbelievable."

"You're the one who's unbelievable," she spits, turning toward the counter. Before I can react to her dismissal, she whirls back around and throws something at me. I flinch, waiting for the pain, but only a wall of cold slaps me. I sputter as water soaks my face, and when my vision clears, I register an odd expression marring her features. It's unreadable save for the thread of disappointment hovering behind her eyes, and my memory flashes to her greeting. For a moment, she seemed excited to see me, a concept so unfathomable that I initially ignored it. What did I miss?

"I found water," Serling says without emotion, and then she storms out of the cafeteria.

SERLING

To think I was excited when I first heard his voice pisses me off. I was convinced Driver had died out there in this heat. He never made contact, and he's been gone for days. I hate the man, even if my subconscious finds him captivating, but I'd still rather he live than leave me alone.

Now I wish he hadn't. I can't believe I hoped he would return. I can't believe I wanted to share my findings with him. No one has ever spoken to me that way, and it took everything in me not to slap him. I did throw water in his face, which felt amazing, but now I'm pissed at my lack of self-control. Returning that water to The Bellator was no easy feat.

After my fever cleared, I filled a large pack with food, a water bottle, and a tester. I also found sealable bags in the cafeteria. We'll need to find more efficient means of transportation, but at the moment, bags were the best option. Their light weight barely took up room in the pack, and I could fill them with water for the return climb if the oasis proved safe.

I then planned a route over the dual cliffs, mapping out a less direct path, and while it took longer, it reduced the time spent on the vertical cliff face. It made traveling with a heavy pack significantly easier, and the less strenuous terrain helped me move faster.

Seeing the oasis in the middle of the sharp rocks still felt like a fever dream, but when I dipped the test into the gentle ripples, and it confirmed the water was safe for consumption, I cried. Big, fat, ugly, happy tears, but this time, I let myself sob. I let myself feel giddy with hope, and then I cupped my hands in the coolness and drank until my stomach was full. The taste wasn't entirely pleasant. The test proved it was harmless to drink and bathe in, but it also registered a high mineral count. It wasn't the filtered water I was accustomed to, but I didn't care. The pool was huge and clean and cool. The Bellator's filters would improve the taste, but that was barely a concern as I stripped off my sweaty clothes and took a swim. I'd found water, and shocking as it was, I wished Driver was there as I floated under the sun. I wanted him to be alive, to see that I wasn't as useless as he believed. That I had helped, and we wouldn't die of dehydration. I also needed his strength to help me figure out how to transport the water to the ship, but after his outburst, I regret wishing him a safe return. I understand why he assumed I depleted our supply. We've had no contact, so I couldn't warn him about the leak. Based on his appearance, he's been through hell, but to come at me like that without asking what happened makes the darker parts of me wish he'd died out there.

"What do you mean, you found water?" He captures my biceps and spins me to face him before I can escape the cafeteria.

"Get your hands off me." I rip my arm from his grasp, but he reaches out with his other hand and grabs my wrist. He's gentle, making sure not to hurt me, but there's no escaping his hold.

"What do you mean you found water?" he repeats.

"Exactly what it sounds like, Driver!" I shout. "I found water. Safe, clean drinking water. I found it! That's why I'm sunburnt, and I'm not as stupid as you think. When I didn't hear from you, I assumed you died, and now I kind of wish you had." I yank my wrist from his hold, and this time he lets me go. "Then a pipe burst. Tank 10 lost most of its supply, so I've been out there doing what you couldn't. I found water within walking distance. Me! The self-absorbed, stupid heiress." I throw his words back in his face. "I saved us, so fuck you."

"What do you mean you didn't hear from me?" he asks.

"Stop asking that!" I scream. "I mean exactly what I said. You never contacted me."

"But I did," he says. "Twice."

"Well, I never got your messages. I thought you were dead, so I went outside. I know you like to control everything I do, but one of us had to save us."

"I'm not controlling you," he says. "I'm trying to keep you safe."

"That's what they all say. 'Serling, we're just trying to protect you. We're just trying to preserve your reputation. *We're just, we're just, we're just...*' Well, do me a favor. Stop trying. I don't need your help. Seems the selfish princess is good enough on her own."

"Serling..." his voice softens as regret floods his features, but his guilt only fuels my hatred.

"Leave me alone." I storm to the water bags and shove three at him. "And wash up. You smell putrid."

"Serling, wait." He chases after me, but I speed up. I don't want his apology because I don't want to forgive him. I realize how this situation looked to him. I also noticed the massive wounds on his arm and the paleness of his skin. Something horrible happened out there. He looks like he barely survived, so I understand how returning to no water made him unreasonable, but I'm in no mood to concede.

"Serling."

"Leave me alone."

"Serling, stop walking." His command is so full of authority that I freeze in my tracks, and I despise how my body reacts to the way he dominates the room, especially since I know he's trying to beg forgiveness.

"Don't bother," I say, regaining control of the conversation because if he begs, I might forgive him. I don't want to hate the only other person on this planet, but my pride is too injured to admit that. "I don't care. Just clean up so I don't have to look at you. It's disgusting."

Only he's not disgusting. I forgot how captivating Driver is. His appearance is unique, and even filthy, he's magnetic. He's too rugged, too angular and untraditional to be handsome, yet he's incredibly tall and powerful. His black hair frames his face in a way my fingers crave, and his full lips warn his kiss would ruin me. He is all dominance and strength and power. He's annoyingly yet refreshingly authentic, and he doesn't take my shit. Driver isn't pretty, yet he's the most attractive man I've ever seen, and the longer I'm around him the more I'm reminded that he represents everything I can never have. It's why I detest him, why I want to destroy him. Because if I don't hate him, I'll have to admit the truth. It's easier to fight with this pilot. Easier to let him think I'm the devil than allow him to see the ugliness my family name bred inside me. To glimpse the fear of my future being around him inspires.

"Take me to it." His redirect surprises me. I expected him to apologize despite my orders, to backtrack and take back those cruel words he can never undo, but he completely avoids any attempt at an apology. I can't decide if that makes me furious, or if his willingness to stick to his hatred makes me respect him.

I've never gone toe to toe with a man who doesn't cower at my name, and maybe it was the week of solitude, but his fight is preferable to his groveling. I've seen hundreds of men beg and bow and bend. I've never experienced one battle my fire with a blaze of his own, and I almost like it.

"Take me to the water," he repeats.

"No. I'm tired."

"Serling." He steps forward until he's towering over me. "Take me to the water, now."

CHAPTER 15

DRIVER

Y ou're in no condition to climb, old man." Serling uses her words like knives, and if I hadn't just eviscerated her with words of my own, I might take offense at the insult.

"That's enough. Let's go." I open the corner of one of the water bags and take a drink, gagging slightly at the taste, and she smirks with smug satisfaction.

"It's safe, but the mineral content is high," she explains. "It'll taste odd until we run it through filtration."

"It tastes fine," I lie as I drink the entire bag. I don't give a shit about the unpleasant flavor. My insides are screaming for water, and drinking feels better than I could have imagined. I can't believe Serling found water, but I'm thankful she did. I still want to see the oasis for myself, though, since I'll need to design a more efficient means of transportation. Carting a few dozen plastic bags on our backs every day will put too much of a strain on our bodies and time. We aren't out of danger yet.

"Are you going to at least wash up first, or are you going to make me smell you the entire climb?" She asks as she moves to her pack and removes the rest of the water bags, draining them into larger bottles for easier storage.

"I'll clean up there so we can save this water," I say. She opens her mouth to protest, but I raise my hands to silence her. "I'll wash far enough away from the source so I won't contaminate the water, but no point wasting what little you brought back."

"You try climbing two cliffs sunburnt with a heavy pack digging into your shoulders," she mutters under her breath. I'm not sure if she meant me to hear it, but I hear it all the same as she digs through the fridge and pulls out a package of cured meats and cheese. They're cured to last for months, so we thankfully have an abundance, but she doesn't so much as offer me a single bite as she eats. Instead, she just watches me as if she expects me to croak from old age. That or yell at her again.

"I'll get a pack and more plastic bags," I grab a protein pack to eat as I search. "We'll leave as soon as I get back."

She doesn't dignify me with a response. She simply stands there chewing, and it's annoying how gorgeous she is, even sunburnt and pissed. It's even more annoying that she saved our asses.

We make quick work of the dual cliffs thanks to Serling's mapped route. I'm exhausted from the lack of sleep, blood loss, and infection, but the moment my eyes land on the oasis, every physical ailment evaporates from my body. The sight is shocking, yet breathtakingly beautiful, for here, nestled among the endlessly jagged and tan rocks, is a crystal pool surrounded on three sides by thick, tropical vegetation. The plants are unlike anything I've seen in the known galaxy, but judging by their vibrance and proximity to safe water, I assume that some of them are edible. The pool is dozens of yards long and almost as wide. A pale beach sits below the cliff, and hope flickers to life within me for the first time since we crashed. We may never get off this planet, but this will ensure our survival.

Serling lies on the sand with her bare feet submerged below the waves while I fill the bags. I'll take them into the rocks to wash so that my filth doesn't pollute the source and so she won't see my scars. Then I'll refill them before we return to the ship. Tomorrow, after I've slept, I'll start working on a plan to streamline transportation, but for now, Serling's solution of filling plastic bags inside our packs is the best option. I study her pink skin and almost feel guilty for making her travel here again. Judging by her appearance, she's endured a lot over the past few days. She surprised me, and I wonder if I judged her too harshly. She is cruel and selfish, but she risked her life to find water. Was I wrong about Serling Ambrose?

"Are you just going to stand there gawking, old man?" she asks with an icy tone, and I have my answer.

"Stay here. I'll be back."

"Where else would I go?" she mutters under her breath as I disappear into the rocks. I should be the bigger person and be nicer to her, but goddamn it, she makes it so difficult. Maybe I'll be more tolerant tomorrow after I've slept.

I make quick work of washing with medical-grade antiseptic, and when I finally pull on a clean pair of clothes, I feel almost human again. My body still aches, my arm desperately needs stitches, and I most likely need another dose of antibiotics, but I—

A roar shatters the silence moments before Serling screams, and for a split second, I freeze because I recognize that sound. I know what creature that voice heralds. It followed me here, and it found Serling.

I seize my weapon from its perch on the rocks and launch into a run, thankful I had the foresight to bring it with me. When I heard this monster in the swamp, I assumed it would hunt me until I left the water's borders. Any animal native to the dark and damp terrain would undoubtedly suffer in this rocky and dry landscape, but it seems vengeance urged it onward. I wonder if it's the mother of the beast I killed, and that thought pushes me faster. If a mother is on the path of revenge, Serling doesn't stand a chance.

As if to confirm my suspicions, the creature roars again, and Serling answers with a cry of her own. I explode from the rocks and survey the oasis with military-honed efficiency. The beast is perched on the cliffs to my left, watching Serling run for our supplies as its claws dig into the stone. It's calculating her trajectory, measuring how far it needs to jump to reach her soft body, and terror floods me at the sight. It's a replica of the beast I killed in those rancid waters. It wears the same black scales, although their shine has dulled in this heat. The same talons, same tail, same all-seeing eyes, but with one alarming difference. The animal I killed stood four feet tall at most. This monster stands at least fifteen feet. My blade did nothing against the child in our fight. Will my gun be equally useless against the mother?

The creature blinks, and that small movement sets off a chain reaction. It leaps down the rocks, its movements too fast as its claws crack the stones.

"Serling, leave it!" I scream as she tries to grab her pack, and her eyes fly to mine. I extend a hand and open my mouth to order her to run, but she understands my wordless meaning and bolts for me. She reaches me in seconds, and I pull her into the rocks. This pool is our only chance of survival, and we cannot let a decaying carcass poison our only water supply. We need to lead the animal away from the oasis before we kill it… if we can kill it.

The creature takes the bait and changes course, its talons digging deep wounds into the sand. Serling holds my hand with a death grip, but I shove her ahead of me, forcing her to lose her hold on my fingers.

"Whatever you do, don't stop moving," I shout as we disappear into the uneven and jagged rocks that form the first cliff. "Get back to the Bellator. Get to the big guns."

"I don't know how to use those," she cries, the creature's screech drowning out her voice.

"You're smart." I catch her as she trips. "You'll figure it out. Just get to the ship and lock yourself inside."

"Wait…" Her voice breaks. "Why? What are you going to do?"

"Run, Serling!" I push her forward as the monster's head comes into view. I twist, aim between its eyes, and shoot. The blast explodes against its scales, and I swear I see them crack as its head snaps backward. They're brittle. Without water, this monster's exoskeleton is brittle. My gun's power will do little against its scales, but The Bellator's blasters?

"What are you going to do?" Serling repeats as I use my shoulders to shove her up the cliff. The creature screams a blood-thirsty rage, but I ignore her question because we both aren't making it back to the ship alive. That monster is gaining on us despite the blast to the face, and it'll keep coming. I killed its offspring, and it's hellbent on revenge. The best outcome I can hope for is to give Serling a fighting chance. To force our predator clear of the oasis and into the Bellator's line of sight. If anyone is coming to rescue us, they're coming for her. She's who the Federation wants to survive. She has a life to return to. As a soldier, I've always known I would die on the battlefield. My end was always going to be violent.

"What are you planning?" She screams above the monster's rage. "You understand The Bellator's defenses better than me. You're coming with me, right?"

The creature leaps over the cliff, and I shoot it in the neck. It stumbles, and I shoot it in the jaw, then the chest, then the stomach. It slips out of sight, and grabbing Serling's hips, I shove her into a hidden alcove.

"Once it passes, you run for the ship. You don't stop, no

matter what," I order, and she grabs my wrists as if she means to follow me, but I force her back into the shadows. "Lock yourself inside and get to the long-range guns. You know how to shoot. I know you do, so get up there, take aim, and fire until that son of a bitch is dead. Then burn the body. You don't want the carcass drawing other predators here."

"Driver, stop." She clings to me, but I peel her fingers off my arms.

"Lock yourself inside. Shoot it. Burn it. Say you understand."

"Driver…"

"Say you understand!"

"I understand."

"Good girl." I study her for a split second. She's proved herself stronger than I expected. Smarter than I thought. She'll be fine. At least the last face I'll see is beautiful. She has been difficult, but she's undeniably lovely, and her beauty will deliver me to peace.

"Stay hidden until it passes and then run like hell," I say, and then I leave her behind.

CHAPTER 16

SERLING

Driver takes off running, leaving me in the shadows as his shouts taunt the beast, and as the creature crests the jagged rocks, it spots him and only him. Tears flood my eyes, but I slam my hand over my mouth to contain my sobs. He's drawing the monster's attention away from me to give me a fighting chance, and I realize I've never witnessed a person die before. Not like this. Not bloody and brutal. Driver is going to die to save me, and a visceral emotion wracks my body. No one, not even the overpaid Ambrose guards, would sacrifice their life like this for mine, and with that terrified thought, I burst from the rocks' shelter. I have to get to the ship's guns.

I race over our newly mapped path through the dual cliffs as fast as my exhausted body can carry me. It's less of a climb and more like giant stepping stones, and without a heavy pack, I fly over the harsh ground. The beast screams, and I watch it lunge for Driver. Its fangs could rip a man in half, and I brace for Driver's death scream, but a shot rings out instead. The monster stumbles backward before it dives again. Its talons collide with the stone, and the sound is so loud it echoes endlessly. My tears come harder as I scramble over the roughness. My palms sting as they scrape over the sharp edges, but I don't stop. The beast's constant violence tells me it hasn't gotten Driver yet, but it'll only be a matter of time. Its strength is breaking the rocks apart. It'll extract Driver from his hiding spot before I can make it to the guns, and judging by its ferocity, it will shred him to pieces with those fangs.

"Hey!" I shout. I don't know what possesses me to do it. I can't fight that monster, but the thought of a hostile alien eating the only other person on this planet nauseates me. It was one thing when I assumed Driver died alone out in the wilderness, but to witness his violent death is something I'll never recover from. My feelings for this man don't matter. I won't survive watching that beast eat him alive.

"Hey! Over here, asshole!" I scream as I push my burning muscles until I'm racing through the small valley between the cliffs. It can't see me down here, so I use the rocks' echoing effect to confuse my voice. "Here! I'm here! Come and get me."

I force my adrenaline-drugged body up the second cliff. My fingers are bleeding. The scrapes on my knees sting. I can't breathe. I can't think. I can't see. *I can't. I can't. I can't.* The gun goes off again, and that monster roars. I've never heard anything scream like that, and the sound will haunt my nightmares until my death. I cannot describe the noise. It's unlike anything mankind has ever experienced. It's a combination of rage and pain and fear and hunger. It's the battle cry of the Mors Expanse. It's the mourning of a mother and the vengeance of inhuman blood thirst.

Another gunshot rings out, and Driver's scream joins the booming echoes. I trip at the sound because it isn't a challenge. He isn't trying to draw the creature away. His voice was fueled by pain. Raw, unfiltered pain.

"Leave him alone, you asshole!" I reach the top of the second cliff, and The Bellator finally comes into view. I've never been so happy to see a crash in my life, but in my haste, I don't notice the hooked rock in front of my boot. I trip over it and fall a few feet before crashing onto a flat ledge, screaming as the impact bruises my shoulder. My vision blurs with tears. The pain begs me to lie here, but I force myself to roll off the rock and down to the next. I catch sight of the creature out of the corner of my eye, its multi-eyed face searching for me. Its massive black talons tap the stone, and I try to slip unseen through the shadows. The sun is setting, the encroaching darkness offering me her protection, but just when I think I'll reach the bottom safely, its eyes find mine. We stare locked together for a moment, and then it screams its hunger.

I leap off the rocks, ignoring the fire of pain burning my ankle, and force myself to keep moving. I groan with every foot-fall, but the monster already knows where I am. There's no need for silence now. My only hope is to reach the ship, but the creature jumps off the cliff and lands feet from me. Its jaws snap, and its talons click as it readies to make me its meal. Paralyzing fear coils in my chest. I don't want to die. Not like this. Not in some monster's jaws. I should've listened to Driver. I should've escaped, but something inside me refused to abandon him. Not when he so selflessly sacrificed his life for mine. I don't think my own father would do that for me. No, I know my own father wouldn't do that for me. He sent me through the Mors, after all.

I stumble as I reach the bottom of the cliff, but I regain my balance before my knees hit the stone. I run with every ounce of my waning strength, but the creature is too fast. Its roar heralds my death, but just as it lunges for me, powerful arms capture my waist. Driver and I careen sideways, crashing to our backs as the creature's fangs bite down on empty rocks. It howls in pain. Or maybe it's Driver who's screaming? I can't tell.

"Go!" Driver orders as he hauls me off the ground and

shoves me forward. He settles his body between me and the predator, but the monster glares past him to watch my escape as if it can't be bothered with the soldier. It stares at me as if it wants my flesh instead, and I wonder if it assumes I'm special to Driver. He's sacrificing himself to save me, and this beast believes I'm important. Maybe it thinks ripping me to shreds first will punish Driver.

The gunshot is so loud, I almost trip as the blast lands between its eyes. That gets its attention, and it leaps for him. "Run, Serling!" He shouts. "Don't look back!"

And I don't. I keep moving as I wait for Driver to die. I wait for his final breath, but all I hear is the shriek of the beast and the blast of the gun. Driver roars, both in pain and anger, but his voice doesn't silence. As long as I hear him, he's alive, and I push faster. I don't know how I manage it, but I'm suddenly at the Bellator, sealing the airlocks behind me as I sprint for the guns. Before we ran out of water, Driver reconfigured their defense parameters to work planet-side, and screw him, but he was right. I pray he holds out for a few more minutes, and I race up the level and collapse into the shooter's perch.

I flip on the machines and swivel the guns toward the monster. Through the sights I watch Driver aim, but nothing happens. He's out of ammo, and I swallow my fear as the creature dives for him. I refuse to react. I refuse to cry or shout or panic. Instead, I breathe in slowly, and as I exhale, I pull the trigger.

The monster's head explodes in a terrifying display of firepower. Nothing remains but blood and pulp, and the headless body teeters for a second before crashing to the stones. I almost throw up at the macabre vibrance painted across the pale and monotone landscape, but I force myself to swallow the bile as I aim again. I shoot it in the chest for good measure. I realize it's dead. Nothing could have survived that decapitation, but I can't stop myself from pulling the trigger. Its chest cavity disintegrates upon impact, and I slide out of my seat and rush back down to the ground level, clenching my teeth to keep from vomiting at my actions. I saw how close that creature came to Driver, and I'm terrified it killed him. I'm afraid my salvation was too little too late, so when I explode out into the sunset, a strangled cry escapes my lips at the sight.

"Driver!" I race for him, and his eyes find mine with an unhinged expression.

"Are you okay?" He seizes my face, and I flinch at his urgency, at his concern. "Are you hurt? Did it get you?"

"No." I sob, but seeing the blood on my hands, he scans my body.

"I scraped myself," I explain. "I'm fine. Really."

"Good, good." He releases my cheeks and gives me the oddest expression. "You did..." He trails off and something about his slurred words terrifies me. "You..."

His voice dies in his throat as he collapses, and for the first time, I notice the blood pouring from his stomach.

"Driver!" I drop to my knees, pressing my palms against the wound carved through his abdomen, but my fingers do nothing to stop the blood pumping from his veins. I look around as if something to bandage his wound will magically appear, but I only find a second gash sliced deep into his thigh. He's bleeding out. He's bleeding out in my hands because he saved my life, and I don't know how to help.

"Driver!" My efforts to staunch the blood flow are useless. "Wake up. Please, get up!"

He doesn't move. I need to get him to the Med Bay, but he's almost double my weight. I can't carry him, but I can't let him bleed out. Not after he sacrificed himself to save my life.

"Don't you die on me, old man." I release his bloody stomach and scramble to his head, wedging my hands under his armpits. I pull with all my strength, but he's so goddam heavy that my slick fingers slip, and I fall on my ass. "Screw you," I growl at his unconscious body as I wipe my palms on my pants. I re-grip his arms and throw all my weight into my movements. Adrenaline and fear lend me their aid, and together, we haul his powerful frame onto the ship. Once his back slides onto the smooth floors, it's significantly easier to drag him, but I still fall twice before we make it to the Med Bay. A trail of gore lies in our wake, and I pray he doesn't bleed out before I place him in the emergency pod. Most ships employ human doctors, but they always come equipped with an emergency surgery pod. Run by artificial intelligence, it can diagnose and treat most ailments from infections to massive bodily trauma. It should be able to handle his wounds, but I need to get him into it first.

I slip on the blood-smeared tiles, screaming as I fight to lift him, but he's solid muscle. I'm too tired to pick him up. I haven't had enough to eat or drink, and we collapse in a slick heap.

"What do I do?" I sob. "Tell me what to do." He doesn't answer, and I cling to his limp body as I cry. I don't know what to do. I'm not a doctor or a soldier. My only hope is to get him in that pod, but he's too big for my exhausted frame to lift.

"Come on, asshole." I stand up, determined to save him, even if it kills me. I won't let him die.

Inch by painfully slow inch, I pull until his torso slides onto the pod's mattress, and then I push until his legs settle into place. Relief washes over me when I notice the subtle rise and fall of his chest. He's alive. There's still hope, and I search every drawer until I find medical scissors. I cut the bloody clothes from his body and then initiate the emergency surgery protocol, praying it's not too late.

It's been hours since I shoved Driver inside the emergency pod, and he's still unconscious as the machine operates on him. I watched over him at first, but when I realized how long the road ahead of us was, my anxiety refused to let me stay still.

I found the Bellator's reserve fuel and doused the creature's corpse with some before setting it on fire. Spacecraft fuel is noxious, and it covers the scent of burning flesh, although I'm not sure that's a blessing. If another creature smells the flames, they won't know what we're burning. All they'll smell is the chemical fumes and steer clear, and while I'm thankful predators won't be drawn to the charred carcass, I gag repeatedly at the toxic, black smoke.

The blaze burned well into the night, guiding my way, and after strapping a gun to my waist, I climbed back to the oasis. I filled as many water bags as I could carry and returned to the Bellator long after nightfall. I then spent the next hours scrubbing the blood from both me and the floor. The crimson sight made it impossible to eat, so I worked until I could barely stand, which is why I'm hovering in a daze above Driver's unconscious body.

The machine finally finished his stitches and administered fluids, pain medication, and antibiotics. All I can do now is wait, but both he and the pod are filthy. Anxiety won't let me sleep, and I can't stomach the idea of food, so I do the only thing I can. I grab a bottle of medical antiseptic and start at his feet.

I lose track of how long it takes to meticulously scrub the blood off him, my body on autopilot as I care for him in the only way I know how. He hates me, yet he was prepared to die so I would live. He sacrificed his life for mine, and no one has ever done that for me. Not even the people who claim to love me. I don't know what drove a man who despises me to place my life above his own, but everything inside me breaks. Who is Driver Thorne? How can one person be so brave and selfless? I don't deserve such intense protection, but I'm grateful for his bravery.

Limbs numb with exhaustion, I dispose of the bloody rags and examine his bare body. The machine did an excellent job stitching up his stomach, leg, and arm, but without the blood coating his skin, I see the severity of the scars he wears. These new and horrific wounds are nothing compared to what already mars his flesh, and I can't stop my fingers from pressing against his side.

I researched Driver Thorne when my father first chartered The Bellator. A legendary military hero, Driver saved his men's lives by sacrificing his own. According to the articles, he almost didn't survive the attack, and his recovery was extensive. Doctors had to replace a few of his organs with synthetics, and his entire right side was destroyed, forcing surgeons to perform dozens of reconstructions. From his ribs down to his calf, he is nothing but deep and angry scars, and I understand now why I've never seen him remove his shirt despite the heat. They're brutal, a canvas of pain permanently carved into his flesh, and I'm sure many women have recoiled at this sight.

But I, too, have scars, only mine are hidden. They mark my soul and make me ugly, and as my fingers trace his jagged edges, I can't bring myself to be disgusted by him. If anything, they add to his beauty. He's perfectly flawed. His blemishes are his strength, and my fingers move to his hips. I caress every mark, every gnarled disfigurement, as if I'm trying to memorize the feel of him. No one has ever done what he did for me, and I want to worship every ugly part of his body because he isn't ugly. He's beautiful. Authentically and powerfully beautiful, and I hope he never hides these from me again. I want him to wear his scars with pride because I don't see flaws in them. I see the only person who genuinely cares if I live or die. Driver Thorne has irrevocably changed me. He has altered my soul, my very DNA, and the Serling I was is dead. He killed her, and I'm glad because she wasn't worthy of this man's sacrifice. But this new Serling? She will be worthy. I swear it.

My fingers move to his powerful thighs, the scars dancing beneath my skin, and Driver grunts. His fist shoots out, capturing mine, and I freeze, expecting him to toss it aside for touching the parts of him he desperately tries to hide, but he doesn't. He simply tightens his grip and pulls my hand to his chest, trapping my palm over his thundering heart.

DRIVER

A featherlight touch tickles my thigh, pulling me toward consciousness, and my hand captures the intruder, forcing its movements to halt. It's soft and warm and comforting. Instinct urges me to clutch it to my chest, and I fall back into pleasant oblivion with its warmth trapped in my fist.

I don't know how long I was unconscious, but when I finally come to, the softness is still clutched in my hand. I groan as I adjust myself, my body incredibly stiff, but it lacks the pain my subconscious tells me I should feel, which means I'm on heavy medication. For a moment, that confuses me, but then something tickles my stomach. It feels like hair, and that confuses me even more.

My eyes blink open to find black hair spread across my bare abdomen, the tangled locks covering my scars. My gaze shifts to my fist, and I realize what I'm clutching. A hand. Serling's hand, and she's currently asleep sitting on a chair beside the emergency pod with her head resting on my abs. Her cheeks are pressed against my scars, and my stomach clenches at the realization that she's seen me. She's seen all of me judging by my state of undress and multiple bandages, yet she's sleeping on my damaged skin. This infuriating woman is full of surprises.

"Serling?" I whisper, squeezing her fingers gently to wake her up without alarm, but she jerks upright anyway with eyes so wide they might swallow me. Seems I'm not the only one shocked by the realization that we're still holding hands.

"You're awake." She rubs her face with her free hand, but she makes no attempt to pull her fingers from my grasp. "How do you feel? Are you in pain?" Her voice is rough with sleep, and I like the sound. It's natural. Human and relatable, not like her normally hostile or curated tone. If Serling were a kinder woman, I might enjoy waking daily to it.

"Are you all right?" I ignore her questions as I scan her body for signs of injury. The girl is a mess. Blood streaks her hair. Dirt stains her skin, and sweat darkens her clothes. She looks exhausted and utterly miserable, but I find no wounds.

"Just some scrapes on my hands and knees," she says, her eyes catching on my scars as she studies my bandaged stomach. I wait for her to recoil at the sight, but she surprises me by touching one of the larger disfigurations. She traces it as if she can't help herself, and I realize it must have been her outlining my marks that woke me earlier. "We don't have much water left," she continues, lifting her gaze to my face. "I need to make another oasis trip, but I cleaned you and the ship instead, since I can't climb anymore. I'm too sore. Oh, and I burned the creature, but thankfully, there's been no sign of anything else."

"It was the mother," I explain. "In the swamp, I ran into one of those creatures. It was about four feet tall, which leads me to believe it was a juvenile and the creature that attacked us was its parent. If the mother had a mate or a pack, they could come for us, but I'm praying only it followed me here because I killed its offspring. When I shot it, its scales cracked. It needs water to survive, which is good for us."

"The oasis." Her concern causes her to press her palm against my scars, and her nearness to what I try so hard to keep hidden makes it difficult to concentrate.

"I doubt those creatures know it's here. The swamp is highly toxic, whereas this water is fresh. If they thrive in the swamp, they won't survive here." I capture her wandering hand and pull it to my chest alongside her other. No one has willingly touched my scars in so long that I can't function with her hands on me. Most women I've been with since the attack prefer me with the lights off and my shirt still on. "You don't have to do that," I say pointedly, and her expression turns serious.

"I wanted to," she whispers, and I've never detected such humility in her voice before. It scares me to see Serling so docile, and I wonder if I was closer to death than I thought.

"Thank you," she says, and her eyes drop to my scars. Not because they disgust her, I realize, but because I suspect she's uncomfortable admitting the words readying to fall from her lips. "No one has ever done anything like that for me. You could have... You almost died."

I don't like the brokenness in her voice. I would rather she shout and call me an asshole for nearly dying and leaving her alone, but I paste a smile on my face and inject a tease into my tone. "Well, I'm sure your dad will give me a huge reward for saving your life. Kind of hard to collect the money if you're dead."

I expect her to roll her eyes or insult me, but instead, she struggles not to cry. I was trying to lighten the mood, but she looks like I just carved her heart out. She must know I was joking, but then I replay her words, realizing I'm one hundred percent the asshole she thinks I am. She thanked me for risking my life to save her. She's shocked anyone would help her, and I made a joke about being in it for the money. I figured she would laugh, but she's crestfallen.

"Ser—" I open my mouth to apologize, but she stands up, pulling her hands from mine. I never thought I would miss Serling Ambrose's touch, but the absence of her warmth feels monumental. For a moment, the heiress and I made peace. We were on common ground, and I fucked it up.

"Well, now that you're awake, and I know you'll live, I'm

going to go clean up and eat." She steps back, putting distance between us that seems more expansive than the Mors itself. "We're almost out of water, and you're in no condition to move. I need to climb to the oasis, but you shouldn't need me now that you're conscious."

And with that, she leaves the Med Bay, signaling our cease-fire is over.

CHAPTER 17

SERLING

I clutch my hand to my chest to keep the blood from dripping onto the floor. I slipped on the return from the oasis, slicing open my palm, and it stings from having to grip the sharp rocks for the rest of the trip. It's not a serious injury, but it also shouldn't have happened. I've made that climb every day, sometimes twice, since Driver returned. I've memorized those cliffs, their every curve and direction, but exhaustion is taking its toll. I shouldn't have risked being out in this heat, not after waking this morning in pain, but I couldn't stay on the ship. I can't be around him.

I enter the Med Bay, resolved to see Driver as I search for a bandage, but his bed is empty. Concern bubbles in my chest against my will, and I hate that I'm worried for his life now. I hate that I'm invested in his welfare when I'm just a payout to him.

"Driver?" I call as I sanitize my hand and then wrap it in gauze, but he doesn't answer. I grab a water bottle, swallow a pain relief pill, and head to the control room, but he isn't there either. Nor is he in his quarters.

"Driver?" I move into the corridor and shout, my concern

morphing into fear. Where is he? Why can't I find him? "Driver—"

"Tanks!" His deep voice echoes through the hallways, and I scowl at how my heart rate calms at his answer.

"What are you doing in here?" I ask as I enter the water storage.

"Fixing the leak." He gestures to the pipe above him where he replaced my temporary fix with an expert welding job. "I'm running diagnostics on the rest of the system as well. Figured I would repair all potential problems so that we could store water in these tanks again."

"Oh…" I trail off as I study him. He's wearing a loose-fitting shirt, so I can't see his wounds. His skin's color is a healthy shade, though, and it's been a week since the attack. With modern medicine, his recovery should be nearly complete, but I want to examine him. I want to check his healing, but I refuse to let him witness my concern. "I can't carry that much water," I say instead, my customary bite returning to my tone. "Even with your help, we'll never fill these tanks, so I don't see the point of fixing them."

"I have an idea for that." He studies the bruising on my shoulder from the pack straps, my sunburnt skin, and finally my bandaged palm. "Carrying the water isn't an efficient long-term solution. It's also…" he reaches out as if to touch my bruises, but then thinks better of it and pulls his hand back. It makes me angry that I wish he followed through.

"The crash destroyed the escape pods designed for space travel," he continues. "But some of the all-terrain rovers survived. They sustained damage, but one is mostly intact. I plan to strip the damaged ones for parts and hopefully use them to fix it. It'll make water transportation significantly easier, and we can fill these tanks so we don't encounter another emergency. I was also thinking of designing a collector for when it rains. My guess is this planet has two seasons. We crashed at the end of the rainy, which means we most likely won't experience precipitation for months during the dry, but when it rolls back around, I want to be prepared. Our food stores won't last forever either, so we should examine the vegetation at the oasis for edible plants. With some luck, we could farm them to ensure we have enough crops, and I think it's best if we reinforce this ship. If the rainy season is as bad as I suspect, we'll need The Bellator sealed tight."

"Months?" I repeat when he finally stops talking. He barely took a breath as he rattled off a list of daunting tasks, but my brain fixates on that single word. "You think we'll still be here months from now? I don't know, Driver, these preparations seem incredibly permanent."

"I understand it's a ton of work, but I can't do it all myself," he says. "I need your help."

"Collecting water is one thing, but you're talking like we're never leaving this planet," I argue. "I don't see the point in building a farm and home just to be rescued."

"We need to be prepared, Serling," he says as if he's speaking to a stubborn child, and I bristle at his tone. "Look at what happened with our water supply. You got lucky finding that oasis, but we cannot leave our survival up to luck. It'll eventually run out."

"Be prepared for what, though? To grow old in this hateful place? Because that's what it sounds like you're planning for, and I'm not settling for that. You can plan and work and suffer all you want, but I refuse to act like this is our life."

"But it is our life now."

"Until my father comes for me."

"Oh my god, wake up, Serling!" Driver shouts, and I flinch involuntarily at the volume. "I'm planning for a permanent life here because this is our future. No one is rescuing us. Not the military. Not headquarters. Not your father. We're alone here."

"You don't know that," I say, fear clogging my throat at the idea that my future is tied to this man.

"I do know that." He steps forward, forcing me to look up as he towers over me. "You need to stop trusting that daddy dearest is coming for you, because he's not. He thinks you're dead, and yes, you're his sole heir, but it's cheaper these days to father another successor with a surrogate than to comb the Mors for someone who's been confirmed deceased."

"He would never," I snarl, but Driver leans closer, meeting my anger with indignation of his own.

"Think about it, Princess. The missile that hit The Bellator. That was no pirate weapon. It was military grade and expensive, and it was aimed at the passenger levels. Out of all the passengers onboard, you're the only one worth assassinating. The Federation's most important heir. That missile was meant for you. You're the reason everyone is dead."

"Fuck you." I try to leave the room, but he grabs my wrist and tugs me back to face him.

"You might not like it, but your presence was a death sentence for my entire crew. I realize you didn't order the hit, but those deaths were because I accepted your father's charter. My guess is whichever rebellious faction sent that missile is boasting about assassinating the Ambrose heir. No one is coming for you, Serling. No one knows we're alive. I'm all you have now, so yes, I'm making permanent plans. I'm a stubborn bastard that way. I refuse to surrender, and if I have to live on this fucking planet, then you're going to stay with me. You don't get to check out. I won't be left alone here. I almost died rescuing you, so you have to survive."

"I didn't ask you to save me," I spit, my emotions raging out of control. I don't want to be stuck here. This can't be my future, but if Driver's convinced that we're never leaving this planet, then his comment about saving me for the reward money must have been a joke. And if he made those words in jest, then he sacrificed himself to that monster for no other reason than to protect me. I don't know how to process that information, so I do what I do best. I fight.

"Well, next time, I'll step aside and let this planet kill you," he growls, pulling my wrist until my chest is a hair's breadth away from his, and my traitorous body reacts to his nearness. My heart thunders so violently that I know he feels my pulse, but he says nothing. Instead, he slips his thumb to press against my wrist, staring at me with a challenge in his eyes. He wants to study my reaction. To see if I'll back down in embarrassment.

"I don't know, old man." I move closer until my lips hover just out of his reach, his thumb still monitoring my racing heart-beat. "You're hurt. You're older. You'll be slower than me. I would be careful how you speak to me because who knows? Next time you might need my help, and it would be a shame if I stepped aside and let this planet kill you."

DRIVER

I need you to hold it steady," I grunt as Serling, once again, lets the part slip, and it smacks me in the forehead. After stripping the damaged rovers for usable parts, I enlisted her to help me repair this somewhat whole vehicle, but after an hour of her complaints and faulty aid, I'm about ready to lose my mind. I keep telling myself that until a few months ago, Serling probably never even wiped up a counter after herself, so to throw her into the deep end of manual labor is a steep learning curve, but she will not shut up. She's trying. The bruises on her shoulders from carrying the water prove it, but sometimes, her incessant noise makes me grind my teeth.

"It's ungodly hot in here," she fires back. "My hands are too sweaty to hold on, and I can't see where you are under there."

"We can't turn on the cooling system with our current water supply." I roll out from under the rover and peer up at her. "It needs a full tank to operate, and the only way we'll fill these tanks is if we repair this."

"Well then, don't complain when I drop parts on your face." She glares at me as she leans back, and that's when I notice she has sweat through her shirt. She's wearing that tiny white top again, and I swear this woman doesn't believe in bras. The damp fabric is completely see-through, her pink nipples straining against the flimsy material.

"Serling, I'm not trying to be a dick." I sit up and peel my soaked shirt off, the sight of her perfection sending my overheated body into the furnace. She's already slept with her face pressed against my scars. There's no use hiding my disfigurements from her anymore, but when I stand to grab my water bottle, the way her eyes dip to my chest surprises me. She isn't looking at my scars. She's studying my muscles. I'm a big guy. Tall and broad and muscular, but most women can't get past the deformities. Serling, on the other hand, seems unable to see them as her gaze lingers on the attractive parts of me.

"Really?" she spits back, all bark and bite, recovering from her momentary lapse of appreciation. "Because you certainly come off like an asshole. You're lucky I'm even helping you. If you were stranded here with my father, he would force you to do everything yourself while he sat in his quarters."

"Yes, I'm so lucky I'm not here with Daddy Ambrose," I deadpan, my dick reminding me I am, in fact, very fortunate to be stuck with this stunning creature. The Imperator in a sheer tank top would make this situation unbearable, but on her, it almost makes her fight worth it. Her current attitude is a different type of fight, though. When we first met, Serling was all venom and hostility. Now her combativeness seems habit rather than cruelty. It's as if she doesn't understand how to be kind, so she's offering me the only thing she has. The only company she's capable of. Her combat. I don't know what kind of sick bastard it makes me, but I honestly prefer the confrontation to the shell of a woman she'd become. The week after I made that stupid joke about collecting a reward was hell. She shut down and ignored me. She wouldn't look at me, wouldn't argue. This heat must be getting to me, because as obnoxious as her complaining is, I prefer it to her silence. I'm actually starting to enjoy it.

"I'm just saying, it's hot, and you're lucky I'm even help-ing," she continues, refusing to let me have the last word as she fuels the argument. I know she likes to have the final say, but her refusal to back down has me wondering if she has also fallen down the rabbit hole with me and enjoys our verbal battles. "I doubt that model Meli would have helped. Sure, she had the hots for you, but she probably would've cried in the corner while you worked. You probably would have let her, too."

"Serling," I warn.

"She probably would have fucked you to get out of helping," she continues. "I bet you wouldn't mind her helplessness, but no, you enjoy torturing me. I think you like making an Ambrose your bitch."

"Serling…"

"You know what? I'm done for the day. I'm too hot for this shit."

"Oh my god, do you ever shut up?" I growl. She freezes, eyes wide at my outburst, and I stride across the hangar until I tower over her. "I should just fuck the attitude out of you. Maybe then you would finally stop running that mouth of yours."

Serling stares up at me with shock, her entire body frozen stiff. For a moment, neither of us moves, and I groan internally. I hadn't meant to say that out loud, but she relentlessly pushes my buttons. And now that I've said it, I can't purge the intoxicating image from my mind. I'd tighten my fist around her throat just enough to remind her she isn't in charge here in the dangers of space, then I'd make her take my cock until she couldn't come anymore, until all the fight had drained from her rigid muscles, leaving her blissfully peaceful. I doubt anyone has fucked her like I could, like every woman deserves to be fucked, and suddenly my entire being craves the woman before me.

"Hmm," she grunts, and a challenge replaces her shock. Her gaze hardens, and her back straightens, forcing her breasts into my field of vision, and goddamn it, but I look. My sight falls to those pink nipples, and I catch her smile a wicked grin at her triumph. "I'd like to see you try."

The seductive tone in her voice is all the permission I need, and I reach out to fist her hair. Serling gasps in surprise as I twist the black strands around my hand, but I don't allow her to escape. I slam my bare chest against hers and drive her backward until she's pressed against the wall. She feels so fucking good, and I pull her ponytail to force her to stare up at me. Her expression almost makes my knees buckle, for the hunger in her eyes is predatory. A woman has never gazed at me with this much desire before, especially with my scars visible.

I wind her hair tighter so that she can't look away, and I slowly trace my other hand up her body to grip her throat. My hold is gentle, but I need Serling to understand she's no longer in control. I expect her to fight my dominance, to resist my every touch, but she simply inhales a shaking breath. It causes her breasts to strain against the flimsy fabric, and I lose all self-control.

I lean forward and capture her lips in a kiss, and the second my mouth finds hers, she moans. It's the most beautiful sound I've ever heard, and an odd sensation burns my chest. Before I can decipher the emotion, though, she slides her hands against my abs, her fingers tracing my scars with need, and then she wraps her arms around my waist. She pulls me closer, deepening the kiss, and my tongue traces the seam of her perfect mouth. She opens for me with another intoxicating moan, and my heart falters. The dance of her tongue against mine, the electricity of her breasts and hips pressing against my skin is both heaven and hell. I've never experienced a woman kiss me with such intense longing, and I grind against her. I need her to witness what she's doing to me. How hard she's made me, and the gasp she releases into my mouth at the feel of my length is a reward I'll cherish forever.

For a moment, she stills as she kisses me, and then she

slowly grinds against the thick bulge in my pants, gasping again. Only it's not with pleasure, but with shock. I smirk as I capture her bottom lip between my teeth. I'm big, my cock matching the rest of me, and the image of Serling working to take every inch tips me over the edge.

Hand still on her throat, I pull my fist from her hair and slide it down into her pants. She practically screams into my mouth as she yanks her hands from my waist. For a moment, I worry I've crossed the line and that she's about to revolt at my touch, but then she slips her fingers into my hair and kisses me harder.

"Fuck, you're so wet, Princess," I growl into our kiss as I slip two fingers inside her.

"Don't call me princess, old man." She bites my lip hard as she thrusts against me, forcing my fingers deeper, and a heady sense of power washes over me, knowing that I'm driving her crazy like this. That I'm the one making her moan so loud, and I thrust a third finger inside her pussy.

"Please," she begs, and I lied. That's the hottest sound I've ever heard. "Please, Driver, fuck me."

"No, Princess." I grind my palm against her clit as I kiss her through my words. "Only good girls get my cock."

"Driver, please. I'm going to come" She pulls my hair to the point of pain, but I don't stop. I love the burn. I love how she kisses. I love how she molds against my body as if she was created just for me.

"Come on my fingers." My voice is rough with need, but I want her pleasure more than my own. "Show me you can be a good girl."

She explodes at my words, and goddamn it, it's glorious. I swallow her moans of bliss with greedy kisses, and she lets me take every sound. She kisses me with a wild abandon I didn't think her capable of, and something about this moment feels monumental. No woman has ever shattered like this for me. I've had my share of decent relationships, but Serling is different.

This experience was a whole body high, and I didn't even come. I'm painfully hard, but just experiencing her shake in my arms destroys me. It's undeniably beautiful. I realize the instant I pull my fingers from her wetness, she'll return to the challenging woman I might almost like, but I never knew what my life was missing until I made her scream.

Serling finally falls still. I wait for her to recoil at my touch, to be disgusted by my scars, by what she let me do to her, but instead, her hands trace my chest down to my abs. She grips my hips, her fingers pressed against my marred skin, and she tilts her head up. I release her throat and cup her jaw, unable to stop myself, and she surprisingly accepts my invitation. She kisses me, not with need, but with a different longing, and I lose track of how long we remain locked in each other's arms. Our lips slow. Our tongues dance. Our hearts beat as one, and when she eventually pulls away breathless, I fear no woman will ever compare to Serling Ambrose.

"What do you say, Princess?" I ask, my voice rough. "You going to lose the attitude?"

She laughs. A full-bellied, throw-her-head-back kind of laugh, and it's the first time I've seen her express joy. It's stunning, and I want her happy like this more often.

"If you think that was fucking the attitude out of me, you have another thing coming, old man." She playfully pushes her palm against my chest, and I get the distinct impression she's copping a feel. "I can be a royal bitch." She winks, the challenge back in her eyes. "You're going to have to try a lot harder than that."

CHAPTER 19

DRIVER

W ake up, Princess." I pull the sheet off her sleeping form and swallow hard at the sight that greets me. Serling's dressed in a flimsy tank top and tiny underwear, and her legs are magnificent. For a split second, I contemplate climbing into bed with her, but she shatters that fantasy when she grabs the sheet and aggressively yanks it back over her body.

"Go away," she groans.

"Not a chance," I chuckle as I adjust my pants. Ever since our encounter in the hangar, all it takes is an ounce of her defiance to make me hard. We've been too busy to explore whatever happened between us, but she's been on point with her aggravating behavior. Some of her complaints and arguments are genuine, but most of the time, I get the sneaking suspicion Serling is challenging me on purpose in the hopes I'll bend her over the worktable and follow through on my promise to improve her attitude. It's had an odd effect on my body since her combativeness used to inspire hate, but now it makes me want to rip that barely-there outfit off her and bury my face between her thighs.

"Fuck off, Driver." She pulls the sheet over her head.

"Okay then." I yank it completely off the bed. "Let's go." I scoop her up and throw her over my shoulder as she squawks in protest. I stride out of her quarters and down the halls as she pounds my back, but I simply tighten my grip on her thighs.

"None of that." I swat her ass, and she freezes with an indignant gasp. "Be a good girl. I just want to show you something."

"You couldn't have waited for a more reasonable hour?" she grunts, but she stops struggling, and we both realize at the same moment that my palm is still cemented to her unreasonably sexy backside. I don't remove it, though, nor does she ask me to.

"Nope," I say.

"Why not? Because you hate me?"

"Nope."

"Then—"

"You'll see." I cut her off as I step out into the new dawn. I move through the pale light and finally set her down on a smooth expanse of stone, instantly missing the warmth of her body draped over mine. "Look." I spin her around.

"You got it to work!" She grabs my forearm with a gasp, her feet jumping with tiny hops of excitement before she picks her way over the rocks to the rover. "It runs?"

"It runs," I confirm.

"Oh my god, I didn't think you would pull this off." She turns back to face me with a smile, and I accept the slightly condescending compliment. Coming from her, it's high praise. "I don't know how a vehicle with wheels will climb twin cliffs, but it'll come in handy for something."

"That's the beauty of this machine." I open the driver's side door and hoist her into the seat. "These were developed for all terrains. I'll teach you how to drive it, but its sensors adjust the wheels for different environments. We'll have to explore to find a less steep entrance, but with its speed and cargo space, travel won't be an issue. We can finally give your shoulders a break." I absent-mindedly trace her bruises from the pack, and she looks up at me with excitement. It's the first time she's offered me a genuinely kind expression, and the urge to kiss her overwhelms me. I force myself not to, though. I don't know how she would react to such an act of affection. I'm not sure how I would either since I thought I hated her, but now I'm not so convinced. Now I'm worried I might like Serling Ambrose, and if that's the truth, this truly is the end of the world.

SERLING

After breakfast, we packed every container we could find into the rover's cargo hold. It runs on solar panels, so as long as there's sun, we'll have fuel, and for once this unbearable heat is a blessing. It might not work as often during the rainy season, but the storms will deliver water to us. Driver plans to build a collection system, which means we're building it since he has this need to include me in every project. I don't mind working as much as I expected to, but I'm not looking forward to this massive undertaking. My palms are hardening with callouses, and old Serling would have thrown a fit about the damaged skin. New Serling still freaks out. I can't change my entire personality overnight, but my tantrums are less meltdown and more antagonistic. If my attitude inspires Driver to pin me against the wall, then I have plenty of defiance for him. No one has ever made me come that hard, and I can't stop fantasizing about his hand between my thighs. This hardened war hero with his midnight black hair, mutilated skin, and powerful body ignites a flame inside me that threatens to burn me alive. I've never craved a man as fiercely as I crave him, and everything I couldn't stand about him is what draws me into his orbit. His rough and masculine features. His refusal to take my bullshit. His willingness to challenge me. He motivates me to be better, and that scares the shit out of me. He makes me want to like him, and that terrifies me even more, which is why I haven't truly pushed him. I'm afraid if he follows through on his promise, if he claims my body, I'll never be the same. It's a foolish fear, though. Even without his skin pressed against mine, he has irrevocably altered my life. The second he sacrificed himself to save me, the old Serling died. Maybe he's right when he says the galaxy believes I'm dead. That woman perished in the stars.

We barely talk as we travel, which gives me too much time to think, too much time to study his profile. He's no model. His features are too unique and rough, but I've never seen someone as handsome as him. I hope we locate a path to the oasis soon because if we don't escape this proximity, I might force him to pull over and climb into his lap.

Much to my disappointment, though, we find nothing to the north. Only taller peaks, and with defeat we turn around. It's early evening when we return to the Bellator, and Driver rubs his face with exhaustion.

"The panels are at full strength since we've been driving in the sun." He twists to study me. "Plus, the rover's cooling system works well, so it's been nice not having to bake in a hot ship. What do you say? Should we try heading south?"

"As long as you feel okay to drive," I say, curling deeper into the seat. "I'm enjoying the cool air."

"It's settled then." He restarts the engine, and we return to our silence, eating our packed dinner as we travel. At some point, I must have fallen asleep because the next thing I know, the moon is high overhead, its rays reflecting off the pool.

I sit up with excitement. He found a path the rover could handle, and I almost cry with joy. My body aches from climbing the twin cliffs every day. This trip in the cool and comfortable vehicle was pleasant, and with water we can easily transport, we'll survive. We won't die on this hellish planet, and I glance at Driver's seat, eager to share this moment with him. Only I find an empty chair. Concern floods my veins until I peer out the front window. A lone figure stands waist-deep in the pool, moonlight illuminating his power, and I open the door. His bare and alluring form beckons me closer, begs me to taste the forbidden fruit that is Driver Thorne, and I slip out into the balmy night air and remove my clothes, following him before I lose my nerve.

DRIVER

The soft splash behind me tells me I'm no longer alone, and I turn to find Serling wading through the water. My heart stops beating at the sight of her skin bathed in the moonlight. She's completely bare, and even though her sheer shirts have teased at what lay underneath, nothing prepares me for the true perfection of her beauty. I wish I could eternally freeze this moment. She's bruised and sunburnt. Her hair is wild from the humidity. Her once-manicured nails are chipped and filthy, but she's never looked more beautiful. When I look at her now, I see the woman who ensured our survival when she found this pool, who saved me when she blew the head off that monster. She's bold and ferocious and a thorn in my side, but the wonderful thing about wounds is they heal and become a permanent part of you. The pain she inflicted when her hatred burrowed into my flesh has subsided, and Serling has infiltrated my very being against my will. She's changed me, and by the gentle smile curving her lips, I've done the same to her. She's so different from the girl who scowled at me as she boarded The Bellator, and that's what makes her moon-kissed skin even more alluring. Her pink nipples are stiff with arousal, like jewelry highlighting her perfect breasts. The curve of her hips swings as she walks. The water barely covers her pussy, but I can still see the outline of her, and it takes every ounce of self-control not to order her to step backward so I can admire her. She's always been beautiful. My traitorous body made me well aware of that fact, but I've never craved her as intensely as I do now because she's no longer just attractive. She's someone I've grown to respect. Heaven forbid it, but she's becoming someone I actually like.

Serling settles before me, but before I can say a word, she throws her arms around my neck. Her movements take me by surprise, and I freeze as her lips find mine. There's no fight in her kiss. No anger. No hatred or resentment. It's a soulful kiss, and something inside me shatters. I no longer belong to myself. I belong to this woman, and that terrifies me. Serling Ambrose could destroy me. She could ruin my life and break my heart, but I don't have the willpower to resist her. So, I give in and capture her waist.

For a few moments, unspoken truths pass between us. The kiss is so raw, so passionate, that my chest aches, and I tug her closer as her fingers dive into my hair. She fits against my large frame as if we were created for each other, and I know I'll always protect this woman with my life. I might fight with her. Her attitude might drive me up a wall, but I'll never let harm befall her. I'll go to my grave ensuring her safety, and as if she reads my promise in my kiss, she moans. It's breathy and desperate and filled with ravenous longing, and my control snaps. I grab her ass with a rough grip and drag her closer. She gasps as my cock slides against her clit to settle between her welcoming thighs, and I seize her parted lips to claim her mouth completely. My tongue tastes every part of her, and within seconds, she's writhing against me, the head of my dick teasing her entrance. Her moans grow louder, her heartbeat quickens, and through a delicious haze of lust, I realize she's on the brink. I haven't slipped inside her, but her body responds to my every move. Pride floods my chest. I do this to her. I make her crazy. God, what would it be like to fuck her? To watch her take me hard and deep. Watching her come on my cock will probably kill me, but I crave it all the same.

Serling wraps her legs tighter around my waist to increase the friction, and I kiss her fiercely as she tenses. She's so close I can feel her ready to fall over the edge, but I say nothing. This moment, this orgasm, feels different from before, and I want to enjoy her pleasure. I don't remain silent, though. I moan into her mouth, encouraging her to move, to use me, to own me, and the second I break my silence, she screams. Her body convulses as she comes, and my knees buckle slightly at the intensity. I kiss her so hard that I worry she'll bruise, but I need her to know how perfect feeling her fall apart was for me. Her pleasure soaks my cock as she continues to writhe, and I realize she wants me to follow her off the cliff. The knowledge almost makes me explode on the spot, but I clench my muscles to halt my bliss because I have plans for my release. I need to see her wear it, and holding her tight against my chest, I stride to the beach.

I don't stop kissing her until I lay her down on the sand, and then I kneel between her thighs, pushing them open so I can finally appreciate just how beautiful she is. She stares up at me in the moonlight, desire evident on her features, and it's stunning to witness. I can't remember the last time a woman truly looked at me like I was perfection, and her expression along with her parted thighs undoes me.

I grip my shaft and stroke it, base to tip. My eyes never leave her face, but her gaze tilts down to watch my thrusts. She studies me with appreciation, her teeth biting her lip with desire, and her observation fuels my need. I pump faster, moaning as the pressure builds. I'm so close. The sensation is too much. Her beauty will be the death of me, and as if to confirm my suspicions, she trails her hands seductively down her body and slips them into her wetness. Her fingers spread her pussy for my enjoyment, revealing every beautiful part of her to me in the soft moonlight, and with a growl, I collapse forward. With one palm in the sand to hold myself up, I erupt. Thick ropes of cum explode from my cock to coat her pussy and thighs, and the sight drags out my climax. It's blissfully endless, and when I somehow finally come down from my high, she's coated in my pleasure. My chest tightens as my release drips down her hand to trail over her clit, and I don't miss how her fingers spread my cum over her sensitive lips. I freeze at the sight, and I worry my heart has stopped beating. Does she understand what she's doing to me? Does she realize how utterly obsessed she's making me?

I glance up at her face, and her eyes tell me she understands exactly the power she holds over me. She says nothing, but her fingers don't stop. They brush against her clit. Her back arches at her enjoyment, and I recognize her lazy movements as a question. She's asking my permission. She wants to know if she can make herself come, if she's allowed to use my release for her own pleasure.

I answer her nonverbal request with actions of my own. My hand is still wrapped around my semi-hard cock, so it's sand-free. It won't hurt her, and I slip three fingers inside her cunt. She gasps as her back comes off the beach, and she fists the sand like it's a bedsheet. Her face is mesmerizing as she enjoys herself, but so is the sight of her fucking herself with my cum. My climax drips down her and onto my knuckles as I thrust deep inside her, and I just might spill in the sand at the image. Who is this woman, and why does she make me feel like I'm suffering a heart attack?

Her free hand slides across the beach to grip mine, and the second our hands join, she screams. Her fingers pinch her clit, and her pussy clenches around me so fiercely that I'm almost worried about fucking her. If she comes on my cock like this, I won't last more than thirty seconds.

Her orgasm is flawless to behold, and she takes her time floating down to earth. Even once she stops fluttering around my fingers, she still rocks back and forth as if she isn't done feeling me inside her. I don't pull out. I let her enjoy herself as long as she needs, and after a few minutes, she stills, releasing her clit to grab my hand. I slowly withdraw from her warmth and accept her affection. We lace our pleasure-soaked fingers together, and she grins up at me with an adorably satisfied smile. Why does she have to do that? Why does she have to be so unbearably sexy one minute and then sweet the next? If she doesn't watch herself, I might end up hopelessly in love with her.

"Serling." I find my voice as I collapse beside her on the beach. It's not lost on me that I land to her left, my scars on full display for her to see, but as if on instinct, she reaches out and places a palm on my disfigured hip. I lose track of how long we lay side by side, but somehow, this vulnerability seems more intimate than what we just did.

"You're fucking beautiful," I finally whisper, gripping her hand that rests on my waist, and I might be mistaken. Her voice is impossibly low, but I swear I hear her say, *"So are you."*

CHAPTER 20

SERLING

The sunrise wakes me, and for a disorienting moment, I'm confused by the brightness until I remember last night. Driver and I fell asleep on the sand, which was probably foolish, but the morning is too beautiful for me to worry. His hand still clutches mine where it rests on his hip. It surprises me we remained hand in hand all night, but the sight of my fingers in his and resting on his naked body fills me with an overwhelming sense of freedom.

I roll onto my side and study his sleeping profile. He looks peaceful, the stress of the world evaporated from his muscles as he inhabits his dreams, and I take this solitary moment to let myself just be. My free hand can't resist tracing his scars, and in this light, I see how extensive they are. It's surprising that he can move as gracefully and powerfully as he does after the considerable damage, but nothing will ever erase these marks. I like them, though. It feels like a lifetime ago, but I used to refuse to even leave the house if my nails were so much as dull. I was so vain, so caught up in being the perfect beauty that my father demanded, that I'd never seen anything so disfigured as Driver Thorne's skin. I've also never seen anything so beautifully freeing. Despite his deformities—the old wounds and the new—, he's beautiful.

It's unnerving, but his conviction that we're never going home has eased my anxiety. I no longer have to be the vapid Serling. I don't have to perform the duty my name requires. My only goal now is to survive, and my soul feels lighter. I don't have to hate Driver anymore. He no longer represents the freedom I'm not permitted to experience. I was cruel to him, in part, because I was unused to people calling me on my bullshit, but my venom went deeper. The moment I laid my eyes on him, I knew I would crave him, so it was easier to despise him. Easier to make him my enemy than admit he was everything I was drawn to but forbidden from tasting. It's why I called him old. It's why I insulted him at every turn. He's anything but old at forty, and despite our eleven-year difference, he's far more alluring than the rich men my age, but if I could convince myself he was undesirable, my bitter life hurt less.

My fingers trail down his powerful thigh, and I can't help but let my eyes wander. I've never seen a man that… blessed before. This pilot is a masterpiece, and I love that he isn't perfect. That he doesn't fit the mold my father set before my feet.

His cock twitches in his sleep as my fingers move along his leg, and wetness pools between my thighs. We're never escaping this planet. I'm no longer the Ambrose heir, and I'm free to forge my own future, to be the version of myself that I choose. I can have this man. This good and brave and infuriating man.

"That tickles." Driver catches my wandering fingers and moves them to rest on his stomach.

"Sorry." I blush that he caught me ogling him.

"You don't have to do that, you know," he says, his voice thick with sleep. "Pretend to like my scars. I know what they look like."

"I'm not pretending."

He squints his eyes open and stares at me as if trying to

decide if I'm picking a fight or being honest. I hold his gaze, letting him see the truth before I pull my hands from his grip. I drag them slowly down his abs to his legs, careful to avoid his hardening length, and his head falls back to the sand with a groan.

"Fuck, Serling. You don't have to do that, but goddamn, your hands feel good."

His words empower me, and I climb over him to settle between his thighs. His eyes fly open in surprise as I lean down, and I grip his legs so tight, my fingers leave indents in his flesh.

"But I want to." Before he can protest, I lower my mouth and suck him deep. He's so large that he hits the back of my throat almost immediately, and the sound he makes as my lips drag across his smooth skin gives me a heady rush of power.

"Fuck." He grips my hair and holds me still, his cock nudging the back of my throat.

I rarely pleasure the men I sleep with. They never seemed worth it, but Driver makes me want to prove my mouth is the best he's ever had, so I push further.

"Serling," he warns. "This is your last chance to stop. If you don't back up, I won't be able to control myself, and I will fuck your perfect little mouth until you're choking on my cum."

Wetness drips down my thighs at his filthy words, and I grab his shaft, pumping him as I suck. I take him as deep as I can before dragging him all the way out. Our gazes meet as I plunge back down, and his expression makes me want to wake him up like this for the rest of my days. No man has ever gazed at me as if I'm life itself, and I'm already addicted to the way Driver looks at me.

"You feel incredible, Princess." He guides me down until he slips even deeper. "Open your throat like a good girl. Swallow me while I fuck you."

I obey, relaxing my throat, and that shoves him over the edge. He thrusts with powerful strokes, holding my head down while never taking his eyes off me. A tear runs down my cheek from how well he chokes me, but I don't let him stop. I want this. I crave him. I'm too afraid to say it out loud, so I let my body speak for me. Our eye contact intensifies the experience, and I know neither of us has ever experienced a connection like this. It's raw and emotional, and within minutes, Driver loses all control, roaring as he explodes down my throat. I drink him down, not wasting a single drop, and when he finally softens, he grabs my biceps and yanks me up onto his chest.

"Kiss me," he demands, and I obey, letting him wrap me in his powerful arms. I lose track of how long we kiss, of how long we lay tangled together in the morning light. At one point, he offers to return the favor, but I don't let him. I want him to, but not now because this experience was monumental for me. I claimed something solely for myself. I let myself have someone I wanted. I let myself become the person I wanted to be. I don't know when it happened, but I've started to hope my father never rescues us because I think this man I hate on this planet I despise might make me happier than I've ever been.

"The day is still early," Driver says as we load the last water container into the rover's cargo hold. "We don't have to rush back, so we should check out the vegetation. The Bellator has a decent provision stock, but it won't last forever. Now that our water situation is under control, we should start thinking about long-term food production."

"I can get used to the work and heat and the crew quarters, but foraging? That's going to be hard to adjust to," I groan. "I like food. Real food. Not alien plants."

Driver leans against the rover with a smirk as he folds his arms across his chiseled chest. He's stopped wearing shirts around me, and it fills me with pride to know he's no longer compelled to hide. It also fills me with intense longing. I've never met someone whose beauty comes from the soul, and while it would normally embarrass me to experience something beyond superficial attraction, he has a way of making me feel safe. Maybe it's because the massive scar healing on his abdomen is proof of just how far he's willing to go to keep me alive.

"I agree," he says, and his response surprises me. I expected him to joke about my princess tendencies and tell me to toughen up. "I've lived off the land before during military missions. Sometimes the native vegetation sucked, and sometimes it was amazing. Other times it made us violently ill, but not even delicious fruit can compare to the food The Bellator served. You cannot replace a masterfully grilled steak paired with roasted grain."

"Hmmm," I moan, and while my appreciation is for his described meal, his eyes darken at the sound. "I don't know. There's a restaurant in Corr'us Sanctum that bakes this cake with alcohol. They won't tell you what's in it, but the liquor is flavorful and spicy but also decadently sweet. When you cut into it, the gooey center spills out thick and warm, and my god." I shudder at the memory. "Nothing beats that." I pause, suddenly sad that I'll never taste it again, but the look on Driver's face makes me wonder if I said something wrong. "What?"

"Nothing."

"What?" I playfully shove his muscular arm, not at all embarrassed that I linger for a few seconds to appreciate his biceps.

"I'd give anything to watch you eat that cake," he says, and I freeze. I wasn't expecting that answer. "Watching you moan as you take a bite, the thick center coating your lips. Fuck." He shifts his legs, shaking his head with an amused laugh, but I don't miss how aroused he is.

"If we ever get off this planet, I'll take you there. You can order a steak, and I'll eat the cake. I'll moan so loud that you'll be crawling under the table in embarrassment."

He laughs, the sound a music I'll never tire of. "It's a date." He peels himself off the rover and grabs two water bottles, handing me one. "Come on. I also want to check if this pool has any fish. We're running out of meat, and the only animal life I've encountered was at the swamp. I am not going back there."

"Please don't." I fall into step beside him. "Besides, I don't want to eat one of those things."

He laughs a deep belly laugh. "Good god, me neither."

"I'm glad no other creatures followed the first."

"Me too, but we shouldn't make a habit of sleeping outside. There's still so much we don't know about this planet."

"I can't believe we fell asleep on the sand. I used to toss and turn on a mattress if a specific company didn't manufacture it."

"I've slept in weirder places, and I can almost guarantee you that, at some point, you will too." He pauses and holds the scanner up to an odd bulbous plant. It registers as nontoxic, but the second Driver pries it open, we both know it isn't edible.

"Can I…?" I glance at his scars. "Never mind."

"Go ahead," he encourages. "It's just us. We might as well get to know each other."

"The attack." I touch a thin mark on his ribs. "Was it like this crash? When you were lying there missing half your leg, did you feel like it was the end? Was the fear crippling? Because when we crashed, that happened to me. I was afraid that was the end of me, and in a way, it was, I guess. Who I was is gone."

"A little, yes," he says. "That attack felt final. In those last moments, before I fell unconscious, I knew death had come. There was no fear, though. I think the shock to my body stole it, which I'm thankful for. But this crash wasn't like that. I was terrified about how we would survive, but it never felt like the end. I'd lived. We had the tools to survive. I had companionship, even if it was obnoxious." He looks at me with a challenge in his eyes. I slap him, but he catches my wrist as my palm bounces off his chest and pulls me into his arms. "Although it's growing on me." He kisses me, and I melt against him.

"In all honesty, I was more afraid during this crash than the attack," he continues, releasing me to inspect a flowering plant. "Death is easy, but survival is hard. I've also been in intense situations before, though, so I'm wired for this. I'm trained to live rough, but I can see how it seemed like the end for you. This is an impossible life for someone who's never experienced danger, and I feel guilty about how I treated you."

My eyes fly to his in shock that he's willing to admit that. My father would rather die than acknowledge his wrongdoings, and I don't know how to respond to a man who does it willingly.

"Don't get too excited, Princess," he laughs. "You were an absolute bitch, but I also threw you into the deep end. This crash probably felt like death to you, and I should've handled it better, even if you were determined to make my life hell. So, for my part in causing you fear, I'm sorry—"

Pain explodes in my ankle, and my screams silence him. What feels like a hundred fangs digging into my calf rips my legs from under me, and my chest slaps the sand hard as I fall.

"Serling?" He lunges for me, but whatever monster captured my leg pulls me into the underbrush.

"Driver!" I scream as the pain increases. Blood pumps from my veins to stain the ground as I struggle against the iron hold. "Help me!"

"Serling, hold on!" He races after me, but the fangs drag me deep into the bushes and out of his sight.

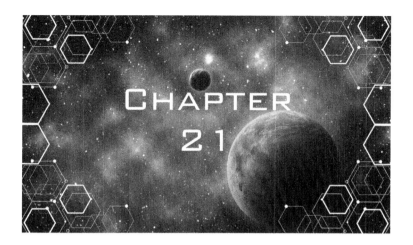

CHAPTER 21

DRIVER

Serling hits the sand hard, and before I know what's happening, something drags her into the underbrush. Terror contorts her face for a split second as she reaches for me, and then she's gone, her screams all that remains.

"Serling!" Fear lodges in my throat as I draw my weapon and race after her. "Serling, hang on!"

"Driver!" She sounds so small, so scared, and an animalistic possessiveness floods my chest. This planet cannot have her.

"Serling, I need to hear you!" I shout as I rush through the underbrush, but the greenery is too thick. I can't see which direction this new predator has dragged her.

"Here!" she calls, her voice weaker than it was a second ago.

"Good girl!" I lunge toward the sound. "Keep talking."

"Driver... please. Help me."

"That's it, Princess." I move faster.

"Driver?" Her words are sluggish, and I panic. Has she been poisoned? Is this creature venomous?

I shove the thick branches aside with frantic movements. Without warning, her arm drags over my foot as the monster pulls her deeper into the jungle, and I dive for her, capturing her wrist and yanking her to a stop. She cries out, but the sound is too soft for how hard I tug her joints. *Please, no. Please don't take her from me. Not now that we've finally made peace. Not now that we've become friends.*

"Serling, stay with me." I pin her to the sandy dirt as my hands slide down her body. The creature has her by the calf and ankle, and the sight is shocking. It's not a monster. It's a plant. A large, green, vine-like plant. Her injured flesh is a dangerous shade of red, and I bring my knife down hard on the stem below her foot. The vine slices apart easily, and I drag her away from the leaking stump and into my lap. The severed section is still suctioned to her skin where it's wrapped around her leg, though, so I dig my fingers beneath it to pry it off.

Serling screams the instant I exert pressure on the plant, and my stomach pitches when I see why it won't budge. The top of the vine is smooth. Gel-like flesh bulges below its soft skin, but its underside is composed of hundreds of razor-sharp needles. They've dug into her muscles, refusing to release their hold even when I use my knife. A few break against the blade, but her screams are unbearable, forcing me to stop. Her silence is worse, though, and she goes suddenly limp in my arms. She passed out, and based on the angry red lines coiling up her leg, it's not pain that's rendered her unconscious but this plant's toxins.

"No, no, no. Serling, stay with me." I grab her face, but her eyes are rolled back into her skull, the whites staring eerily out at me. "Stay with me, Princess." I hoist her into my arms. She needs an anti-toxin, and I pray she survives long enough for me to return to the rover. It's stocked with emergency med packs, and regulation demands they include a basic anti-toxin. I pray it's enough. It needs to be.

I race over the sand, her body limp in my arms, and fear, unlike any I've experienced, chokes me. Being afraid to lose my life is one brand of hell, but this is an entirely new and treacherous one. Watching her hit the ground, watching that thing drag her on her stomach into the darkness, made me sick. I can barely look at her unconscious form because she looks lifeless, and she can't be dead. She can't. I won't allow it.

I skid to a stop and shove her into the rover before grabbing the med pack. My fingers fumble the lock, but I open it without spilling its contents. I find the anti-toxin and rip off the safety seal before plunging the needle into the angry flesh of her calf. The medication releases into her bloodstream, and I lean over her to cup her face.

"Come on, Serling. Please wake up," I beg.

She convulses, and tears involuntarily prick my eyes. I can't watch her like this. I can't watch the woman I've grown to care for die like this. The way her body spasms is unnatural and terrifying, and I climb into the seat and pull her into my arms.

"Come on, Princess." I hold her tight so she won't hurt herself. "You're too much of a bitch to die. You're too fucking stubborn. If you aren't here, who will aggravate me until I'm ready to jump off a cliff, so please wake up? I need you."

Her shaking slows, and after five minutes, she falls still. She doesn't regain consciousness, but her breathing steadies, and color returns to her cheeks. I dare to hope that she's out of immediate danger, but with that vine's fangs still embedded in her leg, she's not safe. I can't remove it without the medical equipment on the Bellator, so I strap her into the passenger seat and climb into the driver's side.

I start the rover and reach over to capture her hand, praying she has the strength to hold on. She has endured harder circumstances on this planet than most soldiers I've fought alongside, so she needs to survive this. I need her to live.

When she asked me if The Bellator's crash triggered the same fear as my attack, I told her the truth. Dying is easy. Living is what's hard, and life on this hostile planet has inspired more fear than my military missions. But what I didn't tell her was my concern wasn't solely for me. I was mistaken about Serling. Lord knows she drives me crazy. She probably always will, but I misjudged her. She rose to the challenge and bloodied her hands in this fight called life. I'm alive because of her. She's proved me wrong about my own prejudice, about her own pride, and I can't hate the woman who challenges me at every step. That's why this fear is so brutal. It's not my life I'm afraid to lose. It's hers. She scares me. She made me want her, long for her, obsess over her, and if she dies, part of me will die too. It has nothing to do with being alone and everything to do with not wanting to live without Serling Ambrose. She wormed her way into my heart, and ripping her free would flay me open and bloody.

"Please hold on." I squeeze her hand and push the rover faster. "You've made my life miserable for months. You can't stop now."

Two days. Serling has been unconscious for two days, and my sanity is slipping. I'm terrified she won't wake up, and it scares me how paralyzing the prospect of her death is. I can't live without her. She proved people can change for the better when the last person I cared to be around transformed into the only person I want, so I need her to survive. I need her to come back to me.

I've taken to sleeping on a medical cot beside the surgery pod since I can't bear to leave her alone. When we first returned to The Bellator, I shot heavy doses of anti-toxins and antibiotics into her bloodstream. When they didn't wake her, the machine operated on the vine wrapped around her calf and ankle. It was a tedious procedure, but it deftly extracted the barbed needles from her mutilated flesh. When she still didn't regain consciousness, the pod started a maintenance dosage of fluids and medication to combat the plant's venom, but after two days, I'm worried she'll never find her way back to me.

Desperate to fill my time with something other than anxiety, I've been studying the vine's remains. If the medical equipment in this Med Bay can identify the toxin's structure, I may be able to create an antidote, but I've had little luck. It's an incredibly complex plant, and its unique properties undoubtedly have many uses, but my frustration only builds as the test reveals everything but how to heal Serling.

"Is that what grabbed me?" A small hand grips my shoulder, and I flinch at the unexpected touch. "A plant?" Serling leans over to peer at the sample. I didn't hear her stand up, yet here she is, alive and well and curious.

"Sorry, I didn't mean to startle you," she continues. "But a plant? A plant almost killed me? This goddamn planet." She stands up, but all I can do is stare at her. She's awake, and not a figment of my anxious imagination.

"I was worried it was another swamp monster," she says, oblivious to my shock. "On one hand, I'm glad those beasts didn't find us, but a plant that can reach out and drag you?" She shudders. "That's freaky—" Serling pauses when she finally registers my expression. "Are you okay?" When I don't answer, she presses a palm to my forehead to test for a fever. "You feel fine. What's wrong?"

I lunge for her before I realize I'm moving and capture her waist. She gasps, but I silence her with a bruising kiss. Her body goes rigid for a few seconds, but then she surrenders to the moment and hugs my neck, the contact turning me feral.

"Two days." I wrap her legs around my hips and set her roughly on the counter before settling between her thighs. "You made me think I was going to lose you for two fucking days," I say as I claim her every moan, as I kiss her with meaning so she understands how her absence terrified me.

"I'm sorry," she whispers, and my brain short circuits. *Did Serling just apologize?*

"You need to be more careful." My voice escalates, and I force her to look at me as I reprimand her, but her eyes are soft. There's no combativeness in her gaze. Only sorrow and relief, as if she regrets torturing me. "You need to watch what you're doing." I'm practically shouting, but I can't stop myself. My fear has been all-consuming. I will not bury her in this god-forsaken Expanse. "This planet is dangerous, and no matter how hard I try, I can't protect you from everything. You need to pay attention. You don't get to fucking leave me."

"I'm sorry." She tugs me closer until her hug is almost suffocating. "I'll be careful. I won't leave you."

"Swear it."

"I promise."

"Fuck." I kiss her until my body burns with an unholy desire. Serling is mine. I crave her with a primal hunger, and I intend to show her who she belongs to.

I scoop her up off the counter, kissing her with intent as I stride to a medical cot. There's no mistaking the meaning behind my kiss, and she claws at my shirt, dragging it off my head in a silent display of consent. Her eagerness fuels my longing, and I set her on the small mattress before stripping my pants off. Her eyes darken at the sight, and I pause to enjoy the way they trace my body. Her obvious appreciation makes me feel all-powerful. Invincible. Both a god and the devil, and when her gaze dips to my erection, her breath hitches. The sound is like a drug injected straight into my veins, and a monster rages to life in my chest. She's so fucking beautiful, and I should go slow. She's injured, healing, and tired, but I need her to know she's never allowed to leave me.

I rip off her clothes with swift movements and then guide her to her back, letting my hands wander over her skin until it flushes pink. She moans as her thighs fall open in a welcoming invitation, and the sight of her glistening pussy is almost too much to bear. She has no right being this stunning.

"That's my girl," I growl as I force her legs apart and push the head of my cock against her opening. "You're so fucking wet, Princess. You can pretend to hate me all you want, but your pussy doesn't lie. You want this old man to fuck you raw and hard until I'm dripping out of you."

"Driver." My name is all she can manage as she pulls my lips to hers. The kiss is rough and primal, and she bites my bottom lip, urging me to claim her. Powerless to resist, I press my cock against her entrance, her soft heat threatening to undo me before we begin, but she shifts below me, releasing the pressure.

"You're too big," she groans. "I can't."

"You can." I kiss her to remind her how much she wants this.

"I can't." She tries to slip away, but I grip her hips to hold her still as I gently push another centimeter inside her. "Oh god." Her hands slam against my chest, but instead of pushing me away, she digs her nails into my pecks until my skin stings. "Please, you're too big. I…" she moans as I roll my hips, her voice contradicting her words.

"You will take me like a good girl." I thrust a little further, and feeling her stretch around the head of my cock is intoxicating. "Relax, Princess. Let me in."

"Driver." She yanks my head up with a snarl until our gazes meet. "Don't call me princess." Her eyes challenge me as her fingers slide into my hair. She pushes me down her body, and for a moment, I resist. I want her to take control. I want to test how forceful she'll be with her desires, and she does not disappoint. She holds my gaze as she shoves me into position, and I can't help but trail my lips over her belly.

"Get me ready, old man," she demands as I settle between her legs. "Lick my pussy until I'm dripping. Maybe then I can take your cock."

"You will take me." I obediently grab her thighs and yank her to the edge of the mattress. "A cunt this beautiful deserves to be worshipped. You deserve more than some small dick man who can't make you come."

"I've been with men who've made me come," she says, and I'm sick in the head because her taunting makes my cock leak precum. Normally, the mention of another partner would turn me savage, but the spark in her eyes confirms she's pushing me to keep my promise, to finally fuck the attitude out of her.

"Oh, Princess, don't lie to yourself. No one makes you come like I do." I waste no time burying my tongue inside her, and we both moan at how beautiful it is. Her arousal floods my mouth, and she tastes so fucking sweet that I know there will never be another woman for me. Not after this.

Her fingers tangle in my hair as she rides my face, and I lick and suck and bite until she's writhing. Her breaths come fast. Her chest heaves, and watching the way her breasts shudder is a high no drug could ever achieve.

Just when she's about to fall over the edge, I pull away and stand up. She yelps in protest, but my kiss silences her.

"Do you see how delicious you taste?" My tongue licks the seam of her mouth before slipping inside. "I could feast on you every day and still never be satisfied. I need more, Serling. Say yes."

"Please," she moans as she reaches between us to grip my shaft, and my heart thunders at her consent. She guides me inside her, her fingers stroking my thickness with unrestrained longing, and this time, she takes me like we're made for one another. "You're so big," she gasps, but appreciation fills her tone, not nerves. "I hope you know how to fuck though, otherwise this will be a waste of the most beautiful cock I've ever seen."

Her compliment goes straight to my head, and I thrust hard until I bottom out. Her breasts bounce with my movements, and I'm obsessed with how her body reacts to mine. "You won't be able to walk when I'm done with you, Princess," I whisper into her ear. "I'm going to ruin you for other men, and you'll crave me for the rest of your life."

"Don't call me princess." She bites my shoulder, and it hurts. Lord, does it hurt, but the pain almost has me spilling inside her. "And I would like to see you try."

Her tease is all the permission I need.

I fuck her hard, and within minutes she's writhing beneath me. Her pleasure is too much to bear, and when she tightens around me in her first orgasm, I have to bite my lip to keep from coming. I can't fill her yet. I need this to last until her love for me replaces her attitude.

"That was beautiful," I praise, as my hand captures her breast to force her nipple into the air. "I fucking love making you come on my cock." I lean down and suck the rosy peak into my mouth until it's stiff with arousal, and only once her moans grow desperate do I stand up. I study her face for any signs that she needs me to stop, but her gaze simply dips to my abs as she grows deliciously wet.

"Eyes on me, Serling," I command, and she instantly obeys. I smirk, giving her a second to watch me lift my hand, and then I thrust deep inside her as I slap her nipple. The impact isn't hard, but it's enough for her nerve endings to spark, and her back arches off the mattress. "No." I grip her jaw and force her gaze back to mine, never breaking our rhythm. "Look at me," I order as I suck her other breast into my mouth. A feral hunger fills her eyes, and her anticipation grants me permission. My tongue circles her nipple one last time for my own pleasure, and then I slap it harder than the first.

Serling's screams echo throughout the ship as she climaxes. Her bliss is like music, and this time, I can't resist. I fall on top of her, thrusting deeper as she rides out her climax. She kisses me as our bodies truly become one. A kiss that confesses she doesn't hate me, and I know my life is forever altered as I come inside her. Her cunt pulses around me, pulling every drop of cum from my sensitive cock, and my pleasure goes on endlessly.

Filling her does something to my emotions, though. I've never fucked a woman bare before, never came so hard that I leaked out of her while I was still buried inside her. The intensity makes me nervous, and I break our eye contact, but Serling grips my chin and forces me to look at her. She says nothing. She just stares at me, trying to decipher her feelings along with me, and I brush her hair from her sweaty face.

"I'll be more careful," she finally says, kissing me so slowly it almost feels loving. "I won't leave you." She smirks, her vulnerability making her shy, but I cherish her promise. "I mean, you're the old man, so you'll probably leave me first."

"Please." I roll my eyes and then kiss her over and over again until she laughs. "With my luck, I'll never die, and I'll be forced to live for decades listening to you."

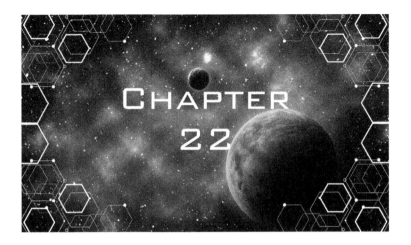

CHAPTER 22

DRIVER

W hat are you working on?" Serling's sleepy voice interrupts the silence, and I twist to watch her shuffle toward me. She looks adorable wearing only my shirt, and I shift my chair to make room for her.

"Come here. It's amazing." I extend a hand, and she accepts my invitation, slipping next to me as I hug her waist. "How's your leg? Are you in pain?"

"A little." She drapes an arm over my shoulders as if we've always been a couple and not two people determined to destroy each other. "But it's a dull ache. You didn't hurt me if that's what you're wondering. I'm just sore."

I smirk as I pull her into my lap, and she settles sideways across my thighs so she can wrap her arms around my neck. She plants a quick kiss on my lips, and if this is what it's like to wake up with her, I want her in my bed every night.

I deepen the kiss, holding her tight against my bare chest, and when I finally pull back, she's flushed and breathless. Her tangled hair frames her face, and I study her for a moment, drinking in the sight of her beauty. I like this Serling. The heiress dressed to annihilate is stunning, but this sleepy, happy, wearing only my shirt Serling stops my heart.

I give her one more quick kiss, and then I lean down, lifting her leg until it rests on the counter. I examine the wound, and while it's still red and tender, she's healing nicely. The color has also returned to her cheeks, and that floods me with intense relief. She managed some food and water after I helped bathe her, and she's been asleep on my medical cot for the past few hours. I seized the opportunity to study the vine, stealing glances at how peaceful she looked, but I'm glad she's awake. I'm eager to show her what I've learned.

"So that's what attacked me?" she asks when I point to my research. "A plant?"

I nod.

"I don't know if it's terrifying or insulting that a vine almost took me out."

"As much as I want to tease you about this, it's terrifying." I kiss her cheek reassuringly. "This plant... It's many things, but first and foremost, it's deadly. Without the anti-toxin in the medical pack, you would've never survived the return trip to The Bellator." I hug her tighter as she shudders at my words. "From what I saw at the oasis, this vine drops thin roots into the dirt as it grows and expands. It's still doing it, even though I severed it from the mother plant." I point to the tiny tendrils, and Serling studies them with a sickened expression. "When its barbed needles sense prey, they wrap around it and deliver a signal to the mother. The vine coils back in on itself, so while it appeared to be pulling you like a predator, it was simply a chain reaction within its fibers, tightening to draw you to the plant's core."

"Let me guess." She looks at me with a horrified expression. "It was going to make a meal of me."

"The emergency pod found two toxins in your bloodstream. The first was a paralytic, and the second was a fatal pre-digestive. One knocks you out and the other breaks down your muscles."

"Oh my god." Serling jerks back until she's flush against my chest. "Why didn't you burn this thing? You cut this section off the plant, and from the looks of it, that didn't harm it. It's still growing."

"This species is remarkably resilient and reproduces at an alarming speed. That sample has doubled in size since the pod removed it from your leg."

"Driver." She jumps off my lap, desperate to put distance between her and this agricultural monster. "Burn it. I don't want that thing on the ship. Do you know how painful the attack was?"

"Come here." I beckon her closer and open the sample case.

"I'm serious, Driver. It tried to eat me."

I smirk as I grab a broken rod from The Bellator's debris. With a wink, I press the metal against the plant, and with lightning speed, the vine chokes it just like it did her leg. Serling screams at the sudden movement and turns to flee, but I capture her wrist.

"Let go of me," she spits.

"It's locked on that bar now. It remains attached indefinitely to organic material, but inanimate objects only hold it for a few hours." I pull her close, and she looks like she might claw my eyes out. "It's safe," I laugh.

"You're an asshole," she growls. "You could have told me."

"That steals all the fun."

"Fuck you."

I kiss her head as I direct her attention to the plant. She fights me, but I slip my arms around her waist and rest my chin on her shoulder. She's so much shorter than me, but she fits perfectly against my body like this. I may never let go.

"Pick up that knife," I say, and she obeys. "The vine is

latched onto that bar. It won't release for a few hours, so as long as you don't touch the barbs, you're safe. Go ahead, slice some off the top."

"What?" She looks over her shoulder at me. "Absolutely not."

"You shot the head off of a reptilian predator. You can cut a plant."

She glares at me, but she takes the bait and presses the blade against the vine. She slices a thick flap off, and her face pinches at the slightly gooey flesh.

"Good girl. Now peel off the rough skin and eat the gel-like interior."

"Okay, now you're fucking with me." She elbows me in the gut. Hard.

"One would think." I wheeze. "But I'm serious."

She searches my features for signs of a trick, but when she sees I mean every word, she lifts the smallest slice to her mouth. She grimaces, staring at me with an expression that warns I'm in danger, and then she shoves it onto her tongue.

"Oh my god." Her eyes widen. "Oh my god!" She laughs and carves another piece from the gooey interior, popping it into her mouth. She moans as she chews, and if I didn't know how much louder she moans when I fuck her, I would be jealous.

"I don't know what this tastes like," she says, "but it might be the best thing I've ever had."

"I told you." I kiss her lips, tasting the juice on her tongue, and when I pull back, she shoves a bite into my mouth with a smile.

"I ran a full spectrum of tests while you were sleeping," I say as I chew. "Not only is it safe for human consumption, but it's filled with nutrients. It tastes like a fruit, but it contains fiber, protein, vitamins, amino acids, and carbs. The list goes on. It's resilient and fast-growing. It's filling and nutritious. Most of our rations survived the crash, but every day, our supplies dwindle. A time will come when nothing remains, but we just found a sustainable food source native to this planet." I kiss her again because while I hate what this did to her, I'm excited about this discovery. "We won't starve."

SERLING

Driver refused to let me do anything that remotely resembled work for the past two weeks. Thankfully, we transported almost a full tank's worth of water after the plant attacked me, so we haven't needed to restock yet. It's been glorious being able to take showers again, even if we can't use the cooling system. It requires more water than we have, and Driver's hesitant to leave the Bellator until he's convinced that I'm no longer in danger. I'm fine. I've been fine for days, but something about his protectiveness warns me not to fight him. He changed after I woke up. He thought I was going to die, and learning my life means so much to him irrevocably altered my opinion of him. He's afraid to lose me, so I listen to his rules and remain within The Bellator's confines. No one's ever been terrified of losing me like he is, and even though I would love the cooling system to be operational, I love knowing he wants me safe more.

A week and a half ago, he began a secret project. He won't let me anywhere near it, arguing I need my rest. I oblige him, but I'm bored out of my mind. Old Serling would've never considered volunteering her help, but as I stand in the cafeteria, I itch to do something other than simple tasks. Driver is also partially to blame for my boredom. We haven't spent a single night apart since I woke, and I've grown attached to his presence, to watching his powerful body flex as he works, to listening to his heroic war stories. He answers every question I ask, yet he understands I can't return the favor. I tell him the simple things about myself. Like the story about the party where an actor got drunk and fell asleep under a couch. When no one could find him, the hosts called the police, and he was declared a missing person for hours until he suddenly rolled out from under the cushions and asked for water. I can share those experiences, but I keep my mouth shut about what it really means to be Serling Ambrose. I can't let him learn about the girl who was forged into hateful cruelty by her own father, about the girl whose duty was more important than her life.

He doesn't push the issue, though, and to make up for my shortcomings, he opens up like a well-loved book. He hides nothing, not even the darkest parts of his past, and between his selflessness, his stories, and the delicious way he kisses me, I miss him when he's working. I miss the weight of his body on mine. I miss the way his rough voice moans when he's inside me, and how its deepness softens when he tells me about his life. I don't understand how it happened, but the man I hated is now the person I crave. We are two people who were never meant to collide, yet we've become unbreakably intertwined.

"What are you working on?" Driver's voice echoes off the walls as he enters the cafeteria, and I hold up the dehydrated vine. I've been playing with different ways of preparing our alternative food source. It's refreshing when juiced, rubbery when boiled, creamy when frozen, and fluffy when baked with flour. My most recent attempt is dehydration, and I push it into his mouth as he approaches.

"That tastes like candy." He grimaces as he chews before capturing me in a possessive kiss.

"That's what makes it so amazing." I smile against his lips.

"It's too sweet." He wraps his arms around my waist and hoists me over his shoulder like a caveman.

"You have no taste, old man." I pound his back as he carries me out of the room, and he slaps my ass hard in response.

"I know. I'm attracted to you."

I pinch his bare waist in retaliation, and he grunts as his spine contorts. He's stopped wearing shirts in this heat since he knows his scars don't bother me, and I love knowing he feels safe in his skin around me. The man is a work of art, a masterpiece of human resilience, but based on how hard I just pinched him, he's probably wishing he'd worn a shirt.

"You ready?" he asks as he kisses my hip before lowering me to the floor.

"Are you finally going to let me see your big secret?"

"What do you think?" He gestures behind me.

I follow his directions, but I have no clue what I'm looking at. A large opening expands before us in a destroyed section of the ship. Sunlight peeks through the damaged hull. Dirt coats what used to be the floor, and pipes hang from the ceiling. It looks like a mess, and I open my mouth to ask him if this disaster is what he's been working on when I recognize it. It's small, but the moment I see green huddling on the far end of the structure, I realize what he built.

"A garden," I whisper in awe. "You built us a garden."

"That plant will save our lives." He wraps an arm around my shoulders, and my body automatically curls against his broad chest. It's amazing how safe I feel in his arms.

"But after watching it almost kill you, I don't want you wandering the oasis to gather it," he continues. "We got lucky, but one day our anti-toxin supply will run dry. Unlike in the wild, I can control this environment. I built wide walkways, and as long as we vigilantly trim the plants, they won't take root in the paths." He directs my vision with his hand. "We'll use rods to activate the vines so they can't latch onto us when we harvest, and if they grow too fast, we'll cut and burn the excess. I hope to diversify our little farm as we locate more edible vegetation, but this is a decent start."

"It's a great start." I smile up at him, and pride warms his features at my praise.

"Thanks, Princess." He kisses my nose. "But please do me a favor when you garden. Wear thick pants."

CHAPTER 23

SERLING

The water lasted another two weeks, and for those fourteen days, I spent every spare second in our new garden. The section of vine that attacked me has flourished, but it's not enough to fill the rows. Driver wanted to wait until the tank ran low to ensure my leg could handle the trip to the oasis, and I didn't have the heart to tell him I didn't need an entire month to heal. His care is unlike anything I've experienced, and I'm afraid to break the spell. It's exhilarating to be revered for what I offer as a person and not as an Ambrose.

While I spent my days in the garden, Driver started working on a water collection system. We've been stranded in the Mors for almost six months now, and while we don't know the cycles this planet abides by, he believes the rainy season should be fast approaching. He wants the Bellator equipped and the crops planted by the time the rains fall since he's nervous about driving the rover during a lightning storm. I'll miss the oasis, but I agree. When those storms finally come, I want to hide inside this ship.

Now that the faint scars on my ankle are only slightly pink, we can finally make a water run. We plan to make multiple trips to fill all the tanks, and after months of heat, I'm dying to use the cooling system. I've forgotten what it's like to not be constantly coated in sweat. I've forgotten a lot of things, though. Like how expensive sheets feel against my skin. What perfectly styled hair looks like. How gourmet food tastes. What dread and oppression do to my soul. Yes, I've forgotten a lot.

As the sun falls through the sky after our second trip, we decided to camp on the beach and use the remaining light to search for edible vegetation. The vine has multiple preparations, but we'll get sick of it when it becomes our only food source. Driver makes me wear thick work pants as we explore, and we carry broken rods from the crash site to trigger the vine's attacks before we cut and gather them. When we find enough to populate our garden, we use the scanner to hunt for different plants. Fortunately, most of the oasis flora is non-toxic to the digestive system. Unfortunately, the jungle is mostly leaves and flowers. They might make decent teas or seasonings, but that's it. Driver is convinced something else of worth hides here, though, and he'll look until he finds it. I've never met someone as determined and resilient as him. His conviction fuels my own, and as we walk back to our campsite for the evening, I pick a strange pink flower. It's beautiful, and while it's too bizarre to be something old Serling would include in her arrangements, new Serling misses floral bouquets regardless of design. The unique petals match the abnormal life I've come to enjoy. I want to plant these in our garden for the color, but I freeze when I pull it out by its roots.

"Driver, you scanned this, right?" I hold it up, and his eyes widen at the bulbous tubers. "It's non-toxic?"

"Yeah, I remember the pink flowers." He brushes the dirt from the roots and pulls a bulb free. He carves it in half with his knife, and crisp white flesh comes into view, reminding me of the vegetable stews I ate one summer while campaigning with my father. We'd traveled to a rural planet, and they served us rustic yet flavorful root vegetables at every meal. My dad wasn't a fan of the earthy notes and humble dining, but I was young. I didn't understand decadence then, so I enjoyed them, and that memory has me instantly recognizing the value of this plant.

"First you find water. Then you go and get attacked by a vine, finding us food, and now you discover this." Driver smiles. "I don't know how it tastes, but it's safe." He slices off a bite and holds it out to me. "You want to try it?"

"No." I shove his hand away. "I'm not testing it."

"It's only fair," he teases. "I tried the vine first."

"Only after it almost killed me!"

"Well, when you put it like that." He pops the slice into his mouth, chews, and then grimaces.

"And you were going to make me eat it!" I slap his arm, and he laughs, cutting into it again. "It's not that bad." He shoves the slice towards my face, but I burst into a run to escape him. He catches me with ease, though, wrapping me in a powerful embrace, and presses the chunk to my lips. "No really, it's not bad." He's laughing so hard that it's infectious, and I can't help but join him. He seizes my temporary weakness as an opportunity, pushing the root into my mouth, and I chew without thinking. The texture is stringy and weird, but the flavor is bland. It's not gross, but I couldn't eat an entire meal of it.

"Fine, you happy?" I say, swallowing it with a scowl.

"Incredibly. Especially since it's mildly unpleasant raw, but it has a starchy consistency, so I have a feeling it'll taste better cooked." He leans forward and kisses my lips with such intensity, I forgive him. I could forgive him for anything when he kisses me like this.

"We should try it back at camp," I say, ripping more flowers out by the roots.

"You really are our good luck charm," he says, following my lead. "Granted, you help us in ways that give me heart attacks, so picking flowers to discover food is a pleasant change of pace." He tucks the plants under his arm and pulls me against him. His sentiments are so different from the ones he expressed when we first crashed here, and it's hard to believe we're the same two miserable people.

"Don't get too comfortable." I nudge his shoulder as we walk back to camp. "I've been thinking. We haven't checked the deeper ends of the pool for fish or seaweed. There's always a chance I'll give you a heart attack then, old man."

"You're never allowed to go swimming." He lowers his arm from my shoulders and smacks my ass. "Shallow waters only for you, Princess."

We pack the vines and most of the flowering plants into the rover, saving a few tubers for dinner, and then Driver builds a fire. We bake the roots until they're soft and steaming, and a smile spreads over my lips when we take our first bite. He was right. It's still stringy and a little bland, but its cooked flesh is significantly better. Some of the leaves growing here might make palatable seasonings, and I'm already picturing ways to prepare this root.

We eat until we're stuffed, and then we lay on the sand side by side to watch the stars. I used to look up at their light and long to return to them; believing life on this occasionally hostile planet with Driver Thorne was a death sentence, but we found food. We found water. I glance across the blanket to where he's falling asleep. We found each other. Maybe I can be different. Maybe I can be honest with him about who I am. Perhaps it's my full belly and the comfortable heat, but this was one of the best days I've lived in my twenty-nine years.

That thought lodges in my brain and refuses to let me sleep. Driver and I moved into the rover for the evening, the seats reclining to allow for a more comfortable night, but while he's fast asleep, I'm wide awake. Today was a good day. One of the best I can remember, and that scares me. I used to rage and panic when life took the slightest detour; my selfishness unable to enjoy anything if even the smallest detail strayed from my ideal, but today was hot, almost unbearably. We spent hours carting water from the oasis to the Bellator, and my body aches from the heavy lifting. Dirt is caked under my broken nails from gathering plants for our garden, and scratches dust my knuckles. I used to have perfectly manicured fingers, and now I look like I went twelve rounds with the mud and lost. I have awkward tan lines, untamed hair, a belly full of a stringy yet starchy root vegetable, and scars on what was once perfect skin. I'm a disaster, sleeping in a warm rover beside a scarred man eleven years older than me and vastly below my station, yet I'm inexplicably happy.

Realizing sleep isn't in my future, I slip outside and cross the sand to the blanket. I'm wearing only Driver's shirt, and the cool night air beneath the starlit sky lulls me into a safe peace. To think I once paid for elaborate versions of this view equipped with state-of-the-art facilities and dozens of staff members, only to find flaws in every aspect. Here, I'm tired, dirty, and dressed in a man's old shirt, yet I can't find a single fault with this moment except my insomnia. My emotions grip my chest with an iron fist, and the realizations dawning on me are overwhelming. It's terrifying when everything that defines you unravels.

The shadows move, and Driver's bare form strides into view. He wordlessly sits beside me and wraps his arms around his knees to join my star gazing. The Mors Expanse is deadly, but from this vantage, it's magical. I could say the same about the ex-soldier sitting beside me.

"No one has ever treated me the way you do," my small voice breaks the silence. "No one has ever put me first or risked their life for mine, not without significant financial compensation. But you? You hated me. I was horrible, yet you've saved my life time and time again. When that creature followed you, you were prepared to die so I would survive." A tear escapes my eye, and I swipe it away, hoping he doesn't notice. "I doubt my own father would sacrifice himself to save me, yet you didn't hesitate. It wasn't even a question in your mind. You saved my life, knowing yours was forfeit, knowing you would never receive a cent for helping me." I finally bring myself to look at him. "I realize we're never getting off this planet. I've accepted that reality, but I want you to know that if we are ever rescued, I choose you."

Driver goes impossibly still, and my stomach cramps at his silence. Admitting even the smallest hint of how I feel is terrifying, and I'm afraid the depth of my emotions is deeper than his.

"I don't know, Princess," he finally says. "I spend more time on transports than I do in my apartment, and when I am home, it's a small and simple existence. You don't think you would miss the glamour and ease of your life?"

"Flying through the Mors on a functional ship will be a luxury after this," I argue. "We're living in a crash site without a cooling system on a planet where vines try to eat you, and I don't miss home. Even sunburnt and dirty, I don't miss it. I don't want to go back. I want to stay with you." I'm practically begging him to hear what I truly mean, what I'm too nervous to say. I can't be someone he's simply passing time with. I need to be the woman he wants, regardless if we're rescued. Serling Ambrose is dead and gone. She and her vapid, venomous demeanor are mere memories. He must see it. He must recognize how irrevocably he has changed me.

For a long and uneasy moment, he stares at me as if trying to decide if he believes my declaration, if I would truly sacrifice my millions to live alongside him in the dangers of space. I pray he can read the conviction in my features. I know we're never leaving this planet, but it's important he understands that I'm not with him by default. I am with him by choice.

"So, you want to tie yourself to this old man?" he finally says. "All the wealth, prestige, and beautiful men in the galaxy at your fingertips, and you prefer to bother me instead?"

"Yes."

"And you want the same cock for the rest of your life?" He leans closer until his handsome face hovers inches from mine. "Because I don't share, Princess. On this planet, it's a moot point, but if we get rescued, and you stay, you're mine. I'll kill any man who tries to steal you from me, so you better be certain you want my cock and only mine for as long as I live."

My breath hitches at his words. "I do."

"Then be a good girl and show me how much you want it," Driver growls, gripping my shirt. His demanding tone flushes my skin, and I straddle his powerful thighs, teasing him with the faintest touch. My movements hint at how wet his words made me, but I don't lower myself onto his bare lap just yet. I want to enjoy this moment, to revel in both the power and pleasure of knowing that, while his dominance owns my body and bliss, I'm the one in control. I'm the one driving him wild with only the slightest taste of what he craves.

"Does that mean this cock is mine, then?" I whisper against his mouth as I slip my hand between us to grip his length. "You might be the soldier, but we both know I'm the cruel one. If I catch another woman even looking at you, she'll live to regret ever meeting you."

Driver's fist on my shirt tightens, and he jerks me down until my pussy slides against the underside of his shaft. "Princess, I couldn't get hard for another woman even if I tried. Your beauty knows no equal, but it's more than that. I respect the fuck out of you. You've proved me wrong in so many ways that your cunt is the only one I want to split open on my cock."

I increase my grip's pressure, torturing him as I stroke him from base to tip, and I kiss him with every emotion curling through me as I angle him toward my entrance. My desire is out of control, a wildfire in the driest of summers, and being in his arms, pressed against his scarred skin, isn't enough. It'll never be enough. I need him deeper, harder, faster, and my desperation is alarming. I'm worried about what it means that I crave the same man over and over until I can't breathe.

"Take this shirt off." Driver rips the top off me and then captures the back of my neck. He leans me backward so he can see my body, and his eyes fixate on where we're joined. "I fucking love watching you take me. It's a work of art to watch you slip lower until I bottom out."

I lean back further and rest my hands on his thighs, giving him an uninterrupted view of everything he longs for. I slow down, slipping his incredible size inside me inch by torturous inch as I savor his strained expression. No one will ever compare to how he fills me, and since I have an internal pregnancy blocker, I love letting him take me without anything separating us. There's nothing more arousing than the sight of Driver Thorne stretching me to my limit as he claims me.

"Goddamn it, Serling." He grips my hips and pushes me down hard, seating himself fully inside me. I gasp at the sudden fullness, my pleasure threatening to spill over as he roughly guides my movements. "Answer my question. Is this what you want for the rest of your life because I fucking love watching you bounce on my cock? Tell me I'm who you want. Tell me you're mine."

"Driver," I moan as my building climax consumes me.

"Don't you dare come," he orders. "You aren't allowed to come until you answer me." His pace speeds up, his thrusts making it impossible to do anything but scream. "I told you no, Princess." He releases my hip with one hand and ever so gently slaps my clit. My eyes jerk to his in surprise, but if he was trying to stop the pleasure, he was mistaken. The sting pushes me to fall off the cliff. "Say it, Serling." He slaps me again, and I explode, screaming so loud that my voice echoes off the cliffs.

"Yes!" I shout as I unravel. "I want to stay with you. I don't want anyone else."

Driver releases my hips and slips his arms around my waist. He yanks me flush against his chest, kissing me with a desperation that's different from the emotions I've experienced from him before. He hugs me tight, slowing our movements until it feels alarmingly like making love.

"Say it again. Say you want me," he begs.

"I'm yours, Driver." I slip my fingers into his hair, his slower pace dragging every inch of my body over his powerful form. It's electric. It's where I belong. "Whether we stay on this planet or we get rescued, I'm staying with you."

Driver pulls back from our kiss and gazes longingly into my eyes. The intensity of his stare makes me gasp, and he lifts a hand to my face. He cups my jaw as I take him slow and deep, his expression changing, but I don't recognize the look. Just when I'm about to ask if he's all right, though, he opens his mouth and changes my life.

"I love you too, Serling."

Four words. Four simple, tiny words plus my name. Yet nothing has ever been so significant. It amazes me how he can read me. How he knows I long to return the phrase but am too scared to admit it. He saw the truth behind my admittance of wanting to stay with him. It's why he added that three-lettered word 'too' at the end of his statement. *I love you, too.*

Driver Thorne loves me.

I press my mouth back to his as if I can capture those words. I want to hide them inside me forever, and when I come, he joins me. He spills inside me, filling my pussy until his cum leaks down my thighs. We don't stop moving, though. We don't stop kissing. We remain locked together for the rest of the night until neither of us can keep our eyes open.

Driver Thorne loves me, and I'm terrified. This is the first time I've experienced a love this intense, and I'm afraid that now that I know how it feels, losing him will kill me. My father murdered any love my family had. I grew up with parents who never touched unless it was for the press. I was raised in a home where I was punished for displaying emotions rather than comforted for expressing feelings. My past is void of affection, and I'm frightened that the poison inside me will contaminate the exquisite beauty of being loved. My father isn't here. He never will be, but he's why I can't return those three words to my pilot. My father has a way of poisoning everything, including his own child. I'm worried his venom will somehow cross the Mors Expanse and corrupt the heaven I've found on this hell of a planet.

DRIVER

The weather has started to turn. It won't be long before the rainy season is upon us, and while the water collection system is up and running, the oncoming rain concerns me. We crashed at the end of the last rainy season, so we have no idea how severe the storms will get. Lightning, like the bolt that almost killed Serling, could obliterate the ship's remains, so I've spent every spare second repairing The Bellator's hull. I've made her as watertight as possible, but flooding and electrocution are still a genuine threat. I try not to fear hypothetical disasters, though, and concentrate on the fact that we'll have a constant and immediate supply of water.

When I'm not working on repairs, Serling and I explore our surroundings, searching for anything else of use. We didn't find any animals or fish at the oasis or any other edible plants besides the vines and the pink flower's roots. The endless rocks are void of life, but we found a salt deposit, which is a relief. The human body needs salt to survive.

Serling has taken it upon herself to invent as many dishes as possible so we don't get bored with our garden. We planted a few herbaceous plants that make decent teas and seasonings, so while some of her creations miss the mark, most are borderline genius. It's surprising that a woman who has never touched a stove can cook well, but Serling's adorable to watch when she discovers a new recipe. So far, my favorite is her breakfast cakes. She had the idea to dehydrate the roots and grind them into flour, using the results to make pancakes. She then stews the vine's juice into a syrup, creating an entire meal from this planet's native food source. It's the best breakfast I've had, and I don't know if it's because it's genuinely amazing, if it's because the meal was created from our thriving garden, or if it's because she makes it with so much love. All I know is her smile when I first tasted it was brighter than the sun.

It's strange how we've become this odd domestic couple. You would think living with only one other person would make me sick of her, but I never tire of her company. Whether we're cooking together, riding in the rover, hunting for provisions, or sparingly using the entertainment items we found onboard, I always want to be around her. She enjoys listening to my war stories. She loves it when I talk about my dad, and the way she devours tales of my upbringing makes me wonder what kind of childhood she had. She adores hearing of my dad's adventures yet refuses to discuss her parents, and it breaks my heart. It's as if she's living vicariously through my life to experience what it's like to have a father who cherishes their child's happiness. She still hasn't opened up to me, but I'm learning to read between her lines. She hints at things, sometimes unconsciously, and if I look closely, I understand her meaning. Like when she promised to stay with me if we left this planet. I'm ashamed that I occasionally have a hard time believing she would. Not that I doubt her feelings, but it's difficult to walk away from that much wealth and power. Regardless of what she'd do if faced with that reality, it was her subtext that was important. I saw right through her. She was attempting to express her emotions, and I understood.

It's why I told her I love her. She's a challenge, a beauty, a fighter. She's strong and smart, and she's mine.

Which is why the water run I'm currently on sucks. I asked her to help me with the hull repairs yesterday. I needed her to hold the parts steady, but it took longer than expected. She wasn't paying attention to her water intake, so by the time we finished, she had overheated. Since The Bellator's cooling system requires large amounts of water, we use it sparingly, but after witnessing the severe flush in her cheeks, I turned it on. It ran all night, and after breakfast this morning, I left for the oasis. I want to keep the cooling system on until I know she's safe. We have limited medical supplies, so it's safer to err on the side of caution. I don't want too much sun to turn into something serious.

Serling wanted to accompany me, promising to rest in the rover, but I asked her to stay in bed. She fought me on it, but her argument lacked conviction. Conflict is her love language, and I think it was her odd way of telling me she loves me and to be safe, but in the end, she conceded. She's still a little weak, and as much as I miss her company, losing her would be a death sentence.

I move as fast as possible. The oasis pool looks lower than usual, so it's good the weather is changing. Whatever challenges the rain brings will be worth it. We need the water.

It's midday by the time I return to the Bellator, and the second I step out of the rover, I know something's wrong. Everything looks normal, but uneasiness pricks my soldier's intuition.

"Serling?" I shout. *Please be okay. I need you to be okay.* "Serling?" She doesn't answer, and I jog through the ship for the cafeteria. I don't find her there, nor is she in our room or the garden. Did she go outside? I didn't see her when I parked, so maybe boredom drove her to search the crew's belongings in the hopes of finding fresh entertainment.

"Serling?" I race through the halls, but the stillness confirms the ship is empty. She isn't here, and my heart thunders so hard that my chest feels like it's caving in on itself. I shouldn't have left her. She could be hurt, and I left her alone.

A faint humming breaks through my panic, and I freeze. That sound isn't coming from The Bellator, but it's decidedly mechanical. The whir pulses through the air, and I take off running, weaving through the corridors until I exit the main airlock on the opposite end of the ship. The volume increases the second I step out into the open, and when I see what's causing the disturbance, my body burns hot.

"Serling!" I scream as I race for her, and the instant she hears my voice, she twists her neck to find me, her eyes wide and her limbs rigid.

"Driver!" She bucks wildly against her captor's hold, but my brain can't comprehend what I'm seeing. Two heavily armed soldiers are dragging her for a transport. Humans. Other humans are on this planet, and they have Serling.

The soldiers study me as I race for her, and a third, younger man guarding their ship's entrance hatch grips his weapon as I capture Serling's biceps and drag her free of the strangers. By their expressions, this situation is about to turn ugly, but then Serling throws her arms around my waist. She clings to me, sobbing uncontrollably, and the men relax their stance. They must realize by our intimacy that I mean her no harm, but my heart rate won't slow. I thought I lost her.

"They're here to take us home." Serling finally manages through her tears.

Home. My body flushes cold as I stare at the soldiers, and the one on the ship quirks his eyebrows in sudden recognition.

"Wait a minute." He steps down off the ramp to get a closer look at me. "You're Driver Thorne, aren't you?"

"I am." I pull Serling tighter against my chest.

"No shit. You're the reason I started flying the Mors. You're legendary."

"How are you here?" I ignore his compliment, unable to function at the sight of other people after over six months of solitude.

"Imperator Ambrose hired us to find his daughter." He looks pointedly at Serling.

"Miss Ambrose," one of the older soldiers interrupts. "We need to leave. We have a long journey ahead of us, and your father is waiting."

Serling stiffens in my arms at the mention of her dad, and alarm bells ring through my brain at her instant discomfort.

"But…" she glances at the Bellator. At the life we built together. "We… Can I go back and grab some—"

"Miss Ambrose, now," he says harshly. The soldiers seize her, and a rabid animal rages in my chest. No one puts their hands on her.

"We're under strict instructions from your father," the man continues, pulling Serling from my arms. I lunge for her, but he presses a palm into my chest. Normally, I would break his hand for touching me, for keeping the woman I love from me, but he's heavily armed, and Serling stands between us. I won't risk killing her, so I fall still.

"We thank you for protecting her," the soldier says coldly, as if to remind me I'm unworthy of the Federation's heir. "We'll take it from here. Our orders are to rescue Miss Ambrose and any other survivors, and her father is eager to have her returned to Corr'us Sanctum."

He turns around and drags Serling for the transport, signaling our conversation is over, and I have no choice but to follow. I won't let her get caught in the crossfire, and while the sinking sensation carves my gut hollow, I tell myself this is a good thing. Serling can go home. She'll be safe. I won't have to worry about vines or heat stroke or monsters killing her ever again.

The soldiers lead us into the small transport and strap Serling into a harness. They then claim the seats on either side of her, forcing me to sit across from them. I don't like this sudden expanse between us. I can't read her expression, and it urges me to say something. To assure her everything will be okay and we'll get through this together, but I can't form the words. The way the soldiers cage her in like she's a priceless artifact and not the woman who owns my soul warns this won't end well. In a matter of seconds, our lives changed, and I desperately want to believe we'll survive this. I want to trust she was telling the truth when she promised to stay with me, but except for the young soldier, these men regard me as dirt unworthy of cushioning her steps.

No one speaks as we leave the planet and travel for the military ship waiting to carry us through the Mors. An inexplicable sadness floods me as I watch The Bellator's remains vanish. I hated this planet when we first crashed. I was certain we would die on those rocks, but it became our home. A home where Serling and I were happy, and I almost wish we could return. I wish we'd never been found.

The trip is both the longest and shortest flight of my life, and when we dock on The Victoriam, the soldiers whisk her into the waiting doctors' and attendants' arms. They swarm her, leaving only a single doctor for me, but Serling meets my gaze through the crowd with an overwhelmed expression.

"Serling." I step forward, readying to pull her free. We haven't seen people in six months, and I can read the claustrophobia in her eyes. She's drowning, but before I can reach her, the same rigid soldier grabs my wrist.

"Take your fucking hands off me," I growl, but he settles his weight to block Serling from my view.

"The Imperator thanks you for ensuring his daughter's safety, but we'll take it from here," he says before turning back to the crowd. "Miss Ambrose," he addresses her with respectful authority, letting her know there'll be no arguing with what he's about to say. "Your father requested we contact him the minute you were safely onboard. If you'll come with us, I'll connect the secure link."

"I…" Serling trails off, panic and uncertainty lingering in her eyes as she stares at me for directions. The sight breaks my heart. This sudden rescue. This horde of people. It's too much for her to handle, and I can't make it worse for her. I won't, so I smile despite the knot in my stomach.

"Go," I encourage. "Tell your father you're alive. I'll be here when you're done."

She nods, some of the anxiety lifting from her features, and she allows the soldiers to lead her away. She throws me one last glance before she disappears behind the airlocks, and I have the overwhelming urge to chase after her because, for some reason, I fear this is the last time I'll see her.

SERLING

I feel her creeping back inside me as I speak to my father. The old and venomous Serling. This reunion is not the joyous one I prayed for, but a perfunctory meeting derailing him from the pressing matters demanding his attention. He's polite and expresses the proper sentiments, but if an outsider were to witness our conversation, they would assume I was a member of his staff and not his sole child who'd been missing for six months.

"Your mother will be delighted to hear they found you without issue," he says, signaling our lackluster reunion is at an end. "I'll convey your sentiments to her at dinner."

"Is mom there?" I ask. "I want to see her."

"No, she's at an event. It would disrupt the guests to alert her. I'll tell her about your rescue this evening."

His words are a punch to my gut. How is an event more important than learning I'm alive? The familiar urge to cry surfaces, but the more familiar icy walls erect around my heart. "I understand." My voice is void of emotion. "I'll initiate communication with her when she's available."

"You'll arrive at Corr'us Sanctum in three weeks," my father says. "There's no need to bother her. You'll have plenty of time to catch up once you return."

It takes everything I have within me not to react to his comment. He wants me to wait until I'm home to speak to my own mother? She doesn't care to hear my voice after months of believing I was dead?

"I'm expecting a call," my father says, oblivious to my distress. "I am glad you're relatively well and unharmed. I'll see you when you return."

"How did you find me?" I ask before he terminates the connection. For a man who spent millions searching for me, he seems unenthusiastic about my rescue.

He pauses at my question, staring at me with a bitterness that stills my heart, and then he answers with a coldness in his voice I'd hoped to never hear again. "You think you're clever." His entire demeanor changes. "You thought you could hide it from me, but you forget who I am, Serling. I know why you were on Daankor. You played your role well. Everyone believed your charade, but I saw through your supposed pleasure cruise."

My stomach cramps painfully.

"I will not be trifled with," he continues. "I couldn't allow your petty act of defiance, so I made my own plans. I instructed your contact on Daankor to do as you requested, but to build in a back door access." He studies my face, waiting for me to react, for my shock to show, but I force every part of what makes me human into a locked cage and return his stare. "I control it now, and not only do I control it, but I had a tracker embedded in it. That's how I found you." He lifts a hand to disconnect our call, but I can't move. I can't breathe. I can't function. "It's time to come home, daughter. It's time to fulfill your duty."

CHAPTER 25

DRIVER

I'm not permitted to see Serling during the weeks it takes for The Victoriam to escape the Mors Expanse. Every time I try to cross the airlock to her quarters, the soldiers bar my entrance. The animal in me longs to fight my way through, but that would only end with my blood staining the white floors. I'm outnumbered and outgunned, but I'm desperate. For six months, she was my entire world. Even when we despised each other, my life revolved around her survival, and now I don't know how to exist without her. What's more, I don't want to exist without her, and by the time we reach Corr'us Sanctum, I'm ready to crawl out of my skin.

We land at the capital with incredible fanfare. It seems the entire planet came to witness the return of the Ambrose Heir, and security is overbearing. They're televising Serling's exit from the ship, and the Imperator plans to receive her in person. He'll give a speech, after which I'm expected to make a brief appearance as the war hero who helped Serling survive. I have half a mind to refuse the Imperator's request that I play the show pony, but the knowledge that Serling will be there demands my compliance. I'll endure anything if only to see her. She promised to leave this circus behind and disappear into the stars with me, but with each passing day, my faith in that dream strangles to death. I need to see her. I need to look into her eyes and know she still loves me.

A young stylist comes into my quarters to prepare me for the press conference, but I send her away. I refuse to play their games. Over the years, people's judgments have made me hide my flaws, but Serling's acceptance changed my desire to blend in. I don't care anymore. My scars? My damage? They are signs I survived, so I wait just as I am for the event. Only Serling's opinion matters. Hers are the only eyes I want on me.

Security finally clears us to exit The Victoriam, and the waiting crowd is daunting. Soldiers erected an electronic perimeter to protect the Ambrose family from the sea of humanity, and when the Imperator and his wife climb onto the stage, the spectators surge into a frenzy.

I hover just out of view to watch the man Serling spoke very little about. What she didn't tell me was telling enough, though, and my skin crawls at the sight of him. He makes a dramatic show of waiting anxiously, of pacing and crying at the imminent return of his daughter, but I know what it's like to love Serling. To fear for her life. To believe she was dead, only to experience intense relief when I found her safe and whole. When she woke from that vine attack, a primal emotion took over me. I couldn't control my actions. I needed her in my arms, and while our relationship differs vastly from the one she has with her parents, the raw emotions are the same. And this man is faking his.

The crowd stills as Serling exits The Victoriam. She's dressed simply but expensively, and the three weeks without sun have calmed the angry pink of her skin. Her hair is down, she's wearing minimal makeup, and her shoes are surprisingly sensible, yet she's still the single most stunning thing in this galaxy. My breath catches in my chest. I forgot how gorgeous she is.

She places the entire crowd under her spell, and her parents rush for her with an embarrassing show of affection. I know what it feels like to be embraced by Serling, and I can read the stiffness in her body language at their performance. She does all the right things, makes all the expected expressions, but their charade makes her uncomfortable. She handles it with the grace of a woman well-trained in managing the public's eye, though. She hugs and waves and smiles. She fools everyone but me.

"This is an incredibly joyous day for my family," Imperator Ambrose finally addresses the crowd. "The daughter we believed to be dead has returned." He hugs her close with movements that come across as controlling, not loving. "My wife and I never gave up hope that she would return to us. For six months, brave men and women searched the treacherous Mors Expanse for her, and here she is. Alive and well." The crowd cheers, and Serling gives a rehearsed smile that makes my blood run cold. I recognize that expression. The venom is back.

"I'm indebted to the crew of The Victoriam," her father continues. "They risked their lives to rescue our daughter, but there is another soldier I must mention. Many of you know him from his legendary military career, but I would like to offer my thanks to Pilot Driver Thorne." He extends his hand, my cue to obey, and I step out onto the stage. I barely hear him as he recounts my determination to keep Serling alive because all I can concentrate on is how she won't acknowledge me. For a fraction of a second, her eyes flicked to mine when her father introduced me, but then they returned stoically ahead. Her gaze remains fixated on the crowd, and her avoidance causes me more pain than a blunt and rusted knife carving through my gut.

I step for her, deaf to the Imperator's speech. I need to get to her. To capture her in my arms and remind her how much I love her, but she refuses to look at me. *Why won't she look at me?*

"Sir?" A soldier tugs on my arm, and I almost punch him for stopping my advance before I realize I'm still standing in the camera's shot. "The Imperator finished thanking you. Please exit the stage," he whispers.

I stare at the fool who thinks I can leave Serling. It's the kid from our rescue, the one excited to meet me, and I reign in my anger. I can't get into a fight with the Ambrose family in such close proximity. A sniper would take me out while the galaxy watched.

"Sir." The kid tugs on me again, and I follow him. Now isn't the time to confront her. I'll wait until after the press conference, and then I'll track her down and steal her away from here.

"I would like to seize the opportunity to make a joyous announcement," her father booms just as I step off stage, and the tone of his voice freezes my boots to the floor. "My daughter's disappearance was not only devastating to my wife and I but also to the Sinclair family."

Wariness pricks my brain at the name. The Sinclairs are one of the wealthiest families in the Federation. Why would they be invested in Serling's survival?

The Imperator extends an arm, and a man climbs the steps to the stage. He's my exact opposite with his perfectly styled blond hair. Not a single ounce of body fat sits on his bones, but it's not a form built in the fray. His muscles have never seen the outside of a gym. His clothing is impeccable. He oozes wealth, prestige, softness, and vanity, and when he settles beside Serling, it takes everything within me not to throw her over my shoulder and escape this insanity.

"It is my greatest pleasure to introduce Tiberius Sinclair to you." Imperator Ambrose continues with a sickening smile as he pounds the newcomer on the back. "And my daughter's fiancé."

CHAPTER 26

DRIVER

F*iancé? Serling's fiancé?* That's impossible. She belongs to me. She's my love, my future, not his. The edges of my vision blur, and rage settles over me as Tiberius Sinclair slips an obnoxiously large ring on her finger before wrapping a perfunctory arm around her shoulders. They smile and pose so the media can capture this momentous occasion, and before I realize what I'm doing, I seize the weapon on the kid's hip.

"Sir?" He clutches my wrist, eyes wide and wild. "Mr. Thorne, what are you doing?"

"Let me go."

"Sir." He steps toe-to-toe with me to obscure our struggle from the cameras. "They'll kill you the second they notice what you're doing."

"Let go," I growl.

"The snipers," he says through gritted teeth. "They have every inch of this dock covered. If you do this, they'll shoot you before you make it two steps. They'll kill me, too, since it's my weapon, and I don't want to die."

His words give me pause.

"Mr. Thorne, you were my childhood hero," the soldier continues, pulling me further out of the crowd's sight. "And I'm not blind. I saw the way Miss Ambrose hugged you. The way you looked at her. I can only imagine your pain, but please, let go. I don't want to die."

I release my grip on his gun, and he lunges backward. I hate myself for scaring him, and honestly, I don't know what I was planning to do with the weapon. It's second nature to see Serling in danger and come to her defense, and Tiberius' arms around her set off alarms in my skull. I love her, and another man just put a ring on her finger. To make it worse, she didn't stop him. She didn't resist. She didn't even look at me, and while I refuse to accept this reality, her actions confirm her choice. Serling isn't keeping her word. She isn't choosing me.

"Mr. Thorne." The kid guides me away from the stage. "Now isn't the time. Not when security is so high. Not when the Imperator is present. I understand... at least, I think I do. I've got a girl. She might be the one, and if I watched her get engaged to the wealthiest man in the galaxy, I'd be murderous, too. But this isn't the right time. The Ambroses are scheduled to return to their private residence after this event. You saved Serling's life. You're a Federation hero, especially after this press conference. I'm sure the family would grant you an audience if you visited her privately."

As much as it pains me to admit it, the kid has a point. The soldier in me wants to fight, but the galaxy is singing my praises after the Imperator's speech. The public's hearts belong to me, but their love is fickle. One wrong move, and they'll crucify me, so I concede under duress. I leave Serling behind and return to an apartment I haven't seen in almost a year that no longer feels like home. I spend the following days reactivating my accounts, checking in with Headquarters, dodging the hero-chasing press, and eating foods I thought I missed but now taste like ash. I try to sleep, but it's useless. I've had girlfriends before, but when they ultimately left, I never missed a night's sleep. It's different when you lose the woman you wanted forever with.

It takes a week for the obsession with our return to die down, and the instant I can leave my apartment without being hounded by the star-struck press, I make the journey to the Ambrose private estate. Seeing the exorbitance Serling calls home is a slap to the face. No wonder she accepted Tiberius' ring. My apartment is an insult compared to this excessive luxury.

The perimeter security guards allow me through the gates and escort me to the front door, where a harsh guard greets me. "Mr. Thorne," he says emotionlessly. "Can I help you?"

"I want to see her."

"See who?" he asks, and despite his size, this man needs to be careful. I've killed bigger than him.

"You know who." I step into his personal space. He's tall and thick, but I'm taller, and his meaty neck has to tilt so he can meet my gaze.

"Mr. Thorne, if you—"

"Where is she?" I snarl. "You either tell me, or I'll find her myself."

"Mr. Thorne, the Ambrose family is greatly indebted to you, but you aren't welcome here. Miss Ambrose won't be seeing you, and if you attempt to force your way into the residence, you'll be treated as a hostile intruder."

I glare at him, but he seems to enjoy telling me to fuck off.

"I would leave now, Mr. Thorne, while you're still revered as a war hero and Miss Ambrose's salvation."

"Serling!" I shout, my feet welded where I stand. I can't be a hostile intruder if I never enter the mansion. "Come out and face me yourself!" The guards close in, corralling me toward the exit, but I move along the immaculate drive to a side window instead. "Serling, I need you to look me in the eyes and tell me we're done. I know you, Princess. You're too stubborn to let this go without a fight, so come out here and fight me. Tell me with your own words that we're over because I love you, Serling. Do you hear me? I fucking love you, and unless you convince me you don't feel the same, I'll never give up hope. I'll never stop waiting for you because giving you up is like refusing to breathe. It's impossible."

The guards circle me, slowly forcing my retreat, but I open my mouth one last time.

"I will always fight for you, Serling. Hell, I'll fucking fight with you if that's what you want. Just fight, Princess. Fight for us, or come outside and tell me your promise meant nothing."

The house remains still. I'd foolishly hoped if I came here, she would run into my arms and beg me to steal her away, but the silence kills my dreams. She isn't coming. She might not have even heard me, and with a crushed spirit, I leave the estate.

SERLING

I sit below the window so he can't see me. I can't look at him. I can't do it. I wouldn't survive witnessing his heartbreak. Hearing it is death enough, so I huddle on the floor in a designer dress that would kill my mother if she saw it pressed against dirty tiles, and I listen to his anguish. I listen until his pain paralyzes me, and when I finally pull myself out of the comatose state that his agony drowned me in, the sun has long since set.

CHAPTER 27

DRIVER

In other news, Serling Ambrose was spotted wedding dress shopping earlier today," the reporter says from the hologram in my living room. "With the wedding of the decade a month away, the beautiful bride-to-be has expertly navigated the political criticism surrounding her marriage to billionaire Tiberius Sinclair. Many Federation leaders have voiced concerns over the joining of the Ambrose and Sinclair families. As a member of the founding family, Imperator Ambrose already has an overwhelming amount of power, and many fear with the Sinclair bankroll funding him, he'll overstep his control. This ever-growing concern in the galaxy is to blame for Serling's disappearance in the Mors Expanse. An extremist militia group known as The Aequatores claimed responsibility for the missile strike against The Bellator—the ship Serling was aboard during her Mors crossing. The Aequatores took extreme and terroristic measures to prevent this union, going so far as to carry out an assassination attempt against Miss Ambrose. Their attack murdered The Bellator's crew and passengers, but by a stroke of fate, Serling survived. Kept safe by the legendary war hero

Driver Thorne, she returned to her family after six months, and despite the tragedy she endured, she hasn't let that stop her from planning her dream wedding. The upcoming nuptials trouble many, but this reporter wishes the couple a lifetime of happiness. Miss Ambrose certainly deserves it after surviving a hostile planet."

My communicator rings, stopping me from throwing the hologram across the room. It's been over a month since we returned to Corr'us Sanctum, and three weeks since I made a scene outside Serling's house. Dozens of days have passed as I wait for her to keep her promise, to choose me instead of her family's wealth, but her marriage to Tiberius is fast approaching. The news constantly reports on her wedding planning, and watching her enter the designer boutique shattered my heart. I could never afford to buy her a gown like the ones hanging in that shop, yet I still can't shake the feeling that she should be marrying me. That she should be dress shopping for our wedding.

I want to fight for that future. It's not in my nature to surrender, and if Serling had given me even so much as a look during the press conference, I would have stormed the Ambrose's proverbial castle. If she'd simply come to the window when I shouted outside her home, I would've fought my way through the army guarding their estate. I undoubtedly would've been gunned down before I reached her, but that outcome wouldn't have stopped me. I would wage war against the entire Federation for her, but I can't force her to love me. I won't chase a woman who has no interest in being caught, and since we've returned to Corr'us Sanctum, Serling hasn't once acknowledged my existence.

"Hello?" I answer the communicator, my voice sour.

"Turn off the news," Archer says by way of greeting.

"I'm not—"

"There's no point in torturing yourself," he cuts me off.

"She's a beautiful woman. I can see how easy it was for you to fall for her, but she's an Ambrose. You should understand more than anyone how the rich and powerful use and discard people. She needed you in the Mors, but now she has Tiberius Sinclair to cater to her every whim."

"It wasn't like that," I argue, knowing full well how difficult it was to love her. I also can't bring myself to believe she cared so little that she lied just to use me when her life depended on it.

"Regardless of what it was like, stop torturing yourself and turn off the news. I have a job for you," he says. Archer and I have worked together since I left the military. He runs Headquarters and was overjoyed to find out their best pilot survived.

"Are you giving me a Mors run?" I ask, muting the hologram without turning it off. Archer insisted I take time off when I returned to Corr'us Sanctum, but even though he's cleared me for flight, he's withheld all Mors crossings.

"You know the answer to that," he says. "I'm not letting you cross the Expanse until you have a few flights under your belt. What happened to you was traumatic."

"I'm fine. I'm your best goddamn pilot. Give me a Mors Run."

"No."

"Then I'm hanging up."

"Okay, okay, wait!" Archer shouts. "Do this simple job for me, and then I'll put you back on the Expanse rotation, deal?"

"Fine. What's the job?"

"It's last minute, but it'll take you off planet during the Ambrose-Sinclair wedding. It'll be good for you."

"What's the job?" I repeat.

"The client asked for you specifically," Archer starts.

"Why?"

"Why? Because you're the handsome war hero who saved Serling Ambrose's life, that's why. Women everywhere are losing their minds over you."

"I'm not accepting a flight for some lonely woman who thinks that chartering my ship will get her laid by a war hero."

"Trust me, I know," Archer scoffs. "This isn't like that, though. She understands your skill and discretion and wants your expertise."

"Why?"

"This isn't public knowledge, but between you and me, the client's an actress. Apparently, she had an affair with a married senator, and the media found out. They're running the scandal story tomorrow, and she doesn't want to be anywhere near civilization when the news breaks. She's willing to pay a shit ton of money for you to pilot a few months' cruise along the outskirts of the Federation until the press dies down, and she asked for you specifically. It's an easy job, Driver. Minimal crew. One passenger. A low-stress route. Do this for me, and I'll schedule your next flight through the Expanse."

"Fine," I sigh. "You said it was last minute. When does she want to depart?"

"The story is breaking tomorrow, and she wishes to be long gone when it does," Archer says, and I can hear the apology in his voice. "You leave tonight."

"You know I don't do last-minute flights," I say as I enter the hangar an hour later with my pack slung over one shoulder. "My preflight checks are extensive, and I won't cut corners. Not even for an itinerary this simple. Too much can happen."

"That's why I started them for you." Archer shakes my hand as he leads me to the cruise ship. It's a child's plaything compared to the Bellator, and it's slightly humiliating that I'm piloting it. This single-family luxury craft is intended for leisurely strolls through the outer rim where nothing dangerous ever happens, while I'm a pilot built for war. It's insulting that I survived six months in the Mors only to merit a job a student could perform blindfolded.

"I know that look," Archer chuckles. "Listen, man, I get it. This is way below your skill level, but when the client sent me the payment, I almost shit myself. She's paying a lot of money for you specifically, and I know how thorough you are, which is why I've been here since we signed the contract getting a head start."

"Who's the actress?" I ask, nervous about what kind of woman would pay so much for my services that Archer came down from his office to run pre-flight checks himself. I don't trust others with my ships, but Archer is the exception. Five years my senior, he left the military before me to work at Head-quarters and rose quickly into a position of authority. He's one of the smartest people I know, so his checks are thorough. I've never seen him disregard procedure for a client though, and I wonder what power this actress has to get a married senator and Archer to bend the rules for her.

"Darla Knox," he answers.

"I don't recognize her name."

"You wouldn't. She's a recent breakout star. She was a model before you went missing, and knowing you, you haven't been keeping up on celebrity gossip since your return."

I have been with one celebrity, but I don't tell him that. He already thinks I made a mistake believing an Ambrose.

"How much is the contract worth?" I ask instead. Archer pulls his control tablet out of his back pocket, swipes through a few menus, and then hands it to me. I take one look at the number and nearly choke. "Are you serious?"

"The money cleared. So, it's legit. She paid in full." He points to my portion of the contract. "That's your cut."

"Holy shit. That's a lot of zeros."

"I told you, man." Archer thumps me on the back as we

board the cruise ship. "You want back in the Mors rotation? Do this, and you get your wish. We have a new warship being built to replace The Bellator. It's yours. You name it. You staff it. You run it. Just cart this actress around first. Get off planet, clear your head, and when you return, I'll throw you back into the fray."

"I'm here, aren't I? What's the itinerary?"

"A scenic tour of the outskirt planets." Archer hands me a tablet with the trip's information. "Too easy a flight for you, but you might enjoy it. There are no scheduled stops during the three-month cruise except for two resupply appointments. Miss Knox has requested her privacy, which means she won't be interacting with you or the crew unless it's an emergency. She's asked that all staff members ignore her quarters, using only the automated cleaners and food delivery methods. You're also not cleared for any unauthorized landings or changes to the schedule. It's a straightforward trip. All you have to do is float around the galaxy. You don't even need to see her."

"That's a plus," I say.

"I figured it would be." Archer thumps my back. "Departure is in a few hours, so I'll stay to help you complete the pre-flight checks. All I need is for you to sign the contract, and you're set."

I stare down at the blank line awaiting my name. The second I sign, that money stops being numbers on a screen and becomes real credits in my bank account. The second I sign, Serling stops being mine, if she ever was. This job suddenly feels like a betrayal. I should be here, waiting for her when she comes looking for me.

"If she loved you, she wouldn't have been on the news buying a designer dress for her wedding to another man," Asher says, as if he can read my mind. I've barely talked about Serling to him. I haven't so much as mentioned her to anyone else, but I guess it's obvious how much she meant to me during the months when we were lost. "You don't want to be here for that circus of a wedding. If you love her, you'll let her go so she can be happy."

"The actress, Darla Knox?" I change the subject as I sign the electronic contract, and Asher nods his confirmation. "When will she arrive?"

"She's here," he answers. "She's already onboard."

I'd assumed that Darla Knox's request for isolation would last only twenty-four hours before the socialite got bored and ventured out into the common areas, but we're three weeks into the flight, and I haven't seen her once. I'm half tempted to believe she isn't even on this cruise liner except there's a heat signature coming from her quarters, and some of the crew have seen her hands reach for the deliveries left outside her door. The female members of my staff are dying to catch sight of the actress. They aren't aware of the reason for her sudden and urgent trip. Our contract forbids us from searching the news for her, so we haven't seen the scandal break. Only I'm privy to the truth behind her escape into space, and I keep her secret. I don't approve of infidelity, but I understand loving the wrong person. It's not my place to judge a woman I've never met, nor is it my place to break a contract that's paying me an outrageous sum. Despite my crew's eagerness to glimpse the beautiful entertainer, Miss Knox has refused to so much as twist her face toward the security cameras in the hallways.

"Mr. Thorne?" My navigator knocks on the wall before stepping into the pilot's cockpit. "Miss Knox just made a formal request that we stop at the nearby planet Tasavera."

"I don't know why she would ask," I say. "As per our contract, we aren't authorized for unsanctioned stops."

"I understand, but her request was more like a demand."

I stare at the man with annoyance. Why am I always paired with women who think the galaxy revolves around them? "I don't care how strongly worded her request was," I say. "We aren't stopping. Tell her she can wave at Tasavera as we fly by."

"Yes, sir." The navigator's voice is tinged with nerves, as if he's afraid to relay my verdict.

"Thank you." I turn back to the controls. It seems odd that after three weeks of radio silence, the woman is suddenly demanding we break our contract and risk being fined by Headquarters for an uninspired planet. Many of the planets along our route are remarkably beautiful to witness from space, but Tasavera is not one of those natural beauties. It's an incredibly plain and unimpressive world. I know nothing about it, and I doubt anyone but its residents does. I can't imagine what an actress would want with it.

I push the thoughts of Darla Knox out of my head. Three weeks of this trip have passed. Nine remain. I just need to survive nine more mind-numbing weeks, and then I can baptize my new warship.

"Miss? Miss? You can't be up here!" A crew member's echoes off the walls, and before my brain fully registers what his words mean, a pair of high heels obnoxiously click on the steps to my station.

"No, Miss! You aren't authorized to be on this level." His warning escalates as her footfalls grow closer, and I grind my teeth. It seems Miss Knox is displeased with my answer. I don't have the energy to deal with another diva on my ship, and I exhale my exhaustion as I start to turn around.

"I paid an ungodly amount of money for this trip, so if I request a simple change to the itinerary, I expect to be accommodated, old man," Darla Knox spits at the back of my head, and I freeze, my skin going impossibly cold at her name for me. It can't be. It's impossible. It's my imagination playing tricks, forcing me to hear her voice speak her nickname for me, yet there's no mistaking the emphasized venom in her tone. There's only one woman in this galaxy capable of filling her words with such hostility.

"So why don't you stop being an asshole," she continues, using her other favorite term for me. "And touch down on Tasavera."

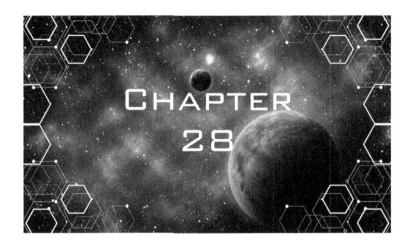

CHAPTER 28

DRIVER

I don't move. I can't bring myself to turn around, to see the truth of who stands behind me, because my mind is surely playing cruel tricks on my heartbreak. It can't be her. It's impossible. She's thousands of miles away, planning her wedding to another man, and I don't possess the strength to face my intruder if it isn't her. For seconds, we exist in silence, my thundering heart the only sound, but she remains quiet for so long, I worry I imagined her words, and that fear forces me to confront the beautiful voice's owner.

"Do you know what's so unique about Tasavera?" she asks, leaning nonchalantly against the doorframe as if this is just a normal conversation, and my system short circuits at the sight of her. She looks different from the girl I love. That version was all sunburns and dirt, but this isn't the woman I first met either. She no longer portrays the heiress, and while her clothing and makeup are expensive, there's a softness to her ensemble, as if she's forgotten to portray the vengeful princess the years forged her into. Warmth graces her face, playfulness dances on her slight smile, and brightness shines through her eyes. The venom in her voice from a moment ago was all an act, and pain slices through my chest to strangle the air from my lungs. Serling Ambrose is impossibly beautiful, and she's here... on my ship.

"It's an agricultural planet on the outskirts of the galaxy," she continues, and I can't move. I'm frozen in my seat as she speaks, confused by her presence, by her topic of conversation, by the fact that her wedding is in one week, yet we're three weeks away from Corr'us Sanctum. Not even the fastest ship could return her in time for the nuptials.

"There's nothing special about it, and as you can see, it's exceptionally plain in its appearance." She gestures out of the cockpit window, but I don't follow her directions. I keep my eyes trained on her face, afraid if I look away, she'll vanish. "The locals don't believe in technology; therefore, they live an agriculturally ruled existence. No military, no factories, no cities. Most travelers pass Tasavera without a second glance, but twenty years ago, a traveler noted the planet's overgrowth of one particular orange and fleshy fruit. It grows out of control all year round and has a bitter and unpleasant taste, but no matter how the locals tried to eradicate it to make space for consumable vegetation, it thrived. They eventually surrendered, allowing the fruit to reign over the land, and the people searched for ways to use its flesh. Most dry it for kindling, though.

"But the traveler recognized its potential. He distilled its juice, and much to everyone's surprise, the liquor was delicious. Convinced he'd struck gold, he bought a distillery and began mass production. Money poured in, and desperate for their dues, the galaxy's leaders declared Tasavera part of the Federation so they could enforce taxation. The alcohol sold well at first, but the fruit's overgrowth created a surplus in the supply, and the price plummeted. It's still widely produced, but the cheap price ensures its consumers are students and lower-class citizens. Officials saw no further need to civilize the planet, but the fact remains. Tasavera is legally a Federation member."

Of all the different reunions I fantasized about, a history

lesson was not among them, and I gawk at Serling. I haven't seen her in two months, and this is how she greets me? With stories of alcohol and the practicality of supply and demand? This woman makes it difficult to love her, and while I'd hoped she would fling herself into my arms and apologize for abandoning me, she's resolved to stand in the doorway. I can feel the remnants of my old agitation rising inside my chest. Why is she here? Is this just another way for her to break my heart?

"It has no military, no governing force with which to detain or deport travelers like us, but as a Federation planet, all rulings made on Tasavera are legally binding throughout the galaxy," she continues. "Every judge's decision. Every arrest. Every signed document." She pauses, suddenly serious, and leans forward as if to ensure I don't misunderstand her next words. "Every wedding. Any marriage performed on Tasavera cannot be annulled, not even by the Imperator. The only way to dissolve a Federation marriage is through divorce. A legal, fought in the courtroom, public divorce. Tasavera weddings are not bonds easily broken."

My skin flushes with ice as my veins burn with molten lava. My chest constricts. My lungs struggle to breathe. I feel too small for my skin, like my own body is suffocating me, and I want to rip my flesh wide and crawl out. The sensation is too much, too overwhelming because I finally understand her choice of topic. Serling Ambrose is asking me to marry her.

I can barely function. I can't bring myself to speak, but somehow, I turn to my controls and alert the crew to our unsanctioned stop. If they protest or question my decision, I don't hear them. I don't recall any of the landing, either. All I know is that we're suddenly grounded, and Serling is gone. She vanished during our descent, and I fear she was a dream. That I landed this ship on an inconsequential planet for a hallucination. My crew bombards me with questions the instant I step out of my cockpit after we dock, but all I can manage is *'not now'* and '*later*' before I'm running. My boots slap the tiles with echoes of desperation until I reach the passenger quarters, and the second I enter the airlock, Serling steps out of her room. She changed. She's no longer wearing the clothes from before, and I skid to a halt at the sight.

Her new outfit is a two-piece dress. The top is an entirely lacy affair. Its long sleeves cover her arms with a delicate floral pattern that descends over her breasts and stops at her ribs, leaving a few inches of her midriff bare. The lace is strategically placed to hide her nipples, but the top reveals much of her skin. It's both elegant and sexy, and normally, the lace would beg me to tug on it just enough to force her nipple to peak through, but her beauty is not what makes me freeze. It's the color. The fabric is white, and the simple skirt is floor-length. It's her wedding dress. The one she hopes to walk down the aisle in as she marries me.

SERLING

"Tell me I'm not too late. Tell me I haven't lost you," I beg, a terrifying breed of horror settling in my chest as Driver stares at my white dress. Until this moment, I was confident in my plan. It's been panicked weeks in the making, and I was so sure of the outcome until this second. I'm suddenly afraid I've ruined the only good thing in my life. That the man I crave more than air hates me because of how I treated him.

"I don't want to rush you, but we don't have much time," I say when he doesn't answer me. "My father's coming for me, but I'm not trying to outrun him. I simply need a head start. It's why I haven't stepped outside of my quarters until now. If your crew knew an Ambrose was onboard, they might have alerted

Headquarters, and my father would've been on us instantly. I have no doubt he's hard on our heels, even with my secrecy, and today's outcome hinges on our timing. If we beat him to the registrar's office, our story will be one of true love's triumph. A fairytale ending for the Federation's princess and the soldier who saved her. But if my father arrives before we sign the license, today will be portrayed as the day a madman stole his daughter. He'll ruin you, which is why we must hurry. I paid news reporters to be at the Tasavera courthouse for an exclusive announcement this afternoon. They'll livestream our wedding, and the world will witness the Federation Heiress marry the civilian who saved her. The public will devour that romance. They're already fans of yours. It's why I didn't fight my father at the press conference, why I didn't look at you. I couldn't bear seeing your pain, but I needed my dad to praise you publicly. If the Imperator named you a hero, the galaxy would not only accept our marriage, but fully support it. My father won't be able to insist on a divorce because, as powerful as he is, the people would crucify him for ripping his daughter from the husband who protected her in the Mors Expanse. He'll be powerless to tear us apart, but only if we beat him to the courtroom."

"How would he know where we are?" Driver asks with a numb voice. "Darla Knox is the only recorded passenger on this cruise." He ignores my proposal and my urgency, fixating on the one thing I don't wish to tell him, but it's time I was honest with the man I hope to marry. I was afraid to share my past's darkness before, but I need him to know everything about me. I need him to understand I'm here for him, no matter the risk.

"Remember when I told you I had a pregnancy blocker?" I ask, and he nods. "I let you assume it was a normal birth control, but it's not." I take a deep breath, trying not to cry, but the tears spill despite my efforts. "My father chartered The Bellator to fly through the Mors because he was angry with my defiance. He didn't want to wait another eight-plus months for me to fulfill my duty. Before you and I met, I'd learned he promised me to Tiberius without my knowledge. I protested the match, and I've never been so terrified of another human being as I was that night."

"Did he hit you?" Driver interrupts so forcefully that I flinch, but I don't respond. I've spent the better part of this year pretending that night never happened. "Serling?"

"Don't make me answer that," I whisper.

Driver clenches his fist so hard that his knuckles turn white, and I fixate on the colorless flesh. It's safer than the icy in his expression. "Did he hurt you?" he repeats.

"He made it clear he would force me to marry," I say instead, and Driver's gaze burns a hole through my chest. He always sees through my words, and now is no different. He understands the monster I call father. He doesn't need me to speak to know what I endured at the hands of a man who is supposed to love me.

"I had no choice, no escape, so I did the only thing I could to regain power over my future." I step closer to Driver. Being near him gives me strength, and there's more he needs to hear. "My father never hid that he wanted a son as his heir, and he doesn't intend for me to inherit his title. He will also never allow Tiberius Sinclair to become Imperator. My marriage was for financial gain, and so I could bear male heirs. As soon as my father had a grandson, he would eliminate Tiberius, undoubtedly, in a way that allowed him to rename my sons as Ambroses so they could succeed him." I wipe my cheeks, unable to stop the sobs constricting my chest. This is the first time I've admitted out loud the magnitude of my father's oppression.

"If I couldn't refuse my marriage, I would refuse him heirs, so I located a doctor," I continue despite Driver's harsh expression. "I paid him to discretely implant a permanent blocker inside me. I had no choice of husband, but I ensured the Ambrose line dies with me. Only my father learned what I'd planned and ordered the doctor to give him backdoor access to the device. My dad now controls it. He decides when it works, when I have children, and he can track it. It's how we were rescued. The Expanse confused the tracker, making it difficult for him to pinpoint our location. It's why we were stranded for months, but in this stretch of the galaxy, he'll know exactly where to find me."

I pause, waiting for him to say something, praying he'll say anything, but Driver just stares at me with an unreadably vacant face. His muscles are rigid, his eyes harsh, and my tears come harder. I'm losing him. I'm losing the only man I've ever loved, and I haven't even been brave enough to confess that to him.

"I know I hurt you." I lunge forward awkwardly, then stop as I detect a thread of rage coiling through his frozen form. "I wasn't lying when I promised to leave my family for you. I want you more than I want my own life, but the moment I learned about the blocker, I understood the depths of my father's control. I could never run away with you. We would barely make it an hour before my father realized we were missing, tracked the device, and fed the news a tale of your abuse and treachery. He would turn you into a criminal of the worst sort, and instead of being worshipped by the Federation, you would end up in a black site prison. He would ensure you died alone and starving, beaten every day until your body gave out for trying to take me. It's why I needed him to declare you a hero before the entire galaxy. If I made the universe love you, the people would root for us, granting us some protection from my father's lies.

"So, I played along. I agreed to marry Sinclair and pretended you were a means to an end. I'm sorry I never told you about my forced engagement. Once we crashed, it didn't seem to matter anymore. I didn't love Tiberius, and being stranded freed me of my duty. So what was the point of confessing I'd destroyed my ability to bear children?

"And I'm sorry I didn't look at you during the press conference, but I couldn't bring myself to witness the pain my betrayal inflicted. I hate myself. I hate my father. I hate everything in my life but you, but the chances of escaping my father's reach were significantly higher if he wasn't expecting me to run. So, I bided my time as the world fell in love with you and waited for a day when he wouldn't notice my escape until it was too late."

I step forward, needing to breathe in the air that he exhales so that part of him becomes a part of me. "I love you, Driver Thorne. I should've said it sooner. I should've said it over and over until you believed me, but I'm saying it now. I hope it isn't too late, because I want to marry you. When you came to my house, I wanted to climb out my window, but the guards would've shot you before we made it ten steps. This plan was our only chance, so I played my father's game until all the pieces were in place, and then I disappeared. We have a head start and a universally televised wedding waiting on Tasavera if you'll have me because I don't want to be an Ambrose anymore. That name has brought so much pain and cruelness to my life. I want to be a Thorne. Serling Thorne."

I fall silent, wiping the tears from my cheeks. I was so afraid to confess my love, but now that I've put a voice to my emotions, I can't stop. I want to scream at the top of my lungs how desperately I ache to be Serling Thorne, but the darkness in Driver's handsome eyes renderers me a mute. We stare at each other for long seconds, and just when I've lost all hope, he steps forward until we're chest to chest.

"Your father better not set foot on this planet," he growls, his voice deadly, and the undertone of protectiveness sends a shiver down my spine.

"He undoubtedly will. He won't let me ruin his plans so easily, and while we have a head start, he'll have figured out where I am."

"Then he better not cross my path." Driver slides his hand up the back of my neck and drags me against his chest with a heated protectiveness. "Because I'll fucking kill him for what he's done to my wife."

And then Driver's lips are on mine. He kisses me with a hunger I've never felt from him before, with a need that threatens to consume me until I'm nothing but burning ash in its wake, but I'll gladly burn in his arms. He can take until nothing remains, for I am his. Solely and completely his. Our kiss is primal, filled with every emotion we've endured over our relationship, but it's different from our others for one defining fact. Love. I've loved him ever since he saved me from that creature, but putting my emotions into words changed everything. It's as if this is our wedding. This is the moment we bind ourselves together. The ceremony will legally join us, but this kiss is our vow. This is when I become his wife.

CHAPTER 29

DRIVER

S ir?" My navigator steps into the passenger quarters with hurried footsteps, only to stop short when he sees who he assumes is Darla Knox wrapped in my embrace. "Oh... excuse me... I..."

"What?" I groan, pressing one last kiss to Serling's lips before acknowledging our intruder. I tighten my arms around her, cementing her to my chest as recognition dawns on the navigator. His mouth gapes as he realizes our one and only passenger was not an actress but the Ambrose Heir herself, but he regains his composure when he registers the harshness swimming in my eyes.

"A warship has locked in on our location." He looks pointedly at Serling, our situation dawning on him.

"He's here." Serling jumps away from me. "How far out?"

"About an hour and a half, maybe less if they push it," he answers.

"We have time." She stares at me with both hope and trepidation. "We can make it to the courthouse if we leave now."

I capture her hand before she even finishes speaking and drag her from the airlock, my force undoubtedly too strong, but she doesn't protest as she chases after me. "You don't know where we went," I shout at the navigator. "And as far as you're concerned, our sole passenger is Darla Knox."

"Yes, sir." He nods as we race past him. "Shall I take care of the docking fees and customs?"

"The ship is yours until my return." I jog backward as I speak because I'll be damned if I let the love of my life slip through my fingers again. "If I return."

"Yes, sir." He eyes me carefully. "I'll see you in a few hours."

I smirk at his faith and drag Serling to the exit hatch. A port official tries to stop us as we disembark, but thankfully my navigator intercepts him, and we race into the rural town. It takes too long to get our bearings. Most modern cities integrate technology into every aspect of life, making navigation easy, but we have no such aid here. The dirt roads don't even have signs, and with every rustic building boasting the same shapes and materials, we make a few wrong turns before we find the right direction.

"I'm sorry," Serling says as I guide her through the teaming market. "I realize I've put you in an impossible position, and you deserve more than a rushed wedding on an outskirt planet."

"Did Serling Ambrose just apologize?" I smile, hoping the tease will ease her anxiety, but her worry lines are etched deep. "Princess, I would marry you with your sunburnt skin wearing only my tee-shirt with the sun as our sole witness." I reach out and brush a thumb over her creased brow. "Although I'm surprised it took your father this long to catch us. How did you escape his attention if he's tracking your movements?"

"I became a nightmare of a bride," she says as we duck under a vendor's low-hanging awning, and I smirk. No one does venom like this woman, and I can only imagine the hell she inflicted on her family and the Sinclairs. I never thought I would appreciate her hostile tendencies, but as we close in on the courthouse, I couldn't be more grateful for her toxic behavior.

"The first part of my plan was to ensure my father publicly glorified you, and the second was to become so unbearable during the wedding planning that he created a separate financial account so I didn't have to involve him. I told him if I was going to participate in his schemes, I wanted a wedding history would remember. He was reluctant to grant me control of the budget, but if you thought I was horrible when we crashed, then you would be appalled by my behavior around my parents. I made him so miserable that there were moments I think he wished I'd died in the Expanse."

I can't help but laugh, and she throws me a please smile. She knows her performance was brilliant, and I wish I'd been there to witness her version of revenge on the man who caused her so much pain.

"After he transferred the funds into my management, I hired an acquaintance to set up false businesses," she continues. "The receipts I submitted to my father looked legitimate, but the money wasn't hiring caterers or musicians, or purchasing a dress or floral arrangements. The payments moved through the bogus accounts and vanished, and when I funneled the exorbitant budget out of my wedding account, I employed you to pilot my escape cruise under Darla Knox's name. I knew when your friend Archer saw the contract, he would force you to take the job. Plus, the transactions became untraceable after I paid those fake businesses, so my father can't reclaim your payment. Legally, he didn't employ you, so while he might be suspicious, there's nothing he can do. There's no proof. That money is yours."

"Is there even a Darla Knox?" I ask.

"Yes. She had her break out after we disappeared. It's why your contract contained a '*no news*' clause. I knew Archer would feed you the tale of Darla's senator, ensuring you enforced that rule onboard, but in reality, it was to keep you from learning there was no such scandal because I needed that lie to encourage your urgency."

"You thought of everything." I drag her up the courthouse steps, my heart pounding with the realization that reporters wait just inside to broadcast our treason. "I wish I had known." I pause before the front doors, seizing this last minute of oblivion to confess my sins. "I love you, Serling, but I haven't seen you in almost two months. I grew angry with you in those weeks. You promised to stay with me, but the moment wealth returned to your life, you abandoned me... or so appearances led me to believe. I wanted to trust in your love, to trust that what we had was unbreakable, but watching you shop for a wedding dress to marry another man broke me."

"I never bought a dress." She cups my face gently, her touch an apology. "The money was gone, already transferred to your contract, so it was all for show. You doubted me, and I understand, but Driver, there wasn't a single moment where I wasn't faithful to us. I couldn't tell you. I was a prisoner in my own home, in my own body. The only time I've experienced freedom was during our months in the Mors." She steps closer, lowering her hands to clutch my shirt. "You set me free, but then my father found us. He resumed control of my life and tried to reduce me to the cruel shell I was when we met, but after learning who I could be with someone who genuinely cared, I couldn't re-inhabit my former life. I've been fighting to get back to you since they discovered us on that planet.

"I have an old school acquaintance whose father is a high-ranking member of the Federation. We both lived under oppressive men, so we formed a pact to always be each other's alibi, no questions asked. On the night we fled Corr'us Sanctum, I made a very public arrival to my exclusive bachelorette party, then donned a disguise before slipping out the back. She put on a wig hours later and pretended to be a very drunk me leaving the party. The plan was for her to tell my father I passed out at her home after the event, buying us an almost twenty-four-hour head start, and since we beat him here, it must have worked. I was worried his warship would overtake the cruise vessel before we reached Tasavera, but it seems not even the Imperator's personal ship can compare to Driver Thorne."

"I am the best damn pilot in this galaxy, and I wish I'd known you were onboard. We would've made it here days ago." I cup her face and lean down until my lips brush hers. "I understand now why we weren't authorized for any stops... Oh, and I know a lot of military doctors. They'll remove that blocker. Your father will never hold you under his thumb again." I kiss her slowly, enjoying this last remnant of privacy. "I swear to always protect you from him... or any other monsters we encounter along the way. I forgive you for the pain your avoidance inflicted on me, and what's more, I thank you for it. You didn't give up, even though I thought you did."

"I'm too stubborn to give up, remember?" She smirks.

"Thank god for that." I release her face to capture her hand. "Thank you, Serling. Thank you for being stubborn. For always fighting, even when I don't realize you are. You did it with the water. You did it now with your father. I've learned my lesson. I'll never doubt you again for as long as I live, and I pray I have many years left because I missed the sound of you arguing with me."

Serling bursts into laughter, and it's like watching chains break apart and fall from her body. She's instantly lighter. "I am younger than you," she teases. "All that youthful energy will fuel my endeavors to drive you crazy."

"Well, when you put it like that, it leaves only one answer to your proposal." I push open the door and tug her inside the courthouse. "Let's get married, wife."

SERLING

The second we push through the courthouse doors, chaos consumes us. Reporters bombard me, confused as to why I called them to such an insignificant planet for this announcement, but I don't let their questions derail us. We are burdened with a life-altering purpose, and I won't rest until I am Serling Thorne. Serling Ambrose died in the Mors Expanse. It's time my name reflects that.

I want to savor our wedding, to gaze into Driver's eyes with longing as we recite tear-filled vows of eternal love, but time is a relentless enemy. She refuses us a romantic ceremony, allowing for only a rushed '*I do,*' followed by document after document of legal forms. We sign the license, submit our fingerprints for the digital records, and pay the rush fees all to the orchestra of reporters broadcasting our elopement for the galaxy to witness. Before the judge began our ceremony, I'd made a small, tele-vised speech explaining that the man who saved my life had also stolen my heart, and I couldn't live without him. The reporters ran with my words, and as Driver and I sign the final electronic form that'll legally bind us, one woman waxes poetic to the camera feed about star-crossed lovers and sacrifice. It's an annoying soundtrack for the most monumental moment of my life, but I can't complain. When she's finished, the public will be obsessed with our romance, ensuring my father will have a bitch of a time convincing people that our marriage should be terminated.

"And that's the last of it," a pretty court official says, tapping the registration button on her tablet. "Your license has officially been entered into the Federation Database. Congratulations Mr. and Mrs. Thorne. You are legally married."

I burst into tears at her words, and the reporters surge for-ward to capture my emotions. Driver has seen me cry more times than I can count, but this is the first time anyone else has witnessed tears grace my face. I've been called a heartless bitch often by the gossip tabloids, and the sight of me sobbing is probably more shocking than me surviving the Mors.

"Mr. Thorne," the judge says with a smile, his support of our marriage evident in his warmth. "Kiss your bride."

Driver captures my waist and hoists me into the air, kissing me before I can even take a breath. The crowd erupts with enthusiastic cheers, and the reporters move closer to catch our embrace, but I don't care. Let them see how he kisses me. Let them see how I love him. I learned during the months when we were lost how dangerous living without water is. How it brings life and comfort and joy when it's present, but it kills ruthlessly when it vanishes. Driver is my water. There is no life without him. Only suffering.

"I love you, Serling Thorne," Driver whispers against my lips, kissing me with an intensity too risqué for the news, yet I can't bring myself to be embarrassed. The way he says my new name burns my skin with electricity that threatens to stop my heart, and I want him to say it over and over until the day I die. I am Serling Thorne. I am his wife.

"I love you, old man." I capture his bottom lip between my teeth, and he lets out a deep belly laugh. His head falls back, and it's like watching a weight drop from his shoulder. The stress of our separation, of racing against the clock, turned him into a rigid soldier. But now that not even my father can pull us apart, he is beautifully light.

"So, that's how it's going to be?" He puts me down and reverently tucks my hair behind my ears.

"Just because I'm your wife doesn't mean I'm going to be easy." My fingers trail down his uniform to where his scars sit, and I trace their uneven patterns under the fabric. I've missed him so much that I even crave the way the rough skin feels.

"I don't want easy, Princess. I never want easy." He leans down to kiss me again, but before our lips meet, the courthouse doors fly open so fast that they almost rip off their hinges, and I know who our intruder is.

My father's eyes instantly find mine, and while I know he doesn't love me unconditionally like a parent should, I've never seen murder in his gaze before. His expression betrays his utter hatred for me, for what I've done to foil his plans, and I recoil. His gaze hurts worse than a physical blow, and the soldier emerges from my husband at the sight. Driver goes rigid, his hold on my waist almost too tight, and my memory flashes to our conversation on the cruise ship. He swore to kill my father if they met face to face, and a different breed of terror washes over me. My father cannot undo our marriage, but if Driver kills him, my new husband will bleed out on this floor before we get a chance to enjoy our triumph.

"Driver, no." I tighten my hold on him. "He's not worth it."

The Imperator and his enormous entourage storm into the courthouse, but the second he registers the cameras aimed at him, he softens. Ever the politician, he hides his malice as he moves for us, undoubtedly rethinking his plan of attack, but I know him well. If given too much time to plot, he'll emerge the victor.

Driver steps out of my embrace, and I try to capture his hand, but he escapes my grasp as he stares my father down. He's the only man I know brave enough to go toe to toe with the Imperator, and if I wasn't so terrified, I'd be incredibly turned on. I always admired how he refused to take my shit, and watching him meet the galaxy's leader on his chosen battlefield is both nerve-wracking and awe-inspiring. The sinking in my gut tells me I'm about to watch my husband die, but the entire room stands transfixed by Driver's bravery.

"I would like to say something," Driver says, and every camera zooms in on him. "I realize this small ceremony doesn't fit the version of Serling you all know, but I didn't fall in love with the heiress. I fell for the girl who climbed two cliffs by herself in the unbearable heat to find water. I came to respect the woman who aimed the ship's cannon at the monster hunting me and didn't miss the target. I learned to adore the friend who saw me bleeding out and dragged me to the Med Bay by herself so I wouldn't die. We didn't fall in love during a political event. We fell in love with sunburnt skin, bruised knuckles, and over-whelming joy when we found water. This wedding was perfect for us because we don't need glamour. We just need each other." Driver looks back at me, but I can barely see him through my tears.

"Serling is the most stubborn, resilient, capable, and intelli-gent woman I know. She does not give up. She does not surren-der. Our time in the Mors Expanse didn't change her but refined her, and you will come to admire her as fiercely as I do. Her name may now be Thorne, but she's still the Ambrose heir, and she'll make one hell of an Imperator. I have no doubt that my wife will bring unbridled passion and strength to her role, and I'm so proud to call her my partner in this life." Driver pauses with meaning. I told him my father never intended to let me inherit his title, but with this declaration, he has officially chal-lenged my father's prejudice. He's placed the idea of a woman inheriting the power into the mind of everyone watching, and my feet step forward of their own accord. I close the distance with tears streaming down my face, and he takes my hand with a look of unadulterated love.

"But today wouldn't be possible without Imperator Ambrose," Driver says, and my body goes rigid. What is he doing?

"Serling was engaged," he continues. "But before you judge her too harshly, we never expected to escape that planet. We were prepared to live the rest of our days on that rock. We didn't plan to fall in love either, but you can't stop the heart when it finds its other half. Serling will forever be my soul-mate, and when we were rescued, she tried to do the right thing. She had made a commitment, and she's a woman of honor."

I try to keep a straight face at his words. He knows full well that I wasn't technically engaged, that I was forced and threatened into marrying Tiberius, so I don't understand why he's lying to the galaxy.

"But love is more powerful than duty, and Serling loves me. The dangers we endured bound us together, and we couldn't survive the separation. Not being with the one you love is a fate worse than death, and we realize our marriage disrupted many plans. We offer our sincerest apologies to the Sinclair family, but ours is a romance that cannot be ignored. Imperator Ambrose saw his daughter's suffering. He watched the pain our estrangement inflicted on her, and he is a generous father. He allowed Serling to dissolve her engagement with Tiberius so we could marry. It's because of him that we stand here today as husband and wife."

The room freezes at his declaration. My father pales with fury, and it takes all my strength not to laugh. I've never seen someone humiliate my dad so efficiently, and it's beautiful. I finally understand Driver's lies. He's spinning a tale for the galaxy to devour, and with my father beside him, it only adds legitimacy to his story. He has cornered the great Imperator, and my father faces a silent ultimatum. Agree with my husband and become the champion of this fairytale romance, or arrest him for treason, effectively murdering his own career. Driver has left him with no choice. The only way he emerges from his encounter unscathed is to play along. To bless our marriage, and the second he does that on a live news report, he can't rescind his words. Driver has forced his hand, ensuring my father can never demand our divorce.

"So, I would like to take this opportunity to thank you, Imperator." Driver steps forward and extends a hand, and if I know my dad, this is a fate worse than death. He's the man who controls outcomes, not someone derailed by scarred soldiers. "You cannot imagine what your blessing means to Serling and me, so thank you from the bottom of my heart. I am nothing without your daughter, and I'm honored you found me worthy of her."

For a second, it looks like my father might refuse my husband as the reporters close in like birds of carrion, but then to both my shock and relief, he accepts Driver's hand for the galaxy to witness.

"You're welcome," he says through a strained smile, his eyes cold despite the grin. "Anything to make my daughter happy."

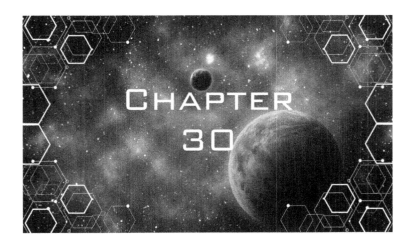

CHAPTER 30

DRIVER

A wise soldier knows when to advance and when to retreat, and after winning this round, I have no intention of remaining in Imperator Ambrose's presence. I backed him into a corner and forced him to bend to my will, and he won't let that go unpunished. If I give him time, he'll find a clever way to turn this triumph bitter, so I slide my fingers through my wife's and pull her back out into the teaming market. We're three weeks into a leisurely cruise, and while I initially moaned the easiness of this journey, I now realize why Serling chartered this course. Most of the outskirt planets are gorgeous and peaceful, and since the flight requires minimal effort on my part, I'll have the time to enjoy our honeymoon.

"I should use that ridiculous salary you paid me to buy you a ring." I lift her fingers to my lips and kiss them as we stroll through the crowd.

"I just want matching bands, nothing fancy," she says, and I gawk at her. Married in a simple dress on a rural planet and absent the desire for jewelry. What have I done to this woman?

"For over a month, I wore another man's engagement ring,

and I couldn't even look at my hand," she explains. "I only want a wedding ring. Your wedding ring."

I wrap my arm around her shoulders and pull her against my chest as a vendor jumps into our path, interrupting my obsession. My first instinct is to defend my new bride, but then he thrusts miniature spiced cakes into our faces, telling us they're a wedding gift. Serling smiles as she accepts the offering and shoves a whole one in her mouth. I watch in awe as she moans in pleasure before snagging a second cake, much to the merchant's delight, and I'm honored that my love helped my beautiful wife break away from her pain. She's so changed from the selfish girl I met who made crew members cry, and seeing her kindness, other vendors surge forward to bless the Federation Heir with their goods.

Serling makes the crowd's day as we move toward our ship. By the time we reach the docks, she's draped in colorful clothes and has tried every food they've given her. She's drank all the offered alcohol, and I can't help but wonder how drunk a wife I'll have by our wedding night. Not that I mind. Whatever makes Serling happy brings me joy.

"I used my father's entire wedding budget to employ your ship, so I have no money left," she says with a heartbreakingly beautiful smile of pure happiness as she gestures to her dress. "So I wore what I already had that was white. I couldn't hire caterers or plan a party, but this crowd just gave us a reception." She hands the plethora of gifts to one of my ship's hospitality members, and because my entire crew came to welcome us onboard, I assume they watched our wedding broadcast. Their presence is an encouraging show of support, but when the woman from hospitality tries to take the spiced cakes from my wife, Serling draws them to her chest with a laugh. The staff stares at her, utterly surprised at this uncharacteristic behavior of the notorious Ambrose heiress, and I cannot wait for the galaxy to see who Serling is when her father isn't crushing the life out of her. Our marriage ceremony didn't allow time for vows, but I silently swear to never crush her spirit like her parents did. She can be difficult and head-strong all she wants, but she will never feel unworthy or unloved. She will never be abused, physically or emotionally. I saw the death glare the Imperator directed at her when he entered the courthouse. I saw the pain it inflicted. I vow I'll do everything in my power to ensure no one looks that cruelly at her again.

"Welcome back, sir." My navigator shakes my hand before turning to Serling. "Mrs. Thorne." Her smile goes nuclear at the term, and the man can't help but return the expression. "I assumed we'll be leaving immediately. I completed the ship's preflight checks, and the docks cleared us for departure."

"You assumed correctly." I thump the man's back good-naturedly. "Come on." I pull Serling behind me. "I want you in the cockpit with me."

She says nothing as she follows along, her mouth full of another cake, and she might be the cutest thing I've ever seen. I'll do everything in my power to ensure her life is always this happy. Whether we're stranded on a planet or flying through the stars or fighting with her father, that smile is never leaving her lips.

"You should eat some of these before I finish them," she says between bites as I take my seat.

"You eat them. I enjoy watching you."

She shrugs and takes another bite. "I'm full, but I can't stop. There's something different about food made with love. My family eats the most expensive meals, yet I keep thinking about those root cakes with the vine syrup I made when we were stranded. Somehow, that primitive meal tasted better than anything I've eaten with my parents, and these spiced cakes are the same. I guess food tastes better when you're happy."

"Are you happy?" I ask as I initiate the takeoff protocol.

"As happy as I can be married to an old man," she fires back, and I reach out and smack her ass.

"Sit down before you go flying like you did when we outran that storm," I chuckle. "You had a lot to drink."

"I've never had Tasavera liquor. Too cheap for my family, but it's good."

"I'll buy you some more after we've put some distance between us and your father." That sobers her, and I instantly regret bringing him up.

"It was nice the locals gave us a reception," she says softly, a hint of nerves in her voice. I can't look at her as I guide the ship out of the atmosphere, but the sound freezes me. "We should save that money I paid you. My father will undoubtedly make life difficult for you after your speech, and I suspect he'll cut me off. Not that I need millions anymore. I got used to living on a crash site, but we might have trouble finding a doctor to help me remove…" she trails off.

"I have a lot of army buddies who work in the medical field," I reassure her. "Trust me, they'll all be clamoring for the opportunity to remove that blocker for free. Don't worry. I'll take care of everything, and then you can have all the babies you want."

"Do you want kids?" she asks.

"With you? Fuck yeah."

"You don't think I would be a bad mom? I can be a bitch sometimes. What if I'm too much like my dad?"

"You're nothing like your father, so never say that again. My kids will be lucky to call you mom."

"I don't know if I'm ready for children yet, though," she says. "My dad will make our lives difficult, and after your announcement, people will be waiting to see if I rise to challenge him for the succession. The next few years will be a fight."

"I thrive in a fight. I think you do too."

"We're a pair, aren't we?" The ship settles into an easy cruising speed, and Serling reaches forward. I can finally give up a hand, and I accept her offering, running my thumb over her soft skin. "Will I really be a good Imperator? Do you even want a wife who's an Imperator?"

"You have the potential to be great," I say honestly. "You've changed, Serling. You evolved. I have no doubt that you'll grow into a woman capable of anything you put your mind to, whether that's motherhood or politics. I won't push you into either path, but I will support whichever you choose. I'll support both if that's what you want too. And as for me? I'm pretty damn secure in myself. I would love a powerful wife. Tell me to get on my knees and worship, Princess. I'll do it gladly."

She laughs as she unbuckles her harness now that the ship's speed is stable. She settles behind me and wraps her arms around my neck, hugging me tight. "I changed because of you. For the first time in twenty-nine years, someone saw the person, not the name. You gave me the strength to be better. I'll probably always be stubborn, but I think I can be good."

"I know you can." I lean back against her chest, and she kisses my temple.

"Thank you for marrying me. I realize choosing me means your life will be difficult. My father will come for you, and come hard, but I belong with you. I couldn't survive a life without you."

"I survived almost losing the entire right side of my body," I say. "I survived a missile to the Bellator, a crash, a hostile planet, a toxic swamp, and a predatory monster. I even survived you." I grab her arm and tug until she rounds my chair and straddles my lap. "But I won't survive losing you, so tell your father to do his worst. I'm never giving you up."

"Do you know how hard it was to stay in my quarters knowing you were only a few airlocks away?" Serling trails her fingertips down my chest, and my hands find her hips. Oh, how I've missed her touch.

"Do you know how pissed I am that you were down there for

three weeks and I didn't figure it out?" I growl as her touch overwhelms my senses. "I sat here thinking of nothing else besides you, counting down the days until you were no longer mine, only for you to be feet away from me."

"I will always be yours," she whispers as her fingers find the hem of my uniform shirt. She pauses, meeting my gaze with a heat that burns me alive, and then she tugs. I reluctantly release her hips and let her peel off my shirt, and when my chest is bared to her, her fingers find my scars. She traces the one I received when I saved her from that monster. I never expected my body to be beautiful to a woman, and there's nothing more intoxicating than my wife finding relief in the touch of my marked skin.

"Why do you like them so much?" I ask as I gently claim her mouth. I move slowly, taking my time with her lips, and for long moments she ignores my question as we savor the intensity. It's soft and sensual, the overwhelming knowledge that this woman is my wife consuming me as our tongues meet. She kisses with her entire soul, with every fiber of her being, and I lift my hand to her chest to feel the thunder of her heart. It beats with the strength of a warrior, and I know it's because her heart no longer beats alone. She stole mine, and I never want it back.

"My life was perfect on the surface," she says against my lips, her words increasing the pressure against my mouth, and I gasp at the intensity. "But I was so scarred on the inside that I became toxic to even myself." She bites my lip, and I curse, lowering my hand from her heart to the swell of her strategically-clad breast. This lace will be my undoing, and if I don't see her bare and beautiful before me soon, I'll turn feral.

"Flaws and emotions were weaknesses," she continues, arching into my touch, and the movement undoes me. I can no longer control myself, and I yank her top until the floral pattern hiding her shifts. Her pink nipple slips out between the threads, and I press my calloused palm against it, rubbing the peeked nub until she gasps.

"It didn't matter how damaged you were on the inside as long as you portrayed the perfect Ambrose image for the galaxy." She pants for breath, but I don't stop. I roll her nipple against my palm, watching her control shatter with rapt attention. "I couldn't even cry without hating myself. I despised myself unless I was perfect, but then you came along and ruined everything. You're too tall, too broad and unique to be beautiful. You're scarred and gruff and confident, and you like who you are despite your visible damage. I think I started falling for you the second I laid eyes on you. I wanted you with a desperation I've never felt. My world would have chewed you up and spit you out for your blemishes, yet you're the best of us. You're good and brave and strong, and you don't give a shit that you aren't perfect because you know what truly matters. These scars taught me so much about who you were and who I was, and they made me love you. They taught me I'd been living my life finding the wrong things important."

"Fuck, Serling." I grab her top and push it up, her full breasts bouncing slightly at the movement. I lean forward, capturing a rosy nipple between my lips, and suck until she moans obscenely. She grinds against my rock-hard cock as she wraps her arms around my neck, forcing her breast further into my mouth. I suck it deeper before letting it go with a wet pop. God, I need to be inside her, to watch my wife's breasts bounce as she rides me.

"I love you, old man." She grabs my face, demanding I meet her gaze. "I fucking love you, scars and all."

"Goddamn it, Serling." I slip my hands up her skirt, gripping her thighs as I speak with a rough voice. "Say it again. Never stop saying it."

"I love you, husband," she moans my new favorite name as my hands slide over her ass... her completely bare ass.

"Oh, Princess," I growl, my fingers finding her soaked opening. "Are you telling me that your pussy was bare this entire time? During our whole wedding?"

"Bare and dripping," she grinds down on my fingers, and I have to agree. She's soaking wet for me. "I haven't had you in almost two months, old man. I think it's time you make me your wife." Her fingers unfasten my pants, and my cock springs free. She takes it in her hands and strokes my shaft, base to tip with teasing force, and I yank her forward. She yelps in surprise, but I don't give her time to recover as I push my swollen dick inside her.

"Oh god," she moans. "I forgot how big you were."

"No, you didn't." I slap her ass before guiding her down slowly. "Lift your skirt, Serling. I want to watch my cock slide inside you as I make you my wife."

She obeys, lifting the white fabric so I can see where we're joined, and we fall silent as I sink in to the hilt. She pauses as I bottom out, acclimating to my size, and when she's adjusted, she gives a cute little thrust of her hips, teasing me with the sight of her pussy stretched around my thickness.

"You're the most beautiful thing I've ever seen." I kiss her deeply, feeling the way she clenches around me as arousal races through her. When I finally release her mouth, I study her flushed cheeks as I bite her nipple. "I was livid when I thought you were planning your wedding with another man, so fuck me in this dress. I want to watch my cock slip in and out of you while you wear my wedding dress."

She tightens her grip on her skirt and starts to move, her hips rising slowly until I almost fall out before she slams back down. She does it over and over, moaning and gasping as she puts on a show. Serling does exactly what I asked her to do. She fucks me in her wedding dress, letting me watch my length split her apart, and I lean back in my chair, enjoying the sight of my wife taking me to the hilt over and over. I listen to her breathing quicken. I savor her moans that turn to screams, and within minutes, her pussy chokes me as she climaxes. Watching her come, witnessing the pleasure on her face and the pink flush on her skin, threatens to shove me off the edge, and I grab her waist and yank her against my chest. She drops her skirt, her arms wrapping tight around my neck, and we lose all coordination and finesse. This isn't sex. This is something deeper, something primal and holy. She's becoming a part of me, and losing her after this would be equivalent to ripping out my own heart. I realize how cliché my thoughts are, but the way she feels on my cock is different from before. She's my wife now. My other half, my partner, my soulmate. She's the one who finds water when I can't and bandages my wounds when I'm injured. I'm the one who steps into a predator's path to save her. We're a team, and that beautiful reality launches me into oblivion.

I come so hard, I almost black out, and as my cum fills her to overflowing, she screams her bliss. Her orgasm fills me with pride, and as she rides out her waves of pleasure, I hold her tight against my heart.

"I love you," I whisper into her ear as she stills. "I don't care what comes our way. I will never allow us to be parted. You are mine, Serling Thorne."

She pushes off my chest with a beautiful yet mischievous smile and slowly rocks on my cock. My oversensitive head sends a jolt of fire through me, and I grip her hips to still her. She smirks as her pussy walls tighten around me, and I wince.

"Always got to be difficult," I laugh, but by her expression, she knows I'm not serious. I may be sensitive, but watching her tease me while I'm overstimulated is hot as hell.

"It's been two months since I had you, and this is our honeymoon. I hope you can keep up, old man, because your young and beautiful wife can't get enough of you."

"Is that a challenge, Princess?"

She nods, the happiness on her face so stunning I want to freeze this moment and live within it forever.

"That was a mistake." I bury my face in her neck and kiss her throat and breasts until she's breathless with laughter. "You shouldn't have said that because you're in trouble now. By the time this honeymoon is over, you'll regret challenging me. I'm not going to let you leave my bed."

I stand up, slipping out of her as I double-check the autopilot, and then rearrange her clothes. When she's fully covered, I throw her over my shoulder and slap her ass so hard she yelps. She pretends to struggle, but I hold her tight and carry her to my room, much to the shocked faces of my crew. But I don't care. Let them look. Let them see how I adore my wife.

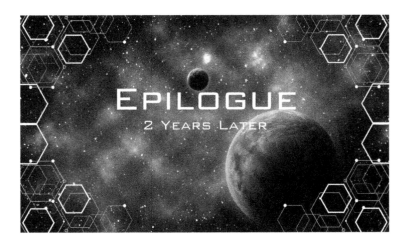

EPILOGUE
2 YEARS LATER

SERLING

I walk into our quarters, take one look at Driver's shirtless form, and face plant into his chest. He grunts a soft chuckle at my dramatics and wraps his powerful arms around my shoulders.

"That bad?" he asks.

"Yes," I mumble into his muscles.

"Do I want to know?"

"Probably, but I'm too tired to repeat it all now." I hug my husband's waist, loving how solid he feels against me. After his declaration that I would make an excellent Imperator, the public has wondered if his words were the misguided faith of a man in love or the shocking truth about the selfish Serling Ambrose. His belief in my potential pushed me to throw myself into Federation politics, and I've been fighting to become the woman my father refused to let me be. It's been a hell of a road, but after two years of proving myself, the public supports me. They're full of hope for what my war hero husband and I can accomplish, but my father has fought us every step of the way. He cut me off from my financial inheritance, publicly claiming that it was at my request. He announced I wished to live as a civilian and make it on my own merit. He hoped it would force me to abandon Driver, but his plan backfired. The people love me for forsaking my wealth and becoming one of them, and after our time in the Mors, our warship is a veritable palace. We have constant running water. What more do I really need?

Headquarters refused to fire Driver when my father strongly suggested they should. A war hero, the Ambrose heir's savior, and an Imperator candidate's husband, he's incredibly popular in the galaxy. He's also one of the few pilots skilled and brave enough to fly the Expanse. After we returned from our honeymoon, Archer gave him control of a brand-new warship and placed him back in the Mors rotation. He named the new beast The Bellator after the ship that brought us together, and it's been our home ever since. We refuse to be parted, so I face the dangers of space alongside him, conducting most of my business from my office with the aid of high-powered communications. It's where I've been sequestered for the past three days as I virtually attended a Federation council meeting. We also just entered the Expanse, so Driver has been busy, making this the first time this week I can hold him without rushing to my next call.

"Come on. Let's get you to bed." He peels my clothes off and helps me under the sheets. He settles nude beside me, content to hold me as I sleep, but I've missed him too much to ignore his warm skin against mine. We make love until I'm shaking in his arms, and then we fall asleep tangled up in each other.

"Princess." Driver kisses my forehead, and I swat him away.

"Go away."

"Get up, wife. Let's go." He tugs off the covers, giving my bare ass a love bite as he exposes me to the cool air.

"You're an asshole," I groan as I sit up and accept my clothes from him. "Why are you making me get up early... and why have we stopped?" Panic floods my system. "What's wrong?"

"Nothing's wrong." He helps me dress and then hands me a steaming mug of delicious caffeine. "I have something for you. Do you want to see it, or are you going to sit here and grumble?"

"I'll come, but I'll grumble the entire time," I say, slapping his incredibly firm ass, and he smirks.

"Finish your drink before I throw you over my shoulder." He says it like a threat, but we both know I enjoy it. I've lost track of the number of times he's thrown me over his shoulder and carried me around this ship. At first, the crew was wary of our affection, but now, they don't even bat an eye. I think they secretly like seeing a marriage that's lived in partnership and love. We aren't perfect. We fight. Lord, how we fight, but we're in this together. I've never loved anyone as much as I love this man, and I can't wait for our children to grow up with him as their father. It saddens me I never got to experience a father's absolute devotion, but I'm comforted knowing that our kids will have parents who place them above duty. Since life has been tumultuous, we decided to enjoy our marriage before starting a family. True to his word, Driver contacted his old military acquaintances, and we found a doctor skilled enough to remove my pregnancy blocker. He then prescribed a less permanent one, which we'll use until we're ready for babies. We aren't there yet, but I suspect we will be soon. I'm not sure we'll be able to fly the Mors once we have kids, but then again, knowing us, our children will be these feral creatures at home in the stars.

"Here." Driver slips a blindfold over my eyes before I realize what he's doing.

"I'm not wearing this."

"You are, so be quiet." He sits me down and straps me into the short-range transport. "No peaking. Promise me."

"Fine," I growl and lean my head back. I listen to my husband prepare for departure, and then we're flying through space. I'm completely disoriented, so I give up trying to guess what he's doing and use the time to relax. The trip is blessedly short, and when we land, Driver guides me to the transport door.

"Are you ready?" he asks, and I nod. "Okay, you can look."

I take off the blindfold, but I don't understand what I'm seeing. I must be hallucinating. This isn't possible.

"Our oasis," I whisper. "How?"

"An ex-military buddy of mine runs a private security firm," Driver says. "I paid him and a construction crew to add something special to our oasis." He extends his hand, and when I take it, he guides me onto the beach where I promised to spend the rest of my life with him.

"See up there?" He points to the circumference of small rods atop the cliffs. "Perimeter fence. It's coded to let us through, but it'll deliver an electric jolt powerful enough to stop any predator's heart to unauthorized intruders. We're completely safe in here, but that's not the surprise." He twists me toward the stretch of open beach. "That is."

I freeze in my tracks as I take in the small house built against the stones. It's simple and almost blends in with the environment, but one resounding fact stands out. It was designed for comfort. Living here would be a luxury vacation compared to the crash site we lived in for those six months on this planet.

"Why is that here?" I ask as I stride for the house and step inside the gorgeous architecture.

"This may sound insane, but I miss it here sometimes," Driver says as he leans against the doorframe to watch me explore. It's a spacious single-room hut with a loft bedroom, a high-tech bathroom, a fully functional kitchen… and a cooling system that works almost too well. "We thought this planet was going to be our home, and this is where we fell in love. This is where I learned I was wrong about you. We left so suddenly that neither of us said goodbye, and we never mourned the life we'd started to enjoy. I don't know… this beach feels special, and I wanted to come back. I want a place that's ours for when we need space to breathe."

"So, you built me a vacation home on our planet... the hostile planet we crashed on in the Mors Expanse?" I ask as I settle before him, my hands on my hips.

"Apparently, yes." He runs a hand through his dark hair that's just started showing signs of grey, but before he can doubt himself, I strip off my clothes and race for the pool.

"After we swim, I'm making pancakes with syrup!" I shout, shifting to run backward so I can watch his magnificent body emerge from his uniform. "You'll have to help me so I don't get eaten by the vines, though." My legs hit the gloriously cool water, and I collapse to stare at the sun. I don't know what's wrong with us, but Driver is right. This place feels like home. Especially since we can now have the luxury of a security system and easy transportation off planet.

I float lazily until Driver joins me, and then I climb into his arms, wrapping my limbs around his torso. "How is it I love you more every day?" I ask.

"So, you like my surprise?"

"I love it." I kiss him fiercely. "It's like coming home."

"I'm always home as long as I'm with you." He tightens his hold on me as we float deeper into the pool. "We don't have to return after this, but we needed closure. Although, after seeing what my buddy did with the place, I think it's a nice spot for us to hide out. Now that we've charted the path here, I'm confident flying this section of the Expanse."

"Only we would pick a romantic getaway in the middle of the Mors."

"So, you agree with this becoming our vacation home?"

"Of course." I shake seductively, drawing his attention to my bare body. "No other resort would tolerate our penchant for skinny dipping."

"Beachfront property without the crowd." He winks at me,

and I kiss him, tasting his mouth, his emotions, his desire. All we do is kiss, but we drag it out, letting the love flow through us as our tongues dance. When we finally break apart, Driver falls to his back, and we float side by side. In a little while, we'll gather the ingredients for dinner, and then after we eat, I'll make love to my husband in that glorious bed as the moon reflects off the water, but for now, I just study his profile. I notice two overwhelming distinctions as I watch his happiness. The first and most obvious is his beauty. He is the most handsome man I've ever seen. I adore him with a fierceness I can't explain, and every time I look at him, I lose my breath. I've committed my life to this man, and every morning when I wake, I'm struck by how lucky I am. He's stunning both inside and out, and he is mine.

The second, and still overwhelmingly obvious, is Driver Thorne is a good and honorable man. He is the best of us, a head above the rest, and he loves me.

THANK YOU FOR READING THE EXPANSE BETWEEN US. IF YOU ENJOYED THIS BOOK AND FEEL COMFORTABLE LEAVING A REVIEW, I WOULD GREATLY APPRECIATE IT. REVIEWS GO A LONG WAY IN HELPING AUTHORS LIKE ME.

Also by N.R. Scarano

A Loyal Betrayal
A Camelot Reimagining Age Gap Romance

Season's Readings
Holiday Romances

Wreck The Halls

X Marks the O's

Tryst or Treat

Happy Hunting (Coming 2025)

Autopsy of a Fairytale
Murder Mysteries Inspired by Fairytales

*As Nicole Scarano

Autopsy of a Fairytale

Forensics of a Fable

Kidnapping of a Myth

Criminology of a Character (Coming Sep 2024)

The Pomegranate Series
A Gender-Swapped Hades & Persephone Reimagining

*As Nicole Scarano

Pomegranate

Pitchfork

Pandora

About the Author

Nicole writes steamy fantasy & sci-fi romance as N.R. Scarano and Mystery Thrillers with fantasy/sci-fi twists as Nicole Scarano. She doesn't like to box herself into one genre, but no matter the book, they all have action, true love, a dog if she can fit it into the plot, swoon-worthy men & absolutely feral females.

In her free time, Nicole is a dog mom to her rescued pitbull, a movie/tv show enthusiast, a film score lover, and sunshine obsessive. She loves to write outside, and she adores pole dancing fitness classes.

For all signed copies, socials, all links & to sign up for her newsletter visit:
linktr.ee/NicoleScarano

Printed in Great Britain
by Amazon

43038064R00148